Malcolm Welshman is a retired vet who was a consultant dealing with exotics. He has written for *The Sunday Times, The Daily Mail* and magazines such as *The Lady*. He was the *My Weekly* vet for fifteen years. He is a BBC Radio panellist and a guest speaker worldwide on cruise ships.

'You'll laugh a lot and thoroughly enjoy reading about the rather hapless Paul Mitchell's escapades. Perfect for animal lovers the world over'
Natasha Harding, *Book Columnist, The Sun*

'Have you ever wondered what your vet gets up to in his or her spare time? Read it here, it's hilarious'
Denise Robertson, *Agony Aunt, ITV's This Morning*

'A romp of a book! Take a loveable goofy vet with a heart of gold, plonk him in some crazy animal situations and laugh out loud as he reacts as only he can. I read the book in a day and annoyed everyone in the house by alternating between giggling and shaking my head. A must-read, highly recommended'
Simon Dawson, *author of Pigs in Clover*

'An entertaining fast-paced bedtime read that any animal lover will enjoy. It provides a humorous insight into the world of a vet'
Sue Parslow, *Editor, Your Cat magazine*

'Living as I do, on a tropical island with a permanently hungry dog and ten raucous chickens tends to produce a few animal-related laughs, but nowhere near as many as this fun book does. Follow the adventures of a young vet as he gets to grips with amusing animals of all shapes and sizes. A great way to spend an entertaining afternoon in a hammock under the palms'
Ian Usher, *traveller, adventurer, writer and speaker*

For my grandson, Rufus, with love from Bup

Malcolm D. Welshman

PETS APLENTY

AUSTIN MACAULEY
PUBLISHERS LTD.

A CIP catalogue record for this title is available from the British Library.

ISBN 978 1 84963 996 5

www.austinmacauley.com

First Published (2014)
Austin Macauley Publishers Ltd.
25 Canada Square
Canary Wharf
London
E14 5LB

Printed and bound in Great Britain

Contents

1

Just Where Does The Buck

Stop?

I'd just hopped across the shopping precinct, perspiration trickling down my spine, and was crouched outside Westcott's Pet Emporium, when two men staggered out from the Crown and Anchor, a local watering hole adjacent to the Pound Shop, and swayed to a halt. One grasped the sleeve of the other.

'Christ, Sean, do you see what I see?' slurred the sleeve holder, pointing at me while bringing his free hand up to rub first his right eye and then his left, shaking his head once he'd done so.

'It's a rabbit, Mick,' declared his mate, attempting to focus his bleary eyes on me, but failing miserably.

'Jesus, I know it's a rabbit, but just look at the bloody size of it.'

''Tis big, to be sure.'

'To think they sell rabbits that big,' said the sleeve holder, looking up at the pet shop sign.

"Tis enough to scare the shit out yer,' said Mick's mate, still in his clutches, both rocking from side to side.

'Hi guys,' I called out from where I was crouched in front of the shop, my voice muffled by the rabbit costume I was wearing.

'Bloody hell, Sean,' spluttered the sleeve holder. 'It can talk too.'

'What did it say, Mick?'

'Don't care what it bloody well said, Sean, I can't be having with a rabbit that talks. Especially one that size.'

'I need another drink,' exclaimed Mick's mate.

'Me too.'

Both men reeled back inside the pub from which they'd just emerged.

By now, I was feeling very hot under the collar. Well, to be more accurate, very hot under the skin of the rabbit outfit I was wearing. A rather grubby, white all-in-one costume complete with whiskers and large pink floppy ears. The heat generated from being encased in synthetic fur was fuelled by the fact that I was crouched down, attempting to hop across the pedestrian precinct of Westcott's shopping centre on a sultry, very humid July afternoon. At the same time I was being snapped by a photographer from the *Westcott Gazette*, a smart young lady called Zara, in tight jeans and a bronzed naked midriff, the latter proving an effective background to the silver stud that gleamed in her navel. A gleam that was reflected in my eye when I first spotted it. A gleam that rapidly faded as my eyes glazed and I started to keel over from heat exhaustion.

I'd spent the first few minutes hopping from the Pound Shop over to Westcott's Pet Emporium. There, I ground to a halt, swaying at eye level with a rabbit hutch, the inmate of which gave a startled twitch of his nostrils, as I snuffled through the mesh at him.

'Not bad, Paul,' shouted Zara, still clicking away. 'But would you mind hopping about a bit more as I'd like to try another angle. An action shot if possible.'

I swung round and was in the process of slowly hopping back when I heard an excited low pitched growl and someone shouting, 'Come here at once, Sammy. Sammy... no... let go... you naughty dog.' I felt myself being dragged backwards, my bum yanked from side to side. As I was pulled past the Pound Shop, I briefly glimpsed a large basket of beach balls before being shunted helplessly into it. Out tipped its contents. Beach balls began bouncing before my bunny-eyes.

'Splendid stuff, Paul. Just the sort of shot I was looking for,' cried Zara. 'Our readers will love it.'

What a load of balls, was all I could think of.

The blame for my current predicament fell squarely on the shoulders of Beryl, our receptionist at Prospect House. She had first mooted the idea as a means of raising funds for WARS – Westcott's Avian Rescue Society – during a tea break in the office.

I walked in just as Eric, one of the senior partners, said, 'Sounds rather fun. I'm sure Paul would be willing to do it.'

'Willing to do what?' I asked, taking my mug of tea across the room to sit in the chair next to Eric.

'We've been discussing ways to raise funds for WARS,' he said.

'And...?'

'We've come up with the idea of a sponsored walk.'

Didn't sound like much of an original idea to me.

'Well actually,..' Beryl intervened, giving me one of her customary owl-eyed looks, 'it's more of a sponsored hop.'

'Hop?' I didn't like the way this was heading. Straight in my direction.

Eric chuckled. 'Beryl's suggesting you should dress up as a rabbit and see how many hops you can do round the shopping precinct.'

It sounded a ghastly idea. And I said so.

'What's this...?' Crystal had just breezed in, a waft of her perfume filling the air.

Eric looked up at his wife. 'We're trying to persuade Paul to do a sponsored hop as a rabbit.'

'Why... Paul, that sounds terrific fun.' Crystal turned her cornflower blue eyes of a Julie Andrews lookalike on me – eyes that when I first started at Prospect House, had me dreaming of sallying on to the Downs with her as my Maria, me as a little goatherd, dancing silly-billy to the tune of *The Sound of Music.*

Now it seems I was being asked to sally round Westcott's shopping precinct to the accompaniment of... what, I wondered – *Run Rabbit Run?*

I couldn't imagine Crystal, as the other senior partner in the practice, slipping into such a costume – well actually I could – an image of her in Bunny Girl gear popped up – fluffy ears nestling in her copper curls and bobtail mounted on her cute little derriere.

'It's a great idea,' said Crystal. 'Don't you think...? Paul...? Are you listening?'

'What? Sorry... was miles away.'

I was suddenly conscious of the funny looks all three were giving me and quickly hopped out of my reverie.

Desperately, I tried to find some way out of the hole into which I felt I was falling – rather like the white rabbit in *Alice's Adventures in Wonderland*. Was Beryl about to organise a Mad Hatter's tea party in front of the Pound Shop? With Crystal as my Queen of Hearts? Eric would be well suited as the Cheshire Cat. And Beryl? Well, with the way I currently felt about her, there was no need for her to have a costume – she'd make a perfect Gryphon just as she was, even in her customary attire – black trousers and top, black cardigan draped across her shoulders.

But with the odds stacked against me, I had no choice but to succumb to Beryl's idea of donning a rabbit outfit and bobbing round Westcott's shopping precinct, making a complete fool of myself.

'It will come as second nature to you,' reasoned Beryl.

Thanks Beryl. Love you too.

As to finding a rabbit outfit to wear, Beryl had already thought of that.

One of the practice's clients, Tim Hutchinson, had such a costume. As Beryl told me, he and his wife, Anna, were employed by the local council to act as guides for visitors to Westcott's Wonderland – one of the tourist attractions down on the seafront – Tim dressed up like a rabbit – Anna trussed up like a chicken. Part of the Wonderland theme, apparently.

'Why can't you ask Tim to do this rabbit thing?' I whinged.

'Because he's getting on a bit and his knees aren't up to it,' explained Beryl. 'So he wouldn't be able to hop about much.'

'Besides, with you doing it,' Crystal interjected, 'it means there's be a bit of free advertising for the practice. That can't be bad can it?'

'How long am I supposed to make a fool of myself?' I asked.

Beryl shrugged. 'Depends.'

'Depends on what?' I persisted.

'How long you can last out.'

Not a very reassuring answer.

In the event, I survived just over half an hour. More than most of the people who sponsored me thought I would.

Still, some funds were raised for WARS.

And Zara managed to get the picture she wanted. One of me being hauled past the Pound Shop by a golden retriever with his teeth in my scut. The shot was featured on the front page of the *Westcott Gazette*. As I suspected, the editor, Finley O'Connor, had great fun concocting suitable headlines – *Rabbiting On for Charity*. And below it, in lower casing – *Local vet, Paul Mitchell, doesn't get off scut-free.*

My association with that rabbit outfit – or at least with its owner, Tim Hutchinson – didn't stop there.

'I say, Paul,' Eric remarked one afternoon just as I was about to start evening surgery, 'there's a very large rabbit and an enormous chicken sitting in the waiting room for you to see them.'

He saw my incredulous look. 'No honest, there is,' he insisted, with a wicked chuckle. 'You'll soon see.'

I did see, but not before I heard.

A commotion suddenly erupted from the waiting room. The sound of dogs growling, voices raised, a 'Give it here.' Then, 'Let go.' Finally, 'Drop it Jasper, drop it.'

What the heck was going on? I rushed through to find two Labradors executing a tug of war over a large rubber chicken's head, its red wattles flapping wildly from side to side as the dogs fought, in a frenzy of growling, to wrench it from each other. Across the room, a spaniel was running round in gleeful circles, vigorously shaking a white rabbit's head clamped in his jaws. Between them, a headless chicken and a headless rabbit were flapping and hopping to and fro in their attempts to regain possession of their heads which, with the aid of the dogs' owners, they eventually succeeded in doing.

The rabbit I recognised as Tim Hutchinson who, when everything and everyone had eventually settled down, introduced me to the chicken – his wife, Anna.

Meanwhile, the reason for their appointment was sitting quietly in a cardboard carton on a chair, nonchalantly washing its whiskers.

Tim explained that having just finished their afternoon stint at Wonderland, they'd popped in on the off chance they could be seen. Beryl had said that though Crystal was solidly booked right through to six o'clock (nothing new there – she had many admiring clients), Paul had got plenty of spare appointments.

Bless you, Beryl.

With their rabbit and chicken heads rescued, it was a rabbit that Tim and Anna lifted from its box on to my consulting table minutes later.

'He's called Munchkin,' said Anna.

'Though he's not doing much munching at the moment,' said Tim. 'That's why we've brought him in.'

I half-expected to be looking at a white rabbit similar to the suit Tim was wearing, but the one I was presented with was far smarter in appearance. Of medium size, but slender build, he did have a short-haired white body but with erect black ears, a black nose, and paws and tail that were also black. But it was to his eyes that I was drawn. Pink and somewhat disturbing in their intensity.

As to breed? I didn't have a clue, not being that familiar with rabbits – apart from dressing up as one. In fact, in doing that, I'd surprised myself as I have this irrational phobia about lagomorphs. Something to do with a surfeit of Beatrix Potter bedtime reading as a boy. The endless doings of Flopsy, Mopsy and Cottontail. Or maybe it was the Tiggy-Winkle doings suggested – but never quite put into practice – by my Uncle Benjamin, sitting at the end of my bed with a lustful look in his eye, whenever he babysat for my parents.

It was Tim who told me the breed. 'It's a Himalayan,' he said. 'They've a super temperament.'

'And Munchkin here is one of the best,' interjected Anna. 'Well at least Tim thinks so, don't you?'

'No question,' he answered and bent over and kissed the rabbit's head. He briefly informed me that he was a bit of a rabbit fancier and had quite a collection at home.

'Whereas I'm more into chickens,' confessed Anna.

Maybe that's why she'd opted to wear the chicken outfit in preference to being a bunny. No problem. Everyone to their own.

And Munchkin's problem?

'It's his teeth,' said Tim. 'I'm afraid they've got a bit overgrown. Guess you might have to clip them.'

While Munchkin sat quietly hunched on the table, Tim gently raised the rabbit's head using his thumb and forefinger and levered open his mouth. He'd guessed right.

Clipping of both upper and lower incisors was required.

Munchkin had an undershoot jaw and the malocclusion had allowed his lower incisors to grow up past his upper ones without getting ground down by them – the usual means by which they stayed in shape. They were now digging into the inside of his upper lip almost pushing into his nostrils.

I ran a finger along the edges of his cheek teeth, checking to see if the malocclusion had caused any problems there. Often spikes of enamel develop which can rub against the mucous membranes of the cheeks and cause ulceration. But no. No such spikes could be felt.

So it was a simple job of clipping the front incisors and advising Tim to bring Munchkin in on a regular basis to have his teeth checked and trimmed.

Before leaving, Tim apologised profusely for the scene he and Anna had caused. I reassured him that it was of no consequence. Already forgotten.

'And by the way,' added Anna, 'if you ever fancy visiting Wonderland, do let us show you round. We're there on Tuesday, Thursday and Friday afternoons and all day Saturdays.'

'Thanks. I may take you up on that,' I replied, in what I hoped was an enthusiastic tone of voice. But Westcott's Wonderland didn't appeal. For a young man in his mid-twenties I couldn't see there being anything there to attract him unless the thought of fulfilling a childhood dream by sitting on a giant toadstool pretending to be a goblin or whirling round in an over-sized teacup was a turn-on. It certainly wasn't my cup of tea. So I never did visit

Wonderland and meet up with the Hutchinsons there.

But I did meet Anna again when she brought some chickens into my surgery – though this time she was not dressed as one.

Beryl had booked them in for me.

Anna was alone. No Tim this time.

She explained his absence by saying she was more interested in chickens than he was. Loved the idea of having freshly laid eggs every day.

She took after my dad in that respect. He'd been keeping six Rhode Island Reds for many years in the back garden of the bungalow in Bournemouth. It was a sloping garden rising up from the patio and at the top of it were a couple of apple trees. Around one of them he'd built a wooden structure to house his small flock. It was more fortress than hen-house, tiered with a ladder running up to the first floor, where there were three nest boxes, above which, on a second floor, were roosting perches. All interwoven between the branches of the apple tree. A masterclass in innovation. And his hens seemed to enjoy a contented life up there, the product of their contentment being a clutch of brown eggs every day, each one carefully dated in fine pencil by Dad before being placed in date-order on the rack inside the fridge door. Heaven forbid if you used one out of the order in which they had been laid – in the fridge that is – though I suspect if he'd been able to monitor the individual bird responsible for production of a particular egg that would have been noted as well. Dad also kept an exercise book recording the number laid each day; and like his birds, he meticulously kept it up to scratch.

I was a little apprehensive about seeing Anna's birds and could happily have chickened out. It wasn't so much the thought of examining the birds, more the mess that might be incurred in doing so. Feathers and droppings on the loose seemed likely. And that would not please Mandy, our senior nurse.

A few months back, I'd treated a sheep in my consulting room. It had scattered piles of droppings, a trail of them leading through from the waiting room. Mandy – a stickler for cleanliness which sometimes bordered on the obsessive – had been sent into a complete tizz. Metaphorical feathers flew then, so I could anticipate a ruffling of Mandy's should I have to admit the chickens for any reason – let alone the foul language it might generate.

The birds arrived in a large cardboard box which Anna heaved on to the consulting table. 'My four Ms,' she declared.

'Yes. Your four hens,' I replied.

'No, Paul, they're my four Ms,' she firmly corrected me. It was the way she said it, combined with the jerking forward of her neck, chin thrust out, that I suddenly had visions of Tim as a hen-pecked husband.

Once she had untied the string wrapped round the box and lifted the lid, four heads promptly popped up and eight beady eyes stared at me quizzically. Anna tapped each one on the head. 'Martha, Mavis, Matilda and Mabel. My four Ms.'

'Er... yes. I see,' I mumbled. Though I didn't really. Each bird looked identical to me. Red comb and wattles. Reddish-brown plumage. I hazarded a guess as to their breed. 'Rhode Island Reds?' That was a mistake if ever there was.

'Warrens.'

Once more put in my place. 'So, Anna, what seems to be the problem with your Warrens?'

Anna pushed a lock of grey hair behind her ear before answering. 'Martha's moulting heavily. Much more than normal. And the others are also losing quite a lot of feathers.'

The chickens jostled against each other, softly clucking, their heads jerking to and fro as they peered over the edge of the box. I couldn't remember which was Martha, took pot luck and lifted one out.

'That's Mavis,' said Anna.

Mavis got bundled back in amidst a cloud of feathers. I lifted up another.

'Matilda,' I was informed.

I dropped her back. The third squawked indignantly as I hoisted her up.

'You've got Mabel.'

I lifted out the last one. 'Martha?'

'Correct.'

The hen flapped her wings wildly. In the torrent of down that erupted into the air, I sneezed and lost my grip on her. She sailed on to the consulting table, skidded across the smooth surface like a drunken ice skater, careered against the side of the box and knocked it off the table as she disappeared over the edge. The other three birds tumbled out of the box, clucking in alarm.

As if a quilt had suddenly burst, the room filled with feathers. In a blinding snowstorm of down, Anna and I careered around attempting to round them up. Suddenly the consulting room door shot open. Through the fog of feathers, I saw the disapproving face of Mandy and heard her loud 'Tut' above the squawks of the hens before the door slammed shut again. So no offer to re-box them. Thank you, Mandy. That decided it. It was me getting my feathers ruffled, not her. In a hissy fit, I decided then and there to admit the hens for further examination and make damn sure it was Mandy who would assist.

With the chickens tipped into a spare kennel, I watched them strut round, their heads twisting to one side as they eyed their reflections in the steel feeding bowls. I then I called Mandy. She appeared, her crisp, white apron crackling against her fresh, green uniform. I pointed to moth-eaten Martha.

'See that rather scraggy one over there? Could you please catch her and bring her through to the prep room.'

Mandy's eyes narrowed. Her lips pursed. A look of thunder clouded her face. 'I'll get Lucy to help you.'

I shook my head. 'No... No... She's only a trainee nurse. You're so much more experienced at dealing with difficult animals. You do it please, if you don't mind.'

Her black look showed she clearly did mind. I smiled sweetly at her and then quickly shot out to the prep room, where I stood listening to the squawks, swear words and rattle of kennel bars as Martha was rounded up. Mandy eventually staggered in, the bird pinned tightly under her arm. She was breathing heavily, her apron creased and smeared, her hair smothered in feather dust. She blew a feather off her lip and levered Martha on to the table, her hand gripping the bird's legs together while her elbow ensured one wing stayed wedged in place while the other was stretched out for me to examine the under-surface. All very expertly done. I have to admit, Mandy did know her stuff. Only I felt perilously close to being the one she'd stuff. When I had finished my examination of Martha's plumage and skin, I allowed Mandy to scoop the bird back up.

'All done then?' she said with a thin smile.

'Er... no. I'd like you to catch up the other hens for me.' If looks could kill, the one Mandy shot me would have had me plucked, stuffed and ready for roasting – especially if she knew that I'd already sussed out what the problem was. But I thought it worth the effort – well Mandy's effort anyway – to check the other three hens just to make sure.

Her lips narrowed until they almost disappeared into her chin.

'Very well, if you insist.'

I nodded.

And yes, they had the same problem. Lice. I'd seen a few crawling through Martha's feathers and had spotted several clusters of nits.

When Anna collected her chickens and the medication to fumigate the hen-house and treat the birds, she presented me with six dark brown, speckled eggs.

That made me feel guilty about how I had treated Mandy. She hadn't really deserved it. Not nice of me. Rather juvenile in fact. So I decided I needed to make amends. Apologise somehow without losing too much face. So that lunch-time, I went down to the newsagent at the bottom of the Green, next to Bert's Bakery, and bought her a box of chocolates. I left this in the tea-room; and with it, a card apologising for being such a nitwit.

After all said and done, like it or not, Mandy really did rule the roost. And that was the problem. It was sometimes difficult to tolerate her rather bossy manner. It had added to the difficulties I'd had with Lucy, affecting my relationship with the junior nurse over the past year. She'd constantly felt she was the underdog. Never fully getting the appreciation she deserved – in her work – clashing with Mandy: and in her love life – clashing with me. However, recently it seems she had gradually found her feet in the hospital. Her working relationship with Mandy had stabilised. They now respected each other's virtues – and worked better together as a result.

As to Lucy's relationship with me? How did she view that? Difficult to tell. She kept very much to herself when working in my presence. Polite. Respectful. Doing her duty. No indication of her feelings towards me. Perhaps she had none. They most likely died the moment she left Willow Wren – the practice cottage we'd shared for seven months – and moved back into the flat over the hospital. Since then, I'd found solace elsewhere. In the arms of Jodie, Crystal and Eric's daughter. Which was fun but I suspected only temporary. Jodie was the sort of girl who had itchy feet. And was likely to do a runner soon – find herself another soulmate.

And then?

Then, maybe I'd find out what was truly missing in my life.

Could it still be Lucy?

The coming months would tell.

2

This Little Piggy Went...

One scorching August afternoon – a Thursday – my half-day off from duty – I was cocooned in a bed of flattened yellow corn on the edge of a vast swathe of wheat that undulated in sheets of rustling swirls across the Downs to the north of Westcott – Downs that heat-haze shimmered under an ultramarine sky. It was a beautiful scene of pastoral bliss.

I was alone – Jodie having wanted to go over to Brigstock with some old six-form friends of hers and spend the time dipping in and out of the sea whilst, in between, sunbathing on the resort's pebbly beach – a beach which would have been packed sardine-like with masses of other sun worshippers intent on doing the same. Not for me. I wanted some peace and quiet. A contemplative time to myself. Even if it meant missing out on a rough and tumble in the corn with Jodie.

But I wasn't to get it – the peace and quiet, I mean.

I'd dropped my rucksack containing a couple of ham sandwiches wrapped in cling film, a packet of peanuts and a bottle of water, dragged off my T-shirt, kicked my sandals to one side, and hesitated for a moment, deliberating whether to yank my shorts and boxers off as well. The spot I'd chosen was off the beaten track, some way from the South Downs Trail with its steady trickle of walkers.

Stretched out naked, I'd be alone, out of sight, and could commune with Mother Nature in whichever way I desired.

Be as one with her.

I could already imagine her saying, 'Feel the warmth of my fingers running down the length of your body.' Mmm...

'Allow me to wrap you in my sultry embrace.'

Mmm...

'Lie back, Paul,' she'd whisper. 'Let my hot breath blow over you.'

Yes...

'Lick your nipples...'

Yes... oh yes.

'Course down your torso and swirl round your...'

I stripped immediately and sank back into the flattened corn with a deep sigh of expectation, waiting for Mother Nature to do her thing.

I don't know what it is about nude sunbathing but it does seem that whenever you bring out something normally kept under wraps, it makes it easier to bare your soul at the same time. And boy, did I need to bare mine. I'd been going through a rough patch of late, what with the heavy work load at Prospect House and my fall-out with Lucy. I felt as threshed as the wheat surrounding me would be in a couple of weeks' time.

Not that I made a habit of habitually exposing myself whenever I reached an emotional low. And definitely not in the company of others wishing to feel liberated from the incumbencies of modern living. That sling-your-hook-zip-toggles, let-it-all-hang-out mentality wasn't for me. A no-go area.

Rather like the section of pebbly beach that the council has cordoned off over in Brigstock for those that wished to air their differences in a stiff sea breeze. Not a place I'd want to hang out in. Bit like being in a geometry lesson: questions of shape, size and relative position with one's protractor encompassing the scene, assessing the variety of triangles from an obtuse angle. All 'pi' in the sky as far as I was concerned.

But here, up on the Downs, in solitary splendour, I felt at ease with myself. Pythagoras eat your heart out.

Above me arced a dazzling ultramarine sky.

The brown, whistling whirling of a skylark.

Tiny white dots of cloud.

White fluffy clouds in a cluster.

Hanging on a breeze to dry.

Those words hung like those clouds in my brain. Drifted through as murmured memories. I closed my eyes and drifted with them. They danced to a tune that sent me spinning back to the time when my gran, who lived with us when I was in my early teens, used to sing one particular song over and over again until it became etched in my mind. A song by one of her favourite singers of the sixties, the light entertainer, Max Bygraves. He'd croon:

'Up there the sun is a big yellow duster

Polishing the blue, blue sky.'

I could hear my gran joining in, her voice crystal clear even though she was, back then, in her early nineties.

'Say what you will, the countryside is still...' she'd chortle.

'The only place where I could settle down...'

Oink.

'Troubles there are so much rarer...'

Oink... Oink...

'OUT of town...'

Plop... Plop... The liquid sound of evacuating faeces.

Oh shit.

Through my drowsy stupor, eyelids struggling to open, I became aware of a twitching disc – a snout – the wrinkled end of which looked like one of those instruments you use to clear blocked drains. Behind it, a pair of golden eyes glinted, and folded black ears drooped down each side of a very black porcine face.

There was another loud serenade of oinks and plops with a few fruity farts thrown in as the pig that had emerged from the corn did a rumba with my rucksack and tossed it into the air. Peanuts showered out to be rapidly hoovered up with further oinks of pleasure. The creature then swung its snout round and started snuffling between my thighs.

'Oh, no you don't missy,' I muttered and rolled out of reach to scrabble to my feet.

The pig then switched to executing a fandango. Like a flamenco dancer, head thrown back, rose clenched tightly in teeth. Only instead of a rose, it was my boxer shorts dangling from her mouth, rhythmically being waved from side to side.

The pig was a medium-sized porker. A 'saddleback'. Female. Black with the characteristic band of sparse white hair over her shoulders and running down both front legs.

'Now, my girl, where the hell have you come from?' I asked myself as her black tail knotted up into a question mark of her own.

As I stood pondering on the porker, looking for an answer, she dropped my boxers – no doubt disappointed at finding no nuts in them (mine were now safely secreted, commando-style, within hastily donned shorts) – and emitted a long, ear splitting squeal. The sound was like a group of bandy-legged flamenco dancers with dodgy castanets. It certainly rattled me.

I began to have an inkling of what pig I was dealing with here.

The Rymans' Miss Piggy. I'd had to attend to her when she'd had difficulty in farrowing. She was a known escapologist. The Houdini of the porcine world. In fact her owners, Jill and Alex Ryman, were rather proud of their pig's capabilities to up sticks – or rather up fence poles, paddock rails and electric netting – in her quests for pastures new. A pig has a great digging and uprooting tool in the disc of its nose. And Miss Piggy was very adept at putting her nose to good use, trenching across the paddocks and out under the fences surrounding them. The POWs of Stalag Luft III, famed for their abilities to escape that 2nd World War camp, had nothing on her tunnelling techniques.

Okay. The question now was, 'What do I do next?'

A plan of action was required.

I gingerly stepped forward again and snatched up my rucksack. Mobile phone in zipped inner pocket was still in situ. Good. I could phone the practice and get Beryl to contact the Rymans and see if their Miss Piggy had gone walkabout. Within five minutes I'd verified that this was indeed the case, and that one of the Rymans would meet me in the car park at the foot of the Downs here as soon as they could. Mind you, there was still the problem of getting Miss Piggy home, whether from up here or down in the car park.

I decided that problem would be best tackled in the car park, assuming I could entice Miss Piggy down. The ham sandwiches in their cling film wrapping were still squashed in the bottom of the rucksack. Excellent.

I pulled them out and waved them at the sow.

'Let's get moving eh, Miss Piggy?'

And move she did.

She suddenly transformed into a black barrage balloon.

A jet of brown, foul smelling sludge burst from her back end, propelling her forward as she launched herself at me. A pig on the loose in every sense of the word.

I managed to side-step her to snatch up my muck-splattered T-shirt and sandals but in the process trod in a very smelly pile of shit, feeling it squirt warmly up between my toes. And the smell. No need for me to raise a stink. Miss Piggy was doing it very nicely on my behalf, thank you.

I lurched along the side of the cornfield, with her close on my heels, prancing from side to side, squealing with apparent delight. I know pigs are highly intelligent and have plenty of character. They make people want to laugh out loud with joy in the way they can skitter along on their tiptoe hooves, tails perkily coiled. But this porcine really did seem to be hamming it up at my expense. And I felt it was no laughing matter.

Once at the top of the field and on to the white chalk path that ran alongside it, I stopped and leaned against a fence post, exhausted from the heat, perspiring heavily. Miss Piggy also stopped and with a grunt, poked the bottom of my rucksack. A slice of ham was clearly required and I duly obliged. 'Well cured, honey roast, no added water,' I muttered as I watched her gulp the sandwich down with further grunts of satisfaction.

I slid my feet into my slippery, smelly sandals and decided the T-shirt was just too rancid to wear;

but with it draped over my shoulders to keep some of the sun off my back, I started to work my way down the steep track.

Miss Piggy hesitated at the top of the path above me, her head swinging from side to side, haloed by the sun behind her. She raised a polished trotter and set it down tentatively on top of a rut. The chalk, dry and crumbly from the heat of the past few days, collapsed under her weight. Her other front trotter flailed in the air, her back legs caved in under her, and suddenly 200 kilos of pork was spinning rapidly down the path towards me. Help! I was about to be flattened by a massive ham roll. There was an urgent need to save my bacon, if not hers.

I've never seen a rotating pig except a hog roast on a spit. So this revolving sow was a revelation as a ball of trotters, snout, tail and ears spun past me and plummeted into a bank of brambles at the bottom of the path. I slithered down to where Miss Piggy lay on her side, flanks heaving like bellows, silent. Surely she must have injured herself? A fractured leg? Internal injuries? But apparently not, as with an almighty snort, she flailed her trotters in the flattened brambles, before heaving herself to her feet, looking none the worse for wear, apart from a graze across her shoulder which oozed a bit of blood. Amazing.

Amazing too that she hadn't forgotten there was another ham sandwich in the offing, since she trotted up to me with a snuffling snort as if to say, 'How about it then?'

So with sandwich held high out of snout reach, the two of us negotiated the remaining stretch of narrow footpath with its banks of brambles and nettles either side. Eventually we stumbled out on to the small gravelled area where I was parked and, in the process, scaring a border collie that had been directing a stream of urine over the front tyre of my car. He raced back to his owners, a middle-aged couple having a picnic next to their silver Toyota, a blanket spread over the grass. Picnic basket open. A Thermos. Two china cups. Two plates – a pork pie on each one. How apt. And too irresistible for Miss Piggy who scooted across and made short work of the pies while the couple barricaded themselves in their car, and looked out aghast as the sow noisily hoovered the blanket and cracked crockery under trotter.

Still, it gave me the chance to unlock my car and swing the boot open where I quickly rummaged through the mountain of vet gear – boots, smock, black bag, plastic gloves – to unearth a rope suitable to throw round the pig's neck and harness her. Well that was my intention. But not Miss Piggy's. No way.

Even though she had her snout buried in a plastic tub of Tesco trifle as I approached, it wasn't a sufficient distraction to prevent her from wheeling away from me, and trotting off down the lane towards the main road, carton wedged firmly on her nose.

Oh Lord, I thought, that's all I need. A pile-up on the main road. Pork chops and spare ribs all round.

It was the collie that came to my rescue. He'd been watching intently, crouched, shoulders down, head forward. Suddenly he swiftly glided forward and slid past Miss Piggy, turning a few feet in front of her to block her way. With a squeal she ground to a halt, flapped her ears and stamped the ground crossly with her front trotters. Clearly the collie had put her snout out of joint. He, meanwhile, had very slowly advanced forward, placing one paw stealthily in front of the other. With another sharp bellow of disgruntlement, Miss Piggy sprang, turned, and came trotting furiously back up the lane, the collie snapping at her hocks.

I was smiling, watching all of this. Great fun. Highly entertaining. But I felt the grin fall from my face as the sow was hustled past me, herded down the side of my car to the open back, where a nip to her ankles made her spring up and land with a crash in the boot. The force of her landing caused the boot to drop shut with a sharp click.

The couple emerged from their car, bemused, bewildered and very bothered. Both were extremely apologetic.

'So, so sorry,' said the man. 'Shep's never done anything like that before.'

His wife smiled weakly. 'At least you've got your piggy back. She seems quite settled.' She nodded in the direction of my car where Miss Piggy, having tossed some of my gear around to make a nest, had sunk in to it, head resting over the front seat. Great.

Just at that moment, a green, mud-splattered Land Rover swept into the car park and out jumped Jill Ryman closely followed by her two children, Emily and Joshua, both still in their green and grey school uniforms. Miss Piggy gave a friendly 'Oink' as Jill and the kids ran up to my car.

'Where did you find her?' asked Jill, who, despite her fuse-wire build, had no difficulty in helping me to haul Miss Piggy out of the boot. The sow rubbed her left shoulder against Jill's overalls and gave another contented grunt as Jill pulled a halter out of her pocket and slipped it over Miss Piggy's head.

'Up there.' I pointed to the chalk path winding down the side of the Downs.

'We've been mithsing you,' lisped Emily, peering at Miss Piggy through metal-rimmed glasses, while reaching out to scratch the sow's right shoulder. 'You're a naughty girl. But we still love you to bits.'

Joshua, the older of the two kids, at around nine years of age, stood back, his dark eyes fixed on the sow, his face serious.

'She'll come a cropper one of these days,' he said.

His words were prophetic.

A few days later there was a call through to the hospital.

'Alex Ryman's on the phone,' said Beryl, cupping her hand over the receiver, 'Miss Piggy's had an accident and is in a bad way. Can he bring her in straightaway?'

I was skimming through my list of Monday morning appointments – booked solid until 10.30 – followed by the customary crop of routine ops – three cat speys, a dog castration and a couple of dentals. Not much leeway to squeeze in a pig. But I knew the Rymans wouldn't have bothered us unless it was something serious.

I nodded. 'Tell him "Yes" but he might have to wait.'

Alex screeched into the hospital car park in his battered Land Rover twenty minutes or so later. To make it in that time from Chawcombe must have meant a high speed drive over the Downs. So things were serious. That 'serious' was etched over his face as he tore in, his tangle of coal-black hair and wild dark eyes adding to the sense of panic that immediately enveloped reception.

'Okay, Alex, let's go and take look,' I said, and dashed out with him to the car park where he threw open the back of the Land Rover. I peered in expecting to see the black-coated shape of Miss

Piggy. But what I saw was a lump of sand. A breathing large lump of sand, piled in one corner.

'Yes, it's Miss Piggy,' said Alex. 'She got out this morning and wandered up to the gravel pits.'

'And... don't tell me... she fell in.'

Alex nodded glumly. 'Some of the guys working there managed to drag her out. But she was in a bad way. And as you can see, still is.'

I clambered into the back of the Land Rover and edged over to the sand-covered sow. She was lying on her right side, neck and front legs stretched out, making soft bubbling snorts with every shallow breath she took; and completely oblivious to my approach. I ran my hand down her bristly flank. It was cold and clammy. All pointed to a very shocked pig. But that was not all.

'Reckon she's done her hock in,' muttered Alex. 'Looks all twisted.'

I'd already seen that her uppermost left hind leg was sticking out at a funny angle from the point of the hock down. It didn't look good. Not good at all.

As if Alex was reading my mind, he said, 'Is she a goner?'

'Well, she's in a pretty bad state.' My voice trailed off, not wishing to admit to the fact. At the same time Emily's voice echoed in my head from when I'd last seen her with Miss Piggy. 'We love you to bits,' she'd said. I turned to Alex. 'Let's see what we can do.'

I levered myself back out of the Land Rover just as Mandy and Lucy appeared at the top of the steps, holding between them the hospital's portable stretcher – a canvas sheet supported by two poles threaded through the sides. They'd obviously been alerted by Beryl to the emergency and, no doubt, had everything geared up, ready and waiting for whatever I decided to do. It was on occasions like this that the two nurses really did pull together.

With the stretcher rolled out on the ground behind the Land Rover, we all braced ourselves for the task ahead – to lever the recumbent Miss Piggy out.

'Look, I tell you what,' said Alex, 'why don't you two girls get in the front and push while Paul and I pull from the back.'

With the sow being the piggy in the middle, I thought as Mandy and Lucy did as instructed and leaned over the front seats to begin pushing against Miss Piggy's back. Alex wrapped his arm over the sow's head and began easing her backwards, with me at her rear end, hands grasping her right leg above the hock, slowly hauling in the same direction. Inch by inch we eased her back, the two nurses clambering over the seats to continue pushing as we got her to the tailgate, ready to lever her down on to the stretcher. All the time, there was barely any recognition from the inert Miss Piggy that she was being pushed and shoved – other than an occasional muted squeal, just audible above her stentorian breathing.

'Now for the difficult bit,' I gasped, pausing to catch my breath.

'Shouldn't be a problem, there's four of us,' declared Mandy giving me one of her customary hard stares. Lucy remained silent though I saw the slight pursing of her lips as she caught my eye and I guessed what she was thinking.

Still, though I might have made a pig's ear of my relationship with her, this was no time to reflect on it with a real live porker to contend with. Well, a pig that was just alive. And in need of prompt treatment to ensure she stayed that way.

With as much grunting as Miss Piggy might have made, the four of us managed to roll her out and ease her down on to the stretcher. Then with each of us crouched down, holding one end of the poles, Alex commanded, 'One... two... three... four. Hey, ho, up she goes.'

And up we went, knees straightening, arms bending. Over the drive, up the steps, into reception to receive a squirt of 'Summer Bouquet' from Beryl, then stagger on past her and down into the X-ray room.

It only needed one radiograph of the hock to reveal what I had suspected. A dislocation. A separation of the end of the tibia from the collection of small bones that made up the hock.

'No breaks that I can see,' said Mandy staring over my shoulder at the X-ray plate on the viewing screen. She pointed to the tarsals below the point of the hock. 'They seem fine.'

'Er... yes, they do,' I said, forcing back a bubble of irritation.

'Crystal would probably splint it. Will you?' Mandy asked.

Another bubble popped.

'Uhm... probably,' I reluctantly agreed.

'Crystal would definitely.'

Two more bubbles popped in rapid succession.

This was just typical of Mandy. The same scenario had cropped up many times in the past twelve months. Crystal this... Crystal that... Dr Crystal Sharpe BVetMed, BSc, PhD, MRCVS – the driving force in the practice. The one with a firm grip on the wheel. If you dared stand your ground with her you were likely to be flattened, with a large tyre mark over you to show for it. So I soon learnt to tread carefully and attempted to keep my distance from any situation that was likely to cause road rage. But it could be difficult when it involved Mandy. She worshipped the ground Crystal drove on and like today was forever telling me what her boss would do when a challenging case arose.

Bubble... Bubble... Bubble... I was fuming now.

Alex cleared his throat. 'I'll leave you to it,' he muttered.

'I'll let you know how things go,' I called out to his rapidly disappearing back.

Meanwhile, Lucy too had vanished, slipping quietly away to the prep room.

'So?' Mandy turned to me. She did have soft, damson eyes with attractively long eyelashes. But they looked more like sour grapes when she was in one of her moods. Like now.

I hesitated a moment and then said, 'I think plastering the hock will do the job.'

Two spots of red appeared on Mandy's cheeks and her mouth twisted open.

She was about to speak when a voice boomed out from the door. 'Beryl tells me we've a porker with a problem.' In bounced Eric, his shirt half-out of his baggy trousers, his semi-bald head pink and gleaming. He rubbed his hands together. 'So this is Miss Piggy.' He looked down at the prostrate pig. Then up at the X-ray of her hock.

'Ah, yep. A dislocation. So you'll be plastering her no doubt?'

He glanced at my glowering face. Then at Mandy's pinched one. 'Whoops... have I said something wrong?' He glanced back down at Miss Piggy again. 'Best if we get her shunted into the prep room eh?' He grabbed two ends of the poles, Mandy and I grabbed the other two ends, and between us we slid the stretcher through to next door where we found Lucy had set out the plastering kit. No sign of any splints. Good girl.

'Okay. Need to get her knocked out now. Yep? What do you reckon she weighs?'

'A good 150 kilos plus,' I suggested.

'Easily. But let's err on the side of caution and go for that.' Eric turned to Mandy, holding out his right hand to take the bottle of anaesthetic solution she was offering.

He peered at the label as she said, 'It's what Crystal would use.'

'I'm not Crystal,' he snapped, clicking his fingers impatiently. 'Ketamine on its own's not going to be very helpful here, is it Paul?' He looked at Mandy as he spoke. 'It won't allow the muscles to relax sufficiently for us to yank the hock back into place.' He continued to stare at Mandy as her cheeks went redder and redder. 'So get us some Diazepam would you? We'll mix up a cocktail.'

Did I detect a slight flounce of the shoulders as Mandy turned sharply and headed over to the medicines cabinet, unlocking it to remove the bottle of muscle relaxant Eric had requested.

I don't know about the pig, I thought, but a shot of Diazepam might have done Mandy some good. She needed relaxing. Boy... was she uptight.

While we waited for the injected cocktail to take effect, Mandy and Lucy washed down Miss Piggy's rear, rinsing off the sand, paying particular attention to the damaged left leg, patting it dry once they had finished.

'Okey-dokey,' said Eric, stuffing his shirt in the waistband of his trousers. 'I'll leave you to it, Paul. If you need any help, just give me a shout. I'll be up in the office.'

Right, I thought. Here we go, Paul. Pull-a-pig time.

With Mandy and Lucy positioned behind Miss Piggy's back – Mandy's arms were linked under

Miss Piggy's left shoulder while Lucy tucked her right arm under the sow's left groin – both nurses tensed, ready for the tug of war that was to ensue. Lucy looked at me and smiled. Mandy remained po-faced.

'Okay, girls, I'm going to start pulling on the leg now. Brace yourselves.' The problem with any dislocation is that with ligaments torn, bones overlap. So I was going to have to stretch that leg out in the hope that the bones in Miss Piggy's hock would snap back into place. In theory it shouldn't have been too difficult. In practice...

Ten minutes later, I felt as if I had been put through a mangle, squeezed dry of energy. I'd pulled, pushed, levered, rotated Miss Piggy's leg through all points of the compass, waiting desperately for that magical sound – a 'clunk' – which would have meant the joint had finally been repositioned. But no. No clunk. Just a leg that remained obstinately floppy.

I leaned back on my heels and sighed. Lucy flashed me a brief smile of sympathy. Mandy said brusquely, 'I'll go and get Eric shall I?'

'Proving a bit of a bugger, is she?' said Eric, when he breezed in. 'She's a well-muscled lady so I'm not too surprised.' He knelt down and tucked up Miss Piggy's front leg. There was no resistance. 'Still well relaxed. Jolly good.' He shuffled along to her damaged hind leg and raised the hock allowing it to rest in his right palm, while taking a firm grip of the fetlock. 'Okay, Lucy, I'm going to start pulling now, so make sure you keep hold of her thigh.' Lucy nodded, her arm once again locked around Miss Piggy's groin. Eric gave a sharp yank. There was a grunt from Miss Piggy and a clunk from her hock. He carefully levered her trotter back and forth, flexing the leg cautiously. No crunching. Everything seemed to be in place.

He scrambled up looking embarrassed at how easy it had been. 'Just had a lucky break,' he declared, and then chuckled when he realised what he'd said. 'That's the way it goes sometimes.'

Okay, I was cross with myself for not having been able to correct the dislocation myself, but I needed now to focus on plastering the leg to ensure the hock didn't dislocate again. Surely I couldn't louse that up. Or could I?

The sour look Mandy gave me before she excused herself and left the prep room to make up some prescriptions suggested I could.

Lucy had made sure everything required was to hand.

'I'll stay to help,' she said quietly.

I have to admit I was a bit shaky. Partially due to the effort I'd just expended, partially due to nerves. It was the first time I'd put a plaster cast on a pig. But it wouldn't be any different to putting a cast on a dog or cat's limb, would it? Of course not. But – confession time – I'd never put a cast on one of them either. This was going to be my first plastering. Hence the jitters. What if I put it on too tight? The leg could swell. Cellulitis could set in, the infection rampaging up the leg leading to septicaemia – meningitis even. Catastrophic. And if applied too loose, Miss Piggy could flick it off and we'd be back to where we'd started. Oh Lordy.

'Paul.' It was Lucy holding out a tube of stockinette.

'Sorry, yes.' I took it from her, bent down and unrolled a sufficient length to slide up past Miss Piggy's trotters and over her hock. Lucy crouched next to me and cut off the end. Her forearm briefly touched mine and I caught the delicate scent of the

41

perfume she always used to apply before leaving me for work each day. *Mystique,* I think it was called. Memories.

'Paul.' Lucy had reached up to the prep table and was now handing me a roll of cast padding. I began to unwind the cotton from the fetlock upwards, pulling it tight and overlapping each turn. As it unfolded so too did more memories of the good times I'd had with Lucy. I forced them back as the cotton was curled over the hock and back down the leg. Another leg presented itself just inches from my face. A slender, trim calf. Lucy's. She had stood up and was leaning across me to reach for a roll of plaster casting which she'd been soaking in warm water. I felt stirred, much like the plaster.

'I'll just give it a squeeze for you,' she murmured, looking down at me.

'What?'

Lucy rolled on to my palm a lump of warm plaster of Paris.

We had thought of spending a weekend in Paris once. See the sights. Eiffel Tower, Seine, *Mona Lisa.* Stop it, Paul.

Concentrate. Concentrate.

I began to apply the plaster roll, slowly unfolding it up her leg, making sure each turn overlapped; and smoothing the plaster flat with my fingers, tracing over the delicate turn of her ankles and the plump swell of her calf.

'Paul.'

With a jolt, I realised I'd reached Miss Piggy's hock and so began retracing my steps in less passionate mode.

'And again?' Lucy was handing me a second roll of warm plaster to repeat the procedure.

'Oh, yes, please.'

Once finished, I got to my feet, feeling very stiff. And that was just from putting the cast on. But I had to admit, I was pleased with myself. I felt I'd done a good job. With no small thanks to Lucy of course. But then we'd always worked well together. Same in our private lives. Just a shame the latter had all recently fallen apart. Something I hoped wouldn't happen to Miss Piggy's plaster in the ensuing days.

With her slid into a large pen down in the ward with the help of Mandy and Eric, it was just a matter of waiting until she came round from the anaesthetic and seeing how she'd cope hobbling around with a plastered hock. She actually did remarkably well. And within twenty-four hours, the Rymans were over to collect her.

She received rapturous greetings from the whole family.

'Mith Piggy... our dear Mith Piggy,' said Emily, throwing her arms round the sow's neck once she'd been led up into reception, under the disapproving eye of Beryl who hovered nearby, a finger on her 'Summer Bouquet'.

Even the serious face of young Joshua creased into a smile as he gave Miss Piggy a tickle under the base of her right ear, to which she responded by twisting her head to one side and emitting grunts of pleasure.

So ecstatic were the Rymans that I half-expected them to burst into song as they had done last year when Miss Piggy had recovered from a difficult farrowing.

Then Emily had skipped round singing:

'Our Mith Piggy goes Oink... Oink... Oink.

Oink... Oink... Oink.' With all the family joining in at that point.

But no such sing-song was forthcoming today, curtailed I felt by the smothering effect of several blasts of 'Summer Bouquet' that were squirted over our heads and which rapidly turned us all into walking lavatory blocks.

As I watched the Rymans drive away with Miss Piggy's snout sticking out from the top of a back window, I did wonder if having a plaster on would curtail her wanderings.

It didn't.

The following week's edition of the *Westcott Gazette* had a picture of her outside Chawcombe village hall into which she'd trotted during a rehearsal of the local rep's production of *A Midsummer Night's Dream*.

Finley O'Connor had been in punning good form yet again with the headline: *Miss Piggy. A New Cast Member.*

Made me think that next time she could perhaps audition for *Ham-let.*

3

Air Way Go

My plastering of Miss Piggy, working in close proximity to Lucy, had stirred memories of our time together. Made me cast my mind back. Not that I was comparing our junior nurse to the likes of a sow. No way. Lucy was a hazel-eyed, blonde-haired elfin creature. Modest. Mild mannered – a delight to work with. Always helpful. The list could have gone on and on. Endless. So why the hell had we split up? I realised now that much of it had been to do with me being me. In fact, too much me... me... me... and not enough of her. Self-centred was how Lucy put it. No consideration of her feelings. Me too busy looking after me. The result? Me ultimately losing her.

Though she had now stormed out of my life, I wasn't entirely bereft of company. Well, initially anyway. Jodie had appeared on the scene in the early part of the summer having just returned from a twelve month voluntary stint doing 'good' out in Caracas or some such place. Now she was doing me 'good'. I had been a bit smitten by her I have to confess. Partially due to the striking resemblance she had to her mother. She had Crystal's copper curls, the dimpled chin, Cupid's bow mouth. Features I'd fallen for in the senior partner when I first started working at Prospect House despite her being twenty or so years older than me. Not that Crystal had the slightest interest in me of course, other than ensuring I got on with my duties – using my hands, not to hold hers, but to whip out wombs, testicles and rotten teeth.

It was no real surprise when Jodie suddenly decided to take off with some mates and head for Goa for the rest of the summer. That was like her. Impulsive. I'd just been a quick fling. A filler-in.

But it left me feeling down as it made me think how stupid I'd been to lose Lucy.

So, for a good part of August I walked under a cloud – and not of the white fluffy Max Bygraves' variety. But a sombre, grey cloud dripping with self-pity. Meanwhile everyone else took advantage of the glorious weather – a series of sun-scorched August days. Office girls in their lunch breaks dotted the parched Green over the road from the animal hospital, sporting themselves to catch the sun's rays while eyes hidden behind dark glasses, feasted on their factored limbs thinking what jolly good sorts they were.

During that period of hot weather, Beryl took it upon herself to act as a jolly good sort herself. Not that she was a 'jolly hockey sticks' sort of woman. Not our Beryl. She of the dyed raven hair, crumpled Kleenex complexion and wart on chin, complete with its solitary hair. I could never have pictured her chasing round a hockey pitch in short grey flannelled skirt, whacking balls with a stick. However, she was a game old girl and, as receptionist of twelve years standing at Prospect House, exercised her ability and know-how to run the practice with a rod of iron; and certainly had the balls to whack anyone she thought wasn't pulling their weight. Besides which, she was a very intuitive lady. She'd have been a good goalie in hockey matches. Nothing seldom got past her.

So it was at her suggestion that she and I took to the Green at lunch times that August, bearing baguettes from Bert's Bakery.

One such Wednesday, found us up at the top end of the Green, away from the far end which overlooked the municipal tennis courts and where the benches were constantly crowded with elderly gentlemen watching the balls in play. No doubt this jogged their memories of the times when they could still toss theirs in the air and serve with long firm strokes.

Beryl and I were sitting next to one of the council's miserable threadbare displays of annual bedding plants. Same as last year – a scattering of red geraniums, punctured by pockets of orange marigolds and a smattering of silver cineraria. All looked rather sickly. Blighted. Rather like I felt.

'You seem a bit down,' said Beryl, taking a bite out of her tuna-mayonnaise baguette.

'No, not really,' I replied, taking a chunk out of mine.

Beryl chewed methodically. The silence said it all.

'Well...' I paused. Did I really want to unburden my feelings on her? No, I didn't feel it was appropriate. Not Beryl's business. I'd keep mum. Not say a word.

'It's Lucy, isn't it?' Beryl raised an eyebrow.

'Yes,' I blurted out.

'Thought as much.'

I hunched my shoulders and snatched another bite of my baguette. Damn.

At that moment fate intervened. Disclosure-time delayed until a later date. It was Mandy on my mobile. An RTA had just been brought in. One of

Lady Derwent's elkhounds. Hit by a car. Looked serious.

'Sure. I'll be right over,' I said, leaving Beryl to finish her baguette and digest what little I'd said. Unspoken words left hanging in the air. *Like white fluffy clouds in a cluster.* Oh piss off Max Bygraves.

It took about five minutes for me to sprint back to Prospect House, nipping across the road that ran parallel to the Green, ignoring the toot of a car I dodged in front of. A dash through the rhododendron tunnel, saw me emerging into the hospital car park, where a sharp turn to the left and a leap up the front steps – three at a time – had me hurtling into reception. There I found a very distraught Lady Derwent, weeping her eyes out, with the consoling arm of Lucy round her shoulder. I had only seen her ladyship once before and then only at a distance – the time when she opened Westcott's new shopping precinct. Though short in stature she wasn't short in sophistication. Well-heeled in a green silk two-piece, she had been a picture of elegance – what little you could see of her diminutive frame over the shoulders of the onlookers. A far cry from her appearance now – the blood-splattered Barbour jacket and smeared cords, floods of tears coursing down her cheeks.

'Fredric's been taken down to the theatre,' whispered Lucy over Lady Derwent's shoulder. The accompanying shake of her head and down-turn of her lips suggested I was probably too late to save the dog.

I found the elkhound stretched out, collapsed on the operating table, a shuddering mound of silver-grey husky-like hair. Mandy had a face mask rammed over his muzzle, oxygen pumping in from the anaesthetic machine alongside.

'It doesn't look good,' she said grimly, as I raced up and skidded to a halt next to him.

It certainly didn't.

Fredric's face was fixed with a glassy-eyed stare.

His chest heaved, frantically fighting for air.

No blink reflex.

No pulse when I pressed my fingertips against his femoral artery.

And when I pulled back his lips, his gums were a sickly shade of blue.

All the signs that Fredric was rapidly dying.

Mandy held up a catheter. 'Eighteen gauge okay?'

'Yep.' I snatched it from her and removed the plastic guard.

Fredric's front left leg had already been clipped. Above his elbow, a tourniquet was ready.

I pumped his paw. No vein appeared. I pumped again. And again. A thin blue outline showed itself. Just.

Catheter held over vein. Needle tip just above the skin. I eased it in. Nothing. Bugger. I tried again. A thin trickle of blood appeared.

We're in.

Tourniquet released. Stylet slid out. Capped off. Catheter taped to leg. Bag of lactated Ringer's solution hooked to drip stand. Air bubbles flushed out of tubing. End handed to me. Plug removed from the catheter and replaced with fluid line. Valve on bag opened. Drip started. Phew.

Now Fredric, my lad. Why this horrendous breathing?

I swung my stethoscope over the side of the dog's chest, pushing the bell down through the dense thick coat.

A saw rasped raggedly to and fro in my ears. The sound of air screeching in and out of Fredric's trachea, rattling up and down his windpipe, drowning out any normal lung sounds.

Shit. If it was what I suspected, we really did have a problem here.

'Do you want an X-ray?' Mandy queried.

I shook my head. 'No time.'

'You're going in then?'

'No choice. He's a goner otherwise.' *Going in* meant piercing Fredric's chest to release the air I felt sure was leaking out of his lungs. To pool round them. Trap them in a vice-like grip and stop them from expanding. It was stopping the dog from breathing and he would end up stop-dead.

Mandy sprang into action.

She shaved a square patch of skin over the side of Fredric's chest, the thick silvery hair curling away from her clippers. The area was then scrubbed with Betadine and rinsed with alcohol rub while I donned a pair of surgical gloves, before a thirty-five millilitre syringe and butterfly catheter were slid out of an opened sterilised pack into my hand – my tools for tapping Fredric's chest.

Never having done this before I was scared stiff. Petrified. What if I punctured his lung? What if I severed an artery? Many 'what ifs' tumbled through my mind, but the one that stood out above them all was 'what if I didn't do it?' No question. No answer required.

I took a deep breath and started.

First I counted back and felt for the space between Fredric's fifth and sixth ribs.

'Lignocane?' Mandy was holding up a bottle of local anaesthetic.

'No time.' If I'd waited for that to have taken effect, Fredric could have been dead. Having located the spot between his ribs, I positioned my finger there and with a deep breath, slowly sank the needle in through the skin and muscle. Fredric didn't flinch. Too far gone.

Mandy had taken the syringe from me and was pulling on the plunger as the needle slipped further in.

Suddenly, the barrel of the syringe filled with air.

Yippee. I'd hit the spot.

I kinked off the tubing and only reconnected it once Mandy had flushed out the syringeful of air.

A second syringeful followed.

Then a third. A fourth. And a fifth.

Meanwhile Fredric's chest continued to rise and fall rapidly, his breathing still laboured, seemingly unaffected by the withdrawal of the trapped air. Surely it should be reducing the pressure on his lungs by now? His breathing should be easier. But it wasn't. Worrying. Very worrying.

A sixth syringeful followed. A seventh.

Still no improvement.

By now Mandy was having to pull harder on the plunger to force it back. 'Sorry Paul, it's stopped,' she eventually said through gritted teeth.

'Okay, let me try higher up,' I said, removing the needle and repositioning it.

A little more air was withdrawn. But only half a syringeful. At that point, I felt a scratching sensation at the tip of the needle. Like it was scoring on sandpaper. I'd touched the lining of the lung. There was no more air that I could remove.

'Stop,' I instructed Mandy, who instantly eased the pressure on the plunger.

I pulled out the needle and we both stood there looking down at Fredric, each holding our breath, hoping and praying he wouldn't hold his.

Only he did.

It was a heart-stopping moment when his ribcage shuddered to a halt. Seconds seemed like minutes, seemed like hours, seemed like days, as that ribcage remained stationary. No movement. Just a twitch of the muscles.

'Come on Fredric, come on boy,' I muttered. 'Breathe.'

Then suddenly there was a deep intake of air. His ribcage expanded. Sank down. Rose again as another intake of oxygen occurred. Then with a big sigh, his breathing settled into a rhythmic rate, his ribs moving slowly up and down with each breath.

Mandy removed the oxygen mask and pulled back his lip to reveal healthy, pink mucous membranes.

Fredric gave a deep sigh, stuck out his tongue – a nice pink one – and licked his lips.

I listened to his lungs.

Soft sounds of air moving through.

I listened to his heart.

Lub... Dub. Lub... Dub. Reassuringly normal.

To think he had only been a heartbeat away from death.

Of course, Fredric wasn't out of the woods yet. With a painkiller given, I raised his right hind leg which was hot and swollen. He growled.

'Sorry, matey, sorry,' I murmured.

'X-ray?' asked Mandy.

This time the answer was, 'Yes.'

It revealed a fractured femur, broken in several places.

I knew what Mandy was going to say before she said it. 'Crystal's?'

I didn't disagree. Crystal's. After all, she did all the orthopaedic work. And after all, Lady Derwent was one of her clients.

So I was happy for her to take over.

Let her pick up the pieces – those slivers of femur that needed wiring and pinning.

I'd done my bit.

Like Fredric was doing now, I could breathe easy.

4

Chi This For A Change...

I drove back over the Downs to Willow Wren that evening in a slightly better frame of mind. My skills as a young vet had been put to the test yet again. And I have to admit, I had come through okay despite bucket-loads of self-doubt. Goodness, there'd even been a hint of praise from Mandy – quite something coming from her. As for Lady Derwent – her thanks had been extremely effusive; and had been backed up by a, 'Well done, Paul,' from Crystal before organising to pin and wire Fredric's femur once he'd been stabilized from the accident. No question that she'd do the operation and that it would be overseen in every precise detail by chief honcho, Mandy. I was no longer involved. No matter. They all realised that if it hadn't been for me there wouldn't have been a dog to operate on.

It was as I arrived at Willow Wren and parked on the small area of hard-standing to the front of the cottage, that my problem hit home. Literally, hit home, here at the cottage. The problem was staring me in the face, the evening sun percolating through from the kitchen at the back of the cottage, lighting up the lounge in a pink glow, framed by the front window and visible from where I was sitting in the car. It might have looked pretty as a picture but it was an empty frame. There was nothing in it. Just a shell. A lifeless interior. Oh dear. Seems my mood was darkening as fast as the evening sky.

That empty cottage just reinforced the fact that I was on my own. There was no one to greet me. No one to discuss the day's events with. Not even a pet. Our dear Jack Russell, Nelson, had been killed – run over by Lucy. And when she left, Queenie, the cat, and Bugsie the rabbit, went with her. In a fit of pique I donated our small flock of elderly budgerigars to Westcott Wildlife Park to join their antiquarian cousins who could only manage short flutters from one branch to another before fluffing up, huddled together, like rows of deck-chaired pensioners on Westcott's promenade. The ferrets found a good home and no doubt were now weaving their way through rabbit warrens with practised ease. I did hesitate when it came to Gertie the goose. After all, she had done us proud when she'd alerted us to an attempted break-in. But she'd been more Lucy's pet than mine and remained a constant reminder of her. Sad as it was to see her go, she went amid much honking. From her and me. To cap it all, the two stray cats, Garfield and Push-in, that had adopted Lucy and me, up-tailed and disappeared – presumably to seek out more family-orientated homes.

So here I was bereft of company – human, canine and feline, indeed of any kind. I definitely needed someone or something to lift my mood and prevent the Black Dog of depression from settling on me.

My neighbour, Eleanor Venables, had been doing her best to keep me buoyant with frequent invites to pop round for a cuppa. 'Have a chat over cha,' as she put it.

I did just that the following day. The Saturday of my weekend off duty. Like an elegant Geisha, she'd just poured a mix of her Assam and Earl Grey, the delicate stream of amber liquid streaming out of the spout of her china teapot – one adorned with pink roses – when she said, 'Do you put down the lid of the toilet seat after you've used it?'

My eyes were still on that stream of amber liquid as she spoke.

'Here.' She handed me my tea.

Was the lady taking the piss in asking such a question? Surely I hadn't been invited round to discuss my toilet seat arrangements? I felt myself flush.

She saw my embarrassment and immediately apologised.

'Sorry, Paul. I do get carried away sometimes.'

As she explained, according to her understanding of feng shui – of which she was an advocate – the relevance of having a loo seat raised or lowered only applied to financial concerns. So in my case, only of use if I fell on hard times. I felt myself going even redder at the thought. I might be emotionally constipated but surely this was taking things too far?

'Whoops,' Eleanor exclaimed. 'Putting my foot in it again.'

But it seems she was no dummy when it came to the art of feng shui. And had put some of it into practice in her own cottage before suggesting it might help in mine. A means to create a harmonious environment. Calm my yin. Prevent my yang from spiralling out of control.

'And did it do any good?' asked Beryl, picking a bit of salami out of her teeth with one of her scarlet claws. We were having another of our lunch breaks over on the Green, with me spouting on about my attempts at feng shui.

'Well... I was hoping it would.'

Certainly, I'd thought it worth trying. 'Get some "chi" circulated throughout Willow Wren,' I told Beryl. 'Blow away the negative vibes.'

'What's wrong with just opening a few more windows?' she commented, clearly not impressed. But then it wasn't her yang out of joint.

'It's called acupuncture of the home,' Eleanor had explained to me.

One of her bright ideas was to fill the cottage with plants. Green plants in particular. She herself was an avid gardener and most days in the spring and summer she could be spotted over the garden fence, snipping this, trimming that. She'd give her roses a delicate squirt of fungicide from green paisley-gloved hands, matching the green paisley-patterned boots she always wore whenever she ventured down her garden; and she'd step cautiously from one stepping stone to another should her neatly manicured lawn show the slightest suggestion of dampness underfoot.

I already had a few potted plants around the cottage. There was the giant cheese plant that I'd had in my room in the hall of residence at Bristol, which went with me to the field station during the last two years of the veterinary course, and which now resided in Willow Wren's little hallway-cum-garden room with its French window on to the back patio. In the shady corner of the living room lurked an aspidistra. Of great sentimental value since the original plant had belonged to my grandmother. This was one of several offshoots successfully cultivated by my dad and was in a cracked green and white porcelain pot embossed with bucolic pastoral scenes of rosy cheeked maidens, draped in white linen, languishing beneath blue skies in which *white fluffy clouds in a cluster were hanging on the breeze.* Oh... No... Max, please piss off.

'Green plants will increase negative ions,' Eleanor told me. 'And make you feel better.'

I wondered whether talking to them a la Prince Charles might also help. However, as I told Beryl, to see me sitting with a takeaway in front of my aspidistra telling it about the difficult dog spay I'd done that morning would be a sure sign I'd gone to pot.

'Maybe,' she replied, lighting up a fag. 'But then you did have one that nearly died on you.'

I did remember. How could I forget? Mrs Little's Bo-Bo. The slipped ligature. The blood pouring out of the wound. Only Crystal's intervention saving the dog's life.

Not a tactful time to mention it though, Beryl. You certainly know how to cheer a chap up.

'To be most effective, you'll need to purchase nine green plants,' Eleanor informed me. 'And they should be purchased fresh.'

When I saw Homebase had a half-price offer on some large dumb canes, I drove over to the store and bought a couple, making up the nine plants required with some spider plants, a philodendron and a mother-in-law's tongue. I thought the green off-white variegated leaves of the dumb canes were quite attractive. But was rattled when wheeling them in the trolley out to my car I was stopped by a lady who warned me they were highly toxic. She'd developed a nasty rash after brushing against some broken leaves and getting sap on her skin.

I promptly went back into Homebase to buy some rubber gloves before I dared to handle the plants any more. Seems I was about to introduce toxic elements into Willow Wren – so adding to the ones that were already there.

Perhaps I should have given the choice of plants more thought. Gone for some peace lilies. Or sweetheart plants. Though if Lucy had still been there in one of her bad moods, a couple of crown of thorns from this spineless yucca would have been more in keeping.

Problem then was where to put them.

'Place as a group of nine near particular irregularities in the room,' Eleanor instructed.

'And did you?' asked Beryl, puffing out a plume of smoke.

'I tried.'

The main 'irregularity' in Willow Wren happened to be the corner at the top of the landing where you had to sidle from the front bedroom immediately through the adjacent door to the tiny second bedroom and then take three steps across to the bathroom. So the nine plants were positioned in a group at the top of the stairs just inside the main bedroom. It may have been a good spot chi-wise, but it was a bad spot body-wise.

After a couple of nights attempting to get to the loo in the dark, blundering past them, stubbing my toes on the philodendron, developing red eczema on my shins from the dumb canes and getting poked in the goolies by the mother-in-law's tongue, the plants were banished to the hallway. Here they could pump out their negative ions to their hearts' content for all I cared.

Hearing about that tickled Beryl. 'You crazy young man,' she gasped, giving a smoker's hack between laughs.

Another of Eleanor's suggestions was discretely mentioned in an email from her, referring me to a website where appropriate paintings could be perused and purchased based on the feng shui notion that you choose bedroom art of images that you want to see happening in your life. Sounded intriguing.

'And did you go on that site?' queried Beryl, her eye agog.

I had to confess that I did.

'Oh...' Beryl gave me one of her bashed-with-a-brick-owl looks. Rather stunned.

I'd found myself hunched over the computer looking at pornographic – or at least very graphic – paintings of couples making love *Karma Sutra*-style. I stared at a painting of a turbaned gentleman inserting his lingam into the yoni of a spread-eagled courtesan. A coupling not without decorum as it was taking place on a grassy mound bedecked with exquisitely painted flowers.

Not that I mentioned any specific details to Beryl. Just that I'd perused some Indian artwork.

'Oh... really?' she said, thoughtfully.

The site had been called 'Art of Legend India'. It had a perfectly credible introduction explaining the meaning of karma as a sensuous love or emotional feeling of attachment – viewed in Western terms as 'erotica'. As I scrolled down, the information given became a bit more specific. Rather graphic. With a touch of the veterinary about it. I learnt that man is divided into three classes according to the size of his lingam: hare, bull, horse. And women: deer, mare or elephant according to the depth of her yoni. I pondered briefly on which category I'd come under and when hamster sprang to mind I quickly scrolled on down, finding myself in a gallery of paintings with titles such as *Arrow of Love, Bull in a Herd of Cows* and very un-Sanskrit – *Big Boobs are our Tools.*

I continued to slowly scroll through the paintings on the lookout for a coupling that wasn't too risqué but fitted my criteria. I shunned *Both Holes are Busy,* was tempted by *Come Inside Babe,* but eventually plumped for and bought *Are You Satisfied?* in the hope that I could put into practice what the picture depicted when the need arose.

The coupling didn't appear that ambitious; and I reckoned it wouldn't require the athleticism of a stallion or mare to go for that particular ride. Even a hamster could have managed it.

'So did you buy anything?' asked Beryl.

'Er... well... yes.' I described the painting I'd purchased leaving out the more lurid details.

When it arrived, I wasn't too sure whether to let Eleanor have a look. Was she broadminded enough? I wondered. In the end I decided to risk it.

She looked dubiously at the *Karma Sutra*-inspired position depicted on the canvas when it arrived. 'Can't make head or tail of it,' she declared holding it at arm's length.

'That's because you're looking at it upside down,' I said, turning it round for her.

I hung it over the bed – apparently the most effective position for such paintings.

But only for a while.

Every time I retired, the sight of it, as I slipped under the duvet, only reminded me of what I was missing. It became a sore point.

Eventually I discreetly wrapped it in brown paper, stuffed it in a Tesco bag and dropped it off at the local Help the Aged charity shop over in Westcott. Seems it caused quite a stir and was apparently bought within thirty minutes of being hung in the window by an excited elderly gentleman.

Through all of this, Beryl had paid keen attention, especially when I described the painting.

'It had a grassy knoll on it you say?'

'Yes.'

'And the courting couple were on top of it?'

'That's right.'

Beryl hesitated before confessing, 'I know the painting you mean. Ernie Entwhistle saw it down in Help the Aged and bought it for me.'

Ernie Entwhistle? Ah... yes... the gentleman who sadly lost his collie, Ben. He and Beryl had had something going for each other ever since. It was my turn to ogle her, both my eyes agog. 'Really?'

'Yes. He's hung it over my bed for me. It's a bit on the big side. But it just fits.'

Hare, bull or horse I wondered.

Nudge nudge, wink wink.

Though my dabbling with Chinese culture didn't bring me any positive results, dabbling with the owner of a Chinese takeaway did.

It started with a phone call.

A fish on the end of the line. Well, strictly speaking, the owner of a fish on the end of the line. All in a flap.

'It's Mr Chang,' hissed Beryl, cupping one hand over the receiver, while hooking me with the other. 'You know – the owner of the Kowloon Chinese Restaurant and Takeaway. Yes... Yes...' she said, having turned back to the phone while I waited with baited breath. 'I'm sure Mr Mitchell will be able to take a look. Can you bring it in?' There was a murmur of voices at the other end. Beryl looked back up at me. 'You're not having a takeaway tonight by any chance are you?'

It had been on my mind. That or a Tesco's *finest*. A meal for one. I wasn't too fussed about what I had these days now I was on my own. So I shrugged and said, 'Can do.'

That's how I found myself ordering Dim Sum, House Special Kung Fu and Yung Chow fried rice – and while it was cooking, staring into a large aquarium which filled the window of the Kowloon Chinese Restaurant and Takeaway, its owner, Mr Chang at my side.

'See, not velly well,' said Mr Chang, running one hand through the hedgehog spikes of his jet-black hair, his hooded eyes creased with concern, as he tapped the front panel of the aquarium, pointing to a goldfish, static in the middle of the tank while a shoal of smaller brightly coloured guppies circled round it.

I'd first met Mr Chang last summer – just after I'd started at Prospect House – when he'd presented himself at the hospital with a large golden orfe slopping around in a plastic bucket. Mr Chang had told me a car had gone out of control and smashed through the restaurant's window.

'Break glass. Like so.'

He'd raised his hand and brought it down in a karate chop on the consulting table.

'Glass shower in tank. All fish velly frightened. This fish sliced.'

I momentarily had a vision of a fish sliced, ready for battering and then served up with chips. But that orfe had been cut by flying glass and needed stitching up.

No such injury this time round.

I peered into the underwater world where multi-coloured shingle sloped from back to front and in which were anchored vivid red and emerald green plastic fronds of seaweed. Crowded on the shingle were plastic green and pink urchins, several lumps of artificial coral in red and purple, two barrels on rocks, some blue clams, a pink and yellow cave with a cannon sticking out of it – and a mini Roman ruin.

Just to add to the rather queasy effect this conglomeration of coloured plastic tat induced in anyone who unwittingly gazed into the aquarium while waiting for their Satay King Prawns, there was underwater lighting that flooded the aquarium in bilious green. One needed a strong constitution and the balls – not of the sweet and sour chicken variety – to avoid dashing out on to the pavement to throw up.

There were a couple of green-faced clients waiting for their orders, as Mr Chang pointed out the fish he was concerned about. If the greenness of the water didn't make you feel ill then seeing the fish in question suspended in the middle of the tank certainly could have put you off your Dim Sum. Not a pretty sight. It was orange with a raspberry like growth on the top of its head.

'She four year old oranda goldfish,' explained Mr Chang. 'She called Felicity. To bring good luck when first open takeaway. Was velly beautiful.'

I could see she was some sort of goldfish and might have been beautiful once. But not now, not with that bubbly-like orange hood over her head.

'How long has she had that hood?' I asked.

'Now three year.'

'Really? That does seem a rather long time.'

'That normal for oranda.'

'It is?' This was all very puzzling.

'Ah so. Wen grow when two year old.'

'Wen?'

'When two year old,' repeated Mr Chang.

'No. You said a "wen".'

Mr Chang's eyes became slits. Then widened. 'Ah, so solly. That hood normal. Call wen.'

65

I felt myself go a colour to match Felicity. Scarlet. Seems the wen – the orange hood that covered Felicity's head – was a characteristic of orandas. See. You learn something every day.

'But fish not good other side,' Mr Chang was saying.

As he spoke, Felicity was turning daintily round, her four lobed tail fin swirling round her like a veil. But it unveiled something far from dainty on her right flank. Here, there was precious little goldfish left. My appetite for the Yung Chow that awaited me suddenly evaporated as I saw the ugly mass sticking out from Felicity's side. A red, raw stalk of cauliflower.

Seems it had been slowly growing these past four months.

'Not velly nice,' said Mr Chang, shaking his head. 'Customers not like. You chop off?'

Difficult question. If I did, there wouldn't be much of Felicity left.

I left clutching my takeaway, thankful it wasn't fish and chips as I felt it might be chips for Felicity when it came to removing that gross tumour. But I promised to give it a go.

I had visions of Mandy, our senior nurse, rattling a tube of Alka-Seltzers at me as she had done when I stitched up the orfe last summer. That experience had left me floundering and I was determined not to repeat it.

Having warned Mandy that an oranda was coming in, I had the satisfaction of seeing the puzzlement on her face. But when I explained it was a goldfish, the puzzlement was replaced by a smug look as she opened the prep room cupboard and waved a tube of Alka-Seltzers at me. Seems she thought I'd use them again to anaesthetise Felicity. Wrong... Mandy... wrong. No way. I'd done some homework since last year. Armed with my new knowledge I felt I could tackle Felicity's anaesthetic without it being so hit and miss as it was then, when, under her instructions ('It's what Crystal would do,' she'd said), I had lobbed tablets into the bucket containing that orfe without knowing how effective they would be. Mind you the operation to remove Felicity's growth was still going to be a challenge. A big... big... big one.

I had read that with tumours such as the one I was going to tackle, it was provident to get some X-rays done to see that it hadn't spread into the spine or vital organs.

Mandy was surprised when I told her that's what we'd do. I could almost see the 'But Crystal wouldn't...' form on her 0-shaped lips. But she acquiesced silently.

Fish don't bark, bite, scratch, defecate, urinate or shed hair all over you, so taking the radiograph was a doddle.

I covered an X-ray plate with plastic and laid Felicity on it.

Her breathing did become a bit more laboured while we made the exposure but soon returned to normal once she'd been popped back into the bucket of water in which she'd arrived.

I'd never examined an X-ray of a fish before but made sure I'd studied some on the Internet before looking at Felicity's.

Mandy pointed to two tiny white specks on the radiograph. They were in Felicity's head.

'Her otoliths,' I said, relishing my smattering of ichthyological knowledge, waiting to see the look of incomprehension on Mandy's face before I enlightened her.

'Her ear stones – used for balance in the water,' she replied without batting one of her innocent-looking doe eyes. Grrr...

'And see her teeth? Not where you'd expect them.' I pointed to the tiny rows of white triangles at the back of her throat. Not in her mouth.

'Pharyngeal,' remarked Mandy. 'That's why she can't bite.'

Another grrr... I began to suspect I wasn't the only one to have done some Internet research. But at least she was showing interest. Brownie points there.

We both could see Felicity's belly was bloated – full of eggs.

And as if to verify the point, once back in the bucket, Felicity squirted out several hundred tiny fish eggs.

As to the tumour, it was all too obvious on the X-ray. A soft, shadowy white mass. But as far as my inexperienced eye could judge, Felicity's skeleton looked fine – no spread to the spine or kidneys.

So, it was worth trying to operate.

But no Alka-Seltzers this time, thank you Mandy.

In fact, the anaesthetic I used was one especially for fish called MS-22. Felicity was placed in a water bath containing the drug and within three minutes was asleep. Please note Mandy – no fizzing of tablets and eruptions of carbon dioxide. Actually she kept very quiet, having secreted the tube of Alka-Seltzers away. I was conscious of her staring at me. Rather like Felicity – whose eyes, un-lidded, looked up at me as she floated there – wide open and unblinking.

Surgery too was different to last summer, when I laboured with what I thought were blunt needles until Mandy, sharp as ever, pointed out that fish had thick tough skin and so Crystal always used the largest of the suturing needles. No needles today. Thermocautery instead. A forceps-like device with which I was able to cut and control bleeding at the same time. The tumour was whipped off with ease and within fifteen minutes Felicity was back in her bucket squirting out another load of eggs. Brilliant. It had all worked a treat.

Mr Chang was also delighted. A big grin lit up his face, his lips almost creasing from ear to ear when he came to collect Felicity.

'Thank you velly, velly much,' he chortled, dropping a fresh pea in her bucket – a titbit she adored apparently – and which she swiftly swallowed.

Though the success of that venture raised my spirits for a while, it wasn't long before I was feeling far more peed off than any amount of legumes Felicity could have swallowed.

And all because I was about to confront my unease, yet again, regarding one particular species of animal – a creature that seemed to have the ability to outwit me on every occasion I encountered it.

5

Stop Horsing Around

Horses are no fools. They can sense when someone is uneasy in their presence. The prick of their ears. Here's one coming. The snort as they look down their nose at you. Wally's arrived. The pawing of the ground. Let's kick him in the nuts.

But they were part and parcel of my veterinary course. Indeed they were the main model for our anatomy practicals held each Tuesday, when groups of four to five students would work their way through an equine carcass over several weeks, eventually tunnelling inside the empty cadaver to trace the vestigial remains of nerves, muscles and arteries. Often the worse for wear after a liquid lunch in the pub opposite the vet school, we'd exhale alcoholic fumes that would form a deadly soporific mix with those of the formaldehyde used to fix the cadavers. Entombed in the horse, I often found myself starting to nod off while rummaging through its lumbar-sacral plexus attempting to shakily dissect out the femoral and sciatic nerves, with the Professor of Anatomy peering over my shoulder watching my wobbly dissection of those nerves while I felt a nervous wreck. It gave a whole new meaning to flogging a dead horse and if it

71

taught me nothing else, I now know they have an awful lot of guts.

As to riding such a beast, that also takes a lot of guts. A belly load of them. I reasoned that if I were ever to be confronted with a horse in practice, then it would be wise to know what it felt like to have one between one's legs. So I embarked on a series of lessons while still at vet school.

'I take it you've not ridden before?' said the tall, sylph-like instructress, eyeing me up and down, the crop in her one hand being tapped thoughtfully in the palm of the other. Very dominatrix. Her body looked as if it had been built from pipe-cleaners dunked in flesh-coloured wax. An illusion heightened by the cream jodhpurs clinging to her so tightly that every crease and crevice of her thin thighs and neat bum were mapped out in minute detail. In similar attire, I'd have been dancing the *Nutcracker* on a rising trot and feeling very 'Ball'shoi.

'I'll put you on Nancy,' she said.

Nancy turned out to be one of the more elderly residents of the riding school. One that should have been turned out to grass years back. Long in the tooth, grey in the muzzle, with a look in her milky glazed eyes that suggested the time was fast approaching when she'd be leaping her final hurdle into the great knacker's yard in the sky should her arthritic old legs ever manage it. Meanwhile she was saddled with the likes of me.

Mindful of how one should approach a horse, exuding confidence in your stride, talking quietly and calmly, holding out your hand to allow the horse to sniff it before you stroke its neck, I did all this to Nancy and was rewarded with two nostril-barrels of snot and a loud fart.

Not a very auspicious start.

Once mounted, it was cue-time to make Nancy walk.

Cue – elbows to my side, reins gathered.

Cue – legs squeezed behind her girth.

Cue – buttocks clenched to push my seat forward.

Cue – testicles squashed.

I was moved to tears. But no move from Nancy. She remained stock still.

'Nudge her with your lower legs. But gently does it,' barked the instructress.

Nancy didn't budge.

'Urge her forward with your heels. Again use the softly, softly approach. Don't kick her. She won't respond to anything too violent.'

Nancy remained stationary.

The instructress marched up to the horse, whacked her rump smartly with her crop and snapped, 'Move your arse you lazy bugger.'

Nancy walked.

Several times she started to decelerate as if running out of gas, though judging from what she let rip from her rear end at regular intervals as she plodded round the sand school, there was plenty in reserve. Each time she slowed down, the instructress bellowed, 'Keep your leg on, Paul. Keep your leg on.' I hadn't the slightest clue what the command meant. Did she think I had a false limb in danger of unscrewing? But in the hope that the right part of my anatomy would obey her instruction, I clenched all heels, calves, knees, thighs and buttocks, the actions of which, instead of keeping Nancy moving as the command had intended, promptly brought her to a shuddering halt with a final fart. Lesson over.

It was with some relief that my encounters of the equine kind since I'd started at Prospect House had been few and far between, Crystal being the vet who usually dealt with them.

It just happened I was on duty one weekend – Crystal and Eric having gone off for a city break to Venice – when the Richardsons' beloved Clementine had difficulty in foaling.

Crystal had warned me how difficult they might be, George Richardson, in particular, imagining all the things that could go wrong – breech presentations, eversion of the womb, heart blocks. I still shake recalling it all. The panic when he called me out at 2.00am, declaring Clementine was dying. The epidural I had to administer – my first ever – George and his wife Hilary, hawk-eyed, watching my every move, suggesting perhaps I ought to get someone in with more experience. The subsequent delivery of a live colt. The elation I felt. To be shared with... and here I pause... to be shared with Lucy. She'd assisted me that night. And it was on the return journey across the Downs as the silver line of the sea beyond Westcott lightened in the dawn, as the sun began to rise, pencils of pink creeping through the clouds, that I stopped the car and turned to thank Lucy. My fingers reached out for hers, entwined them at the start of our life together. That was seven months ago. Time had moved on. And so had she. Back to Prospect House. Making it plain she was no filly for me to horse around with. I could now see that and I was deeply ashamed.

Then, there was a case just a few weeks back.

The call came through late one Friday afternoon, just as evening surgery was finishing.

'It's a Mrs Pattison,' said Beryl. 'She's got a pony that's trying to lie down on the ground and roll.'

We both rolled our eyes – in Beryl's case just the one – she'd lost her right eye as the result of a childhood accident and it was now glass. The word 'colic' hung unspoken in the air between us. It was going to be my responsibility to attend to it as I was duty vet that evening.

'Tell her I'll be out as soon as I can. And meantime make sure she keeps the pony walking as much as possible.'

A quick scan through Mrs Pattison's computer notes told me she had two ponies, a two-year-old colt, Little Joe, and a twenty-five-year-old Shetland, Hoss. Both in good health it seems. Just annual vaccinations and the occasional dental for Hoss. Routine stuff. But not this time. Not for Little Joe anyway – the pony in question. I had a feeling I could be dealing with a difficult problem, a feeling that Little Joe was experiencing right at this moment. A gut feeling that could result in a twisted intestine and his death. The thought was enough to make my guts churn let alone his. I had to get out there asap.

'There' turned out to be along the coastal road from Westcott, heading east towards its larger and more famous and more glitzy cousin – the seaside resort of Brigstock. Between the two, flowed the Ouze, which true to its name, oozed through treacherous reed-lined channels of mud before dispersing into the sea. A flyover built in the seventies ensured you flew over that estuary at a safe height and smell from its bubbling cauldron of marsh gas. Under it and edging the old coastal road, had sprung up a patchwork of paddocks, some small, hardly half an acre or so, others several acres in size. These stretched from the roadside across to the main channel of the Ouze; and formed a ribbon of pasture which wound down alongside the river to end abruptly at the line of bungalows that constituted the outskirts of the little seaside port of Stanport. From the flyover, the endless wooden rails crisscrossing that ribbon of pasture looked like a trellis stretched on its side. And dotted in those sections were scores of equines ranging from small ponies to hacks and hunters, owned by people in town. The variety of horses was matched by the variety of stabling provided for them – small jerry-built field shelters awash with mud through to smart triple stable blocks raised on concrete bases, which secured them from the water that sometimes overflowed from the Ouze when weather conditions caused freak high tides and the river burst its banks.

My destination was Ponderosa – a name conjuring up the ranch of that name in the *Bonanza* TV series of the sixties and seventies. Though before my time, but being a bit of a Western buff, I had seen the boxed sets and knew there was a Little Joe and Hoss in the series. Perhaps Mrs Pattison was a fan and had named her two ponies after them?

Though the light was beginning to fade, I managed to locate the wooden sign swinging from the pole which I had been told to look out for. With the way it swayed and creaked in the sharp breeze blowing up from the estuary, accompanied by tussocks of marram grass that bowled along the sandy track I turned down, I began to imagine I was entering the Wild West territory of the TV series, a sprawling ranch set in its half a million acres ahead of me. That illusion was quickly shattered when I braked in front of a metal field gate, the entrance to a two acre thistle-strewn paddock with a rickety looking row of looseboxes, at each end of which were rusty iron poles angled into the ground to prop them up. No doubt in the hope that it would prevent the 'loose' boxes from living up to their name, become semi-detached and drift apart. Here it seems, I was looking at Stanport's answer to *Bonanza* if the 'Ponderosa' emblazed in burnt wooden lettering along the weather boarding – together with a row of rusty horse shoes above the looseboxes – was to be believed. If not *Bonanza*, the woman who stepped out from one of the boxes as I crossed the paddock could have stepped out from the boxed set of *The Big Valley* – a TV Western that starred Barbara Stanwyck. I loved that actress's TV presence. The strong, smouldering type. A type that was stepping up to me at that moment in the form of Mrs Pattison. Nut brown complexion. Creased. Weather-worn. Hair tied back in a no-nonsense ponytail. Green gilet over jeans. Cowboy boots but no Stetson.

I felt like slipping my hand from under my poncho to remove the cheroot dangling from the corner of my mouth before saying, 'How do, ma'am.'

But she got in first with, 'I'm Gloria.' Holding out her hand she took mine – cheroot-less – in a firm grip. 'You must be the vet.' She looked me up and down, and from the way her eyes narrowed as they bore into mine, I instantly sensed she knew I was no sharpshooter of a vet. Just a novice still wet behind the ears. But she was polite enough not to say anything.

'Little Joe's over there. My daughter's with him.' She pointed to the far side of the paddock adjacent to the end of the looseboxes, where I could see a girl in her mid-teens, holding a lead rope attached to a chestnut-brown pony that was unwillingly shuffling forward as she pulled, his gait unsteady.

'We've managed to keep him going. Just. He's been down twice, trying to roll, poor little lad.'

77

Gloria grimaced. 'Reckon it's a touch of colic. But that's for you to decide.' She gave me a sideways glance as we walked across to the pony that clearly stated, 'But I've already decided.'

As we approached, a very rotund black Shetland ambled over, stretched his head out and leered at me as we passed, his lips lifting to expose a misshapen mouthful of teeth. 'Don't mind Hoss,' said Gloria. 'He sneers at everyone. It's the wry nose that does it.' I made a mental note to look up 'wry nose in horses' when I got home. Obviously there was more to it than Hoss showing displeasure at my arrival. Or so I hoped.

Having been introduced to Gloria's daughter, Sophie, similarly attired to her mum, I turned my attention to Little Joe, who was now stationary, his legs quivering, about to sink down again. He was a cute little pony, a mere nine hands or so, with chestnut head, black mane and tail, and two white socks. But he was clearly in pain. I didn't need too much veterinary expertise to realise that. Nor did Gloria and Sophie, who were now standing waiting for my next move, the first having been to walk up to Little Joe and with what I hoped was a reassuring, 'Hello boy.' Stroking his neck, I hoped he wouldn't sense my apprehension, the first signs of which I could feel in my armpits as they started to sweat. But that was nothing to the darkened patches of matted, sweat-soaked hair evident along Little Joe's flanks and under his shoulders.

There was a standard procedure to clinical examination of cases of colic. I'd mentally been turning the pages of my medical notes in the drive over, and had carried from the car everything I thought I'd need to reach a diagnosis as to why Little Joe was in so much pain.

Right. The scene was set. Take one. Action.

'You won't hear much,' said Gloria as I produced my stethoscope, about to listen for any intestinal movement detectable through his flank. 'I've already listened.' She pulled a stethoscope from her gilet as if brandishing a gun and waved it at me. 'But do check yourself.' Hey. This wasn't in my script.

But I did as I was told. And she was right. Just a few occasional grumbles were audible.

Next scene. Take two. Action.

I whipped a long plastic sleeve from my black bag, half expecting Gloria to whip similar from her gilet. Instead, she marched over to Little Joe's rump, instructed Sophie to shorten the lead rope and hold on tight while she lifted and pulled the pony's tail to one side.

Scene three. An interior shot. One invisible to us three.

Inside Little Joe's arse. Up his rectum. My arm inserted as far as it would go.

He swung to the left. I swung with him. As did Gloria.

He swung to the right. I swung as well. Likewise Gloria.

'Easy, boy, easy,' I muttered, feeling far from easy swinging with Gloria, my hand up her pony's bum.

I could certainly feel a lot of gas – bubbles of it through the plastic sleeve – as I cautiously probed with a cupped hand, conscious of the fact that too much prodding with a finger could inadvertently poke a hole through the pony's rectal wall. Result? Escape of bacteria into the peritoneal cavity leading to septicaemia. Nasty.

Then scene three. Knackers yard.

Cut. Reshoot.

Move arm further up intestine. Arm now fully immersed in faeces. Find small hard mass of dried dung between fingers. Cause of colic. No twist. Relief.

Scene four.

'He's got an impaction,' I said, pronouncing my lines with a dramatic flourish as I withdrew my arm and peeled off the plastic sleeve.

Gloria clutched a hand to her bosom and to the roar of traffic thundering over the flyover, gasped in a trembling voice, 'Can anything be done to save him?'

'Don't worry ma'am,' I replied in a husky voice, pulling down the brim of my black Stetson, 'All is not lost.'

What Gloria actually said was, 'You'll give him a drench then?' and I meekly nodded.

Showdown. Time to loosen up Little Joe's bowels with some shots of liquor from the saloon bar. Well, 500mls of mineral oil from the bottle in the boot of my car. But not tossed down the back of the throat Clint Eastwood-style. But by an orange rubber tube stuck up his nose – Little Joe's nose that is – and pushed down the back of his throat – stomach-tubed – the medication then trickled in.

With a passing shot – an injection of anti-spasmolytic – I rode out of Ponderosa into the setting sun, leaving instructions to call me in three hours should Little Joe not improve. Seems he did since I never heard back, save for a note of grateful thanks a few days later which left me riding high. Gee. Haw.

The following week, Beryl spotted an ad in the *Westcott Gazette*, our local newspaper. It came out on a Thursday and from that lunch-time, when she bought the paper, through to the next afternoon, she would methodically scan through its contents and pick out any stories she thought might be of interest to us. They seldom were. Though the editor, Finley O'Connor, the owner of a basenji and a client of ours, did have a sense of humour, so some of the headlines were often funny – if you liked puns that is.

A local man caught for poaching inevitably had the headline:

Local fisherman gets hooked.

While a local novelist caught for doing thirty-two mph in a thirty mph zone – they're hot on speeding in Westcott – was honoured with:

Local Author gets booked.

The broken headstones at St Augustine's inevitably had:

Churchyard vandals – a grave concern.

But it was the *Don't horse around – Ed Byrnes is coming* that caught Beryl's attention that particular Thursday and she read the headline out loud at tea-break.

'Ed Byrnes? Sorry, who's he?' I said.

'You've never heard of Ed Byrnes?' she replied, eyebrows raised as she looked over the top of the paper at Eric and me sitting opposite her, our mugs of tea perched on our knees.

I shook my head.

'Surely *you* have?' queried Beryl, swivelling her raven-haired head to cast a glinting eye at Eric.

To judge by the rapid reddening of Eric's face – an effect that Beryl had on him whenever she fixed him with that owl-like look of hers – he hadn't either. But he hazarded a guess. 'Er... something to do with horses?' His tea wobbled on his knee.

'Very much to do with horses,' said Beryl, giving hers a quick slurp before continuing. 'He's *only* the most famous horse whisperer in the country.'

'Whisperer?' said Eric glancing from side to side before dropping his voice and leaning forward, his mug between his hands. As he did so, he gave me a sly wink.

'Yes,' said Beryl, whispering back. 'A whisperer.'

'What does he whisper about?'

'He doesn't whisper about anything. He just listens.'

'Listens?' Eric edged his chair closer to Beryl and dropped his voice even further. 'Listens to whom?'

'Horses.'

'Really? He listens to horses?'

'Yes.'

'What do they tell him?'

I began to feel a fit of giggles come on. Though Beryl still hadn't twigged Eric was leading her on, she wasn't far off. In which case, Eric was dangerously close to having his mug smashed – and not the one he was holding. I snorted and bit my tongue. Stop playing silly fillies, I thought and snorted again.

'What's so funny?' snapped Beryl raising her voice and switching her full beaky look to me.

'Nothing, Beryl, nothing.' I was picturing this Ed Byrnes listening to Nancy, that old nag I'd had a lesson on. Two snorts of snot and an explosive release of wind. What would that tell him? That she was just a snotty-nosed old fart. I giggled again.

'Oh do grow up, Paul,' exclaimed Beryl, shaking the outstretched paper at me.'

'Yes, Paul, show some maturity,' echoed Eric, turning to give me a stern look, though his lips could barely restrain themselves from curling up. 'This is serious stuff. A man who can stomach listening to a whole lot of nags. Must be very special. Not many of us can do that, especially when they come from the wife.' It was his turn to snort.

'What's that about nags, Eric?' This from Crystal who had just stepped briskly into the office.

'Oh, hello dear,' gulped Eric, turning an even darker shade of puce.

'Crystal,' said Beryl turning to her. 'Would you believe it, these two have never heard of Ed Byrnes.'

'You haven't?' exclaimed Crystal looking questioningly at us.

We both sat there, necks sunk into our shoulders like deflated rubber ducks and shook our heads.

'Well it's about time you did.'

Beryl flapped her raven's wings in vigorous approval. 'He's giving a demonstration over at the Appledore Equestrian Centre next Saturday.'

'Well, book a couple of tickets for these two. Give them a chance to brush up on their approach to horses. Maybe then...' Crystal paused to glare at us, her cornflower blue eyes flashing, 'maybe then they'd be more enthusiastic about taking on some of the horse work. Lessen the burden on me. What say you, Beryl?'

'Good idea. Good idea.' Beryl stared with her good eye.

Now three eyes flashed at us.

Eric and I turned to look at each other, just one thought flashing between us.

What a couple of nags.

The event at the Appledore Equestrian Centre was huge. A special marquee had been erected, several paddocks turned into car parks, one for coaches of which there were five when Eric and I turned up.

'This Ed what's-his-name must be popular,' commented Eric as we joined the queue filing into the marquee to await the arrival of Ed Byrnes.

When the man duly strode into the arena and positioned himself in the centre, no one could help but be impressed. Any whispering amongst the crowd promptly died away.

He was tall, smartly dressed in a dark suit and tie, with well-polished black brogues – I half expected him to be carrying a briefcase – instead he was holding a thin coil of nylon in one hand. The outfit didn't accord with the cascade of white hair that flowed down to his shoulders, matched by a long, white goatee beard and bushy sideburns, which reminded me of the likes of Buffalo Bill or Wild Bill Hickok. But there was no American drawl when he spoke. It was in a precise, very English tone of voice – clipped, mid-Shire – his words clearly spelling out his objectives through the microphone attached to his jacket lapel, once he had introduced himself. As he spoke, a young frisky palomino was reluctantly led in by two lads to either side of him, each holding a lead rope which they released once the pony was in the arena. The pony immediately bucked and shied away, pawing the ground.

'This is Trigger,' said Ed. 'As you can see, he's a bit overwrought.'

'That was the name of Roy Rogers' horse,' I whispered to Eric.

'Who?' Eric whispered back.

'Roy Rogers. The singing cowboy and movie star,' I said in a lower whisper.

'Never heard of him,' said Eric in an even lower whisper.

I whispered back, 'He starred in the 1952 movie *Son of Paleface* with Bob Hope.'

'Never heard of it,' whispered Eric in return.

'Stop whispering and listen to the whisperer will you,' was uttered in a vehement whisper by the lady sitting next to Eric.

'Sorry.'

'Shh...' A whisper from behind Eric.

'Sorry.'

'Shh... Shh...' echoed the man in front of him, who had turned in his seat to glare at Eric.

'Sorry.'

'Shh... Shh... Shh...' from the second and third rows.

That spawned a whole series of whispered, 'Shh... Shh... Shh...' that shunted up and down the seats like a steam train leaving a station – threatening to derail the show. But they eventually died down, everyone's attention once more focussed on Ed Byrnes. Silence fell. Not a sound. Just that of the palomino's bellows of breath as he continued to circuit the arena while Ed lightly swung the coiled rope in his hand.

'He's going to lasso him,' I felt like whispering but thought better of it in case it provoked another stream of, 'Shh...' And so I contented myself with recalling Will Rogers, the master of the lasso, and that 1922 film of his *The Ropin' Fool*. I wondered if any of his ponies bucked and balled as much as this Trigger did. Boy, did he go wild. Trigger happy? No way.

But I was wrong about Ed lassoing him. He didn't. Instead he kept the rope in his hand and squaring his body up to the pony, lifted his arms a little and spread out his fingers. Trigger immediately tore off round the arena at a breakneck speed.

'Now ladies and gentlemen, I'm going to stare at his shoulders,' said Ed. 'Watch what happens.'

We watched intently, staring as hard as he was.

Gradually Trigger started to slow down. He didn't stop but his pace definitely slowed.

'Now I'm going to look him in the eye. Watch what happens next.'

We watched in hushed silence as Trigger started to increase his speed, gradually building up until he was going at full pelt once more.

'Now,' Ed went on, 'what I'm looking for is for his inside ear to lock on to me.'

We all stared at Trigger's left ear, the one facing Ed as the pony cantered round anti-clockwise. In less than a minute it had twisted and turned towards Ed.

'Trigger's listening now,' said Ed. At which point he snapped the rope out in front of him, causing the pony to swiftly turn and trot in the other direction.

'Now look,' said Ed. 'That right ear's turned towards me. Means he's still listening, folks. And any minute he'll start licking and chewing.'

As if on cue, Trigger did precisely that, pushing his tongue out between his teeth.

'Time to talk,' declared Ed.

'Well I'm blowed,' whispered Eric, prompting a sharp, 'Shh...' from behind.

But Ed wasn't finished. 'Now Trigger, time you dropped your head. Hear me?'

The pony must have heard him because, within a couple of minutes, he was trotting round, his nose just inches from the floor.

'Bugger me,' exclaimed Eric.

More, 'Shh... Shh.'

'There folks, what did I tell you? Trigger's telling me everything's okay,' Ed was saying. 'He trusts me. So I'm now going to ask him to stop.'

At that point, Ed turned his shoulders away and lost eye contact with the pony. The effect was immediate. Trigger ground to a halt.

'Amazing,' murmured Eric.

No, 'Shh,' this time. Everyone was mesmerized.

Trigger took a tentative step towards Ed, who continued to ignore him. There was a snort. Another step. Then another. Within moments he was standing next to Ed, his nose at his shoulder.

Ed then began walking slowly in a circle. Trigger followed.

Ed turned and circled in the other direction. Trigger did the same, his nose close to him.

I felt the hairs on my neck tingle. I reckoned the whole audience felt the same. You could have heard a pin drop.

But Ed hadn't finished. 'Just to prove that Trigger really does trust me, I'm going to give him an examination.' He proceeded to run his hands over Trigger's neck and withers. Then his flanks. Then under his belly. All the while, the pony let him do it. Even allowing Ed to run his hands down his fetlocks and pick up his hooves.

Incredible to think of the transformation that we'd witnessed in less than thirty minutes.

And it didn't stop there.

One of the lads carried in a saddle, bridle, stirrup leathers and lunge line, heaping them in the centre of the arena. This did cause Trigger some concern. He leaned across to the pile of unfamiliar equipment, gave the saddle a snort and wandered away. Only to return to Ed's side, clearly seeking reassurance that all was well.

Gripping stuff. It had me on tenterhooks.

Especially when Ed lifted the saddle on to his back, slid the girth under his belly and buckled it up on the other side, without so much as a murmur from the pony. And this all done without the use of a lead rope attached to his head.

I felt my mouth drop open.

I glanced at Eric.

He too was gob-smacked.

And we remained that way as we watched Trigger being put through his paces with the saddle on, a bridle and bit in place, the same techniques being employed by Ed as before. He spoke with his hands, eyes and body position. Trigger responded with the same ear turning, the licking of the lips, the chewing. They were speaking the same language.

This was crowned when one of the lads walked out, slipped into Trigger's saddle and walked him round the arena without so much as a jig or side-step from the pony. All this achieved with no restraints. No whips. Not a harsh word uttered. Ed and Trigger in tune with each other. Trusting each other in perfect harmony.

Wonderful to witness.

'So?' queried Crystal on our return. 'Did you learn anything?'

'Maybe,' replied Eric, thoughtfully. He had been standing square on, his hands level with his shoulders, fingers apart, staring hard at his wife. He turned sideways and glanced away from her. But she didn't come up and nuzzle his shoulder.

'Guess we'll both need to practise a bit more, eh Paul,' he added, winking at me as Lucy walked into the office, realised she was interrupting something and backed out smartly, nostrils flared.

6

What's In A Name?

People often give pets names which sum up their characters.

Beryl and I were discussing this one coffee break. With mugs of coffee and a couple of blueberry muffins from Bert's Bakery, we were in the back garden of Prospect House – the exercise yard for hospitalised dogs. More a crap yard than back yard. Most of the canine in-patients had had their morning run to do what they needed to do, so we'd side-stepped anything they'd done before sitting at one end of the slightly wonky garden bench – the wooden slats at the other end had been used as a marking post and were saturated with urine. Having thus avoided any evidence of canine bodily functions, we sipped our coffees and tucked into our muffins, munching away merrily.

'It's one reason I smoke out here,' declared Beryl, waving her hand in front of her face. 'Helps mask the pong.' She'd finished muffin-munching and had lit up her customary mid-morning ciggie while watching the departure indoors of a hunched Dalmatian that Lucy had dragged round us three times, dribbles of diarrhoea dripping from his back end.

89

I could have pointed out the other reason was that smoking was strictly prohibited inside the hospital. The one concession to Beryl's nicotine addiction was to allow her to smoke in the back garden. If the weather was inclement or the dog excrement factor too high, Beryl could be found at coffee and tea breaks leaning out of the open back door, right hand holding her fag, blowing the smoke through the gap, left hand cupped at bosom height to catch the ash.

During this particular coffee break, she'd given Crackerjack as an example of an apt name for a cat if ever there was one. 'Crackerjack by name, Crackerjack by nature,' she said. 'You'll see if you ever meet up with him.'

That led on to what ones were the most popular.

'I bet you've had a fair few "Tiddles" over the years,' I ventured to say. Then mentally kicked myself for putting it like that. Could have been misconstrued as me taking the piss. There again it could have been seen an inference to Beryl's advancing years. Not a good idea as she never liked to be reminded of her age however indirect. And certainly not via her annual tally of urinations. It was currently sixty-four – her age that is – but was never usually mentioned until her next birthday came round – 13th of May – when she would be delighted to let everyone know how old she was providing several rum and Cokes were on offer to celebrate it. On those evenings, Tiddles would have been an apt name for her, especially by her third rum which, at her insistence, only had the merest dash of Coke in it.

Mind you, when I was a boy, the cats we owned then all seemed to be black. And their names reflected that. Mum and Dad would ask me what

I'd like each new one to be called. I'd think about it for a bit. But not for long. 'Sooty,' I'd reply.

Subsequently over the years, we had a string of Sooties. I've a small, grainy black and white photograph of me as a four-year-old in Cyprus, standing at the top of some steps, struggling to hold our first Sooty in my arms. I can still recall one incident with that cat.

It was a ferociously hot day. Mum was standing in the kitchen of our bungalow, preparing some salad for lunch, wearing a polka dot dress – white with the dots in deep navy – and singing along to a CD of songs Gran had given her. One song that stands out in my mind was by Max Bygraves (gets in everywhere, doesn't he?). He was singing *You're a Pink Toothbrush*. It's a funny song and always made me giggle when I heard it being sung either by Gran or my mum. Often, they'd sing it together. I can still remember some of the lyrics.

You're a pink toothbrush I'm a blue toothbrush
Have we met somewhere before?
You're a pink toothbrush and I think toothbrush
That we met by the bathroom door.

Only then I wasn't standing by the bathroom door, but by the back door of the kitchen, in baggy, blue short dungarees, bare-footed. Sooty was by my side, looking down the concrete path that divided the parched yellow patch of burnt grass that passed for a lawn, the scene blurred in whorls of shimmering heat. I stretched out my foot and gingerly touched the concrete doorsill with my big toe.

'Ouch, that's really hot,' I exclaimed, pulling back my foot.

Mum laughed. I can remember her laugh. High, tinkling, bell-like, head thrown back, the dark ringlets of her hair, gypsy-tousled over her shoulders. 'Let me show you how hot.'

She took an egg from the fridge, a knife from the drawer, and knelt next to me to crack the shell on the doorstep.

The egg spread out a little, turned white and suddenly began to spit and bubble. Within seconds, it was fried. Seeing the astonished look on my face, Mum laughed again. How young at heart, how carefree she seemed those days. The strains of a brittle marriage yet to come.

Sooty nosed past me and sniffed the still bubbling fried egg. A final 'splish' made him leap sideways and out on to the path. A furnace of a path, the heat of which seared through his paws. With a loud yowl, he hurtled down it, paws flaying from side to side each time they touched the burning concrete. A Tennessee Williams play in the making.

A few weeks after my back garden chat with Beryl, the subject that prompted that discussion reared its ugly head.

'I've booked you a visit for 2.30 this afternoon to vaccinate Crackerjack,' Beryl informed me one cold and blustery late October morning, the wind whipping whirls of fallen leaves round the car park, small clusters of which spiralled into reception whenever the front door opened and another client blew in for an appointment.

I was a bit puzzled. A bit peeved. The practice policy was now to encourage clients to bring their pets in for an appointment rather than make house calls. So I was about to query the fact that this visit had been booked in for me. Especially as it appeared to be just a routine annual booster. But I hesitated. Just as well.

Beryl had tensed up. Her shoulders hunched over her computer, making her look like a crow about to have its feathers ruffled. Only in Beryl's case it wouldn't have been feathers but the black cardigan which was draped across her shoulders now the weather had turned. Its dangling sleeves swayed like folded wings about to unfurl. She had that look in her eye. That tilt of her head. That pursing of her lips. All warning signs that I was in danger of being picked on. Like a lump of flattened road-kill on the tarmac.

Just as well I hesitated. I should have known better. Of course Beryl would have had a good reason for making the booking. And so it proved.

'Miss Jameson's a long standing client of ours,' she explained raising one of her claws (hands). 'She's used to having a house visit.' Beryl shifted on her perch (computer chair). Pulled one of her wings (sleeves) down. 'She lives over in Hamfield. Which is about ten miles as the crow flies.'

Her unfortunate choice of words had me imagining a black-feathered Beryl flying straight over the Downs with an eye open (only the one of course) for a flattened rabbit (vet) to pounce on. Peck. Peck.

'You'll see why he's called "Crackerjack" when you meet him,' Beryl added with a wry smile.

Warning bells began to ring. It suggested the cat might be somewhat high spirited. And so it proved.

Having been ushered into her cottage, Miss Jameson stood at the foot of the stairs, grey shawl drooping from her shoulders, hopping from one foot to another like an agitated heron.

'Crackerjack's upstairs in my bedroom,' she said, fiddling with the pearls round her neck.

Uhm... I hesitated.

Last summer, I'd had to visit a rather curvaceous young lady who had opened the door in a clingy white cotton shift. The sun had been streaming in through the French windows behind her, highlighting her curves in a very revealing way.

'Ah, Mr Mitchell,' she'd crooned. 'I hope you don't mind taking a look at my Fifi up in the bedroom.'

I was looking at those curves.

They were driving me round the bend. Vroom. Vroom.

Setting my pulse racing. Vroom. Vroom.

Formula One winners move aside. I was in pole position here. Ready to do several laps round this lady's curves. Vroom. Vroom.

But that's another story.

Here we had Miss Jameson. I felt safe following her rear bumper up the stairs. After all she was more old banger than Ferrari.

In her bedroom I was confronted by a huge Victorian bedstead.

'Oh dear,' faltered Miss Jameson with another fiddle of her pearls. 'Crackerjack must be under it.' She bobbed her head down level with the bed and addressed the dark shadow lurking beneath it. 'Now Crackerjack, if you behave yourself for Mr Mitchell I've a nice plate of coley for you afterwards.'

Crackerjack's reply was a loud hiss. Clearly he wasn't hungry.

I put down my black bag and peered under. All I could see were two large green eyes. Foolishly, oh so foolishly, I reached under.

HISS... There was a flash of teeth.

I hastily withdrew my hand.

'Perhaps we could move the bed?' I suggested. Another foolish move. A big mistake. A ball of black

94

fur exploded from under the bed, hurled itself across the room and disappeared out of the door.

'Crackerjack's vaccination will just have to wait,' I grumbled, snatching up my black bag. 'And next time perhaps you can keep him downstairs.'

Miss Jameson nodded meekly, twiddling her pearls.

Next time happened to be just a couple of days later. Another blustery October afternoon.

'I'm sorry to call you out,' said Miss Jameson, on the fiddle again – with those pearls of hers. 'But Crackerjack's been out all day and has only just returned. He's not well. In fact...' She faltered, her voice cracking, and pointed upwards.

Dead? Gone to heaven? I wondered.

'He's upstairs,' she said. 'I'm afraid he shot up there as soon as he got in.'

I found Crackerjack not under the bed but lying stretched out on the counterpane. Panting. Mouth open. Eyes glazed. Clearly distressed.

I pressed the toes on one of his paws. Uhm... Just as I suspected. The claws were shredded where he'd scrabbled on a road. I raised his left hind leg. There was a grunt of pain.

I turned to Miss Jameson. 'Crackerjack's been hit by a car,' I said.

Her face went white. Her lips quivered. A tear rolled down her cheek. There was more frantic fiddling with her pearls.

'But he will be all right?' she faltered.

'Well, he's in a state of shock. And there's a problem with his left hip. What I'll do is to take him back to Prospect House and hospitalise him overnight. Then see how he is in the morning.'

Crackerjack seemed much brighter the next day to judge from the way he spat at me from the back of his cage.

But he wasn't putting any weight on his left hind leg.

'Yes. Well. We need to catch him up,' I stated, turning to Lucy, who was on duty that morning.

'All yours, Paul,' she said, shoving away the leather gauntlets I'd been holding out.

'Coward,' I muttered, donning the gauntlets, opening the cage door and subjecting myself to the full fury of Crackerjack's venom. Spits. Growls. Hisses. Claws. Teeth. All intent on inflicting as much damage on me as possible.

But I eventually managed to restrain him and he was sedated with an injection of anaesthetic.

An X-ray revealed that he had dislocated his left hip. It was quite a job manipulating the joint back into place as Crackerjack was such a muscular beast. But I eventually managed it with as much swearing and cursing as he might have done.

There was one more thing I wanted to do. I'd suggested it to Miss Jameson, saying now would be a good time to do it. The big snip. Well two actually. With Crackerjack castrated it might calm him down a bit. Lessen the fighting. Lessen the rampages under the bed. Well one could only hope.

I went round to visit Miss Jameson a week later.

'So how's Crackerjack?'

'Fine... fine...,' she declared with the now familiar fiddle of her pearls. My... My... What a highly strung lady she was.

I hardly dared to ask the next question. 'And where is he?'

'In my bedroom,' she confessed, pointing upwards. She saw me grimace. 'Well, he does so love sleeping on my counterpane. Besides, he's been through such a lot recently. Poor thing.'

She opened the bedroom door.

'Crackerjack. Your nice doctor's here to see you. Crackerjack? Crackerjack? Where are you?'

My heart sank as a familiar snarl came from under the bed.

Clearly Crackerjack was back in fighting form. With more sparks to fly.

Another cat mentioned during that back garden chat with Beryl was Snowflake.

What a lovely name it conjured up. Crystals of snowy fur. Diadems of white lightly swirling before your eyes.

He was owned by Jack and Ruth Frost, who used to make jokes about their name. So it was no surprise when they acquired this white cat and called him Snowflake. It suited him. To start with at least.

He was a Persian, solidly built, with large almond-shaped eyes. Their colour was very distinctive, one being blue the other copper. His coat too was distinctive. Well it used to be. A coat that drew admiring gasps. Thick, white and soft. A coat that willed you to run your hands through its silky strands.

'Right little show-off, isn't he?' Jim would chuckle as Snowflake twirled on my consulting table, in a cloud of white.

But keeping Snowflake's coat in pristine condition proved to be a problem. Caused the Frosts no end of trouble. Despite a battery of grooming equipment, it was a real headache for them. And the reason? Snowflake hated being groomed. The mere sight of a comb transformed him from a Snowflake into a snow storm. His hisses and snarls a clear indication that Jim and Ruth should get knotted. Problem was it was Snowflake that got knotted. Big time.

Hence the ragged ball of matted mog that landed on my consulting table that particular afternoon. He looked distinctly lumpy. And very grumpy.

'I'm sorry he's such a mess,' said Ruth. 'But he's so bad tempered, he simply won't let us run a comb through him.'

To judge from the mass of clits I was looking at, a pair of garden shears, let alone a comb, would have had difficulty cutting through Snowflake's coat.

'Well,' I said. 'We've no choice then. We'll have to sedate him to get the job done.'

With Snowflake admitted to the hospital, he was given an intramuscular injection of Ketamine. I then left Lucy to snip away all the knotted fur taking care not to nick his skin.

I poked my head round the prep room door ten minutes later. 'How's it going?' I asked. Lucy pointed to the pile of clits she'd cut out. 'Going at a rate of knots,' she joked.

But it was no joke when later that afternoon, she rushed through to the office exclaiming, 'Snowflake's escaped.'

Apparently the cat, while still dozy, was being transferred from the recovery cage to his basket, when he managed to claw his way out of her arms and had scrabbled up on to the top of the drugs' cabinet.

It was from there that two eyes – one blue, one copper – now stared defiantly down at us. Any notion of persuading him down with a gently expressed, 'Puss, puss,' died on my lips as another snarl was spat in our direction. In a fit of pique, I snatched a rubber tube from the instrument trolley and flicked it up at Snowflake. A bad move. A mistake. In a whirl of white, Snowflake took a flying leap and sailed down on to the trolley. A tube of ointment was squashed under paw, the green, greasy contents jettisoning over him. He skidded across the surface, knocking over a bottle of blue coloured disinfectant which liberally splattered his coat. And, as a final touch, Snowflake managed to shower himself with tincture of iodine, so adding an extra dollop of purple to his already blue and green coloured coat. What a mess. We finally managed to corner him, but not before the Lucy and I were each left with a welter of red, bleeding scratches.

So no wonder I was feeling decidedly scratchy when the Frosts came to collect their cat. I did apologise for his multi-coloured appearance.

'Never mind,' said Ruth. 'He's still our precious Snowflake.'

Keeping my scratched hands tucked in the sleeves of my white coat, I ushered them out, thankful to see that particular Snowflake melt away.

I suppose the best example of the name-game with cats had to be the one involving Will and Kevin.

Though they were the two hair-stylists who ran Sweeny Todd's down in Westcott's shopping precinct, they reminded me more of *The Two Gentlemen of Verona*. There was a certain Shakespearian air to them. A whiff of theatricality whenever they waltzed into my surgery with their latest cat rescue.

Will was the worst. But then he was the more flamboyant of the duo. A tall, willowy beanpole of a guy in his mid-twenties, with bleached, black streaked, shoulder length hair, black-lined, mascara-lashed eyes and perma-tanned complexion. His partner, Kevin, in contrast, was a pea-stick of a man with a shaved head, pink lidded eyes, rosebud mouth and tiny lobed ears, from the left one of which hung a small silver cross that swung in circles every time he jerked his head – which was often.

Each cat presented, landed on my consulting table with a dramatic flourish, details of its rescue announced in tones clearly meant for those sitting in the Upper Circle; and each was given a name with a Shakespearian connection.

Take Pericles for example. A stocky shorthair with broad black stripes across his back. Very warrior-like.

'Your Prince of Tyre,' I said, giving the cat his vaccination.

'Ooh...so you know your Shakespeare,' exclaimed Will, turning to his partner. 'A man after our own hearts.'

'Someone we can bond with,' enthused Kevin. His shaved head gleamed, his silver cross swung.

Yes... well...

'I've yet to do Pericles,' said Will, running a hand through his floppy hair.

Kevin sniggered. I sighed.

A Russian Blue was next to appear. Another rescue. Flea infested but otherwise healthy.

'He's got rather a large nose,' commented Kevin.

'A Roman nose,' I ventured to say.

'Exactly,' chorused the two men like Tribunes of the People. 'So we've named him Coriolanus.'

When two black and white kittens were acquired, I learnt they were the sole survivors of a litter of five that had been at the centre of a feud between two warring families on the local estate.

'Bit like the Montagues and Capulets,' said Will.

'Only it was the Willetts and Smiths,' said Kevin. 'But thankfully these two sweeties have come through unscathed.'

'So what do you think we've called them?' asked Will, a plucked eyebrow raised.

Easy that. 'Romeo and Juliet,' I replied, pleased with myself.

'He's good at this,' remarked Kevin, nudging Will. 'We'll have to make it harder for him next time.'

With subsequent additions, guessing the names of the cats did get more difficult, the clues given more obscure. Determined not to be beaten, I found myself borrowing Shakespeare's plays from the library. 'Well, it's educational,' I said to myself. 'Been meaning to do it for ages.' Who was I kidding?

The Sphinx-like cat was easy enough, especially when told she liked dipping into saucers of milk. Cleopatra.

So was the ginger tom.

'He likes his pound of flesh – or rather a pound's worth of coley,' said Will, with a wink.

'Shylock,' I declared, smugly.

The squint-eyed half-Siamese was more difficult. He was a lean, twitchy little creature. No Shakespearean character sprang to mind when he was placed on my consulting table. His squint and a hunching of his shoulders gave him a somewhat shifty look. Was he a Richard the Third? Or was the look more of a despairing Hamlet?

I commented on the squint.

'You're getting close,' said Will.

'You're hot,' said Kevin, giving me an admiring look.

I felt myself redden. Yes, I was hot and very bothered. These silly games were getting the better of me.

'Tell him,' Kevin went on.

'I will,' said Will. He turned to me. 'It's that sly look.'

Kevin butted in. 'So we've called him King Lear.' He collapsed in a fit of giggles.

When I heard a voice inside me, all squeaky and petulant saying, 'Oh that's not fair... Far too difficult,' I knew I should put a stop to all this malarkey.

But then came a real show-stopper. An absolute stunner. A long-haired, white Persian with pale, milky-blue eyes and an aloof expression on her pert, snub-nosed face.

'She's named after the wife of Oberon,' said Will, as he held the cat in his arms and planted a kiss on her red-ribboned head.

'Queen of the Fairies,' said Kevin gazing up at his partner.

'Hmm... just as you like it,' I muttered to myself. Out loud I said: 'Titania.' I was right of course – but then I had been tackling *A Midsummer Night's Dream* as a bit of bedtime reading.

That night, I nodded off before the end of 'act two', drifting into a scene where my bottom suddenly sprouted the ears of a donkey.

I woke in a cold sweat, resolving to bring the curtain down on any further acts, Shakespearian or otherwise, before I made a complete ass of myself.

I just brayed I wasn't too late.

Of course apt names didn't just apply to pets. It could equally be applied to their owners.

'Remember Mrs Tidy?' said Beryl, as I drained the dregs of my coffee that morning out in the back garden.

I nodded. Who could possibly forget such a lady? A lady of beefy proportions who could have hod-lifted a stack of bricks with her little finger. Everything about her was tidy. Hair tidied back. Navy skirt in neat, tidy pleats. Even the sand sheet on which her cockatiel had deposited a neat tidy dropping had been secreted away before the bird was presented to me in its tidy cage.

That tidiness extended to her home where, when I visited, I found everything tidied away. Nothing cluttered the work surfaces. Nothing lined the mantelpieces. Everything was where it should be. Even her husband, a meek, silent sort, looked as if he'd been put in his place. They made a tidy pair and were aptly named.

When Beryl told me I had a Mrs Trilling coming in, I was curious to see whether her name was apt. Whether she would ring any bells. I wasn't disappointed.

Mrs Trilling was the epitome of an African dawn chorus. A jungle stuffed with parrots. Every time she opened her mouth a whole flock of them were voiced. Every syllable uttered was a full-blown note. A chorus of crotchets loud enough to make you quaver.

And with the pounding head I had – the result of finishing off a bottle of wine the night before – I certainly quavered on first hearing her. Though her husband, the diminutive man standing next to her in my consulting room, didn't seem to flinch. Maybe he'd found a way of tuning out.

'It's Max, my Siamese,' trilled Mrs Trilling as a large cat basket skidded to a halt on my consulting table. 'He's lost his voice.'

Wish I could say the same of you, I thought darkly.

The pitch of Mrs Trilling's voice – like an out-of-tune violin – was already getting on my nerves. Already a bit over-hung, I didn't need her to tighten my guts.

'Max is named after my favourite entertainer,' she was saying. 'You know... Max Bygraves.'

I inwardly moaned. Oh no, not Max Bygraves yet again. Damn him.

'He had such a lovely voice,' Mrs Trilling was saying. 'My Max here joins in as soon as I put on one of his Singalongamax CDs. And I join in as well, don't I dear?' Mrs Trilling looked down at her husband.

Mr Trilling nodded benignly, his baby face flushed.

His wife scooped out the Siamese, a sleek blue point, and placed him on the consulting table.

Mrs Trilling began singing the cat's praises. How healthy he usually was. So tame. Very vocal.

The lady's praise was very noteworthy. But if only her notes could have been in tune. Less strident. The way she spoke was not music to my ears. I'm not sure it was to Max's either, to judge from the way the cat just sat there, huddled up, a rather dazed expression on his face.

'He's lost his voice you say?' I asked.

'Yes,' verified Mrs Trilling, her double chins wobbling, the hoops in her ear lobes rattling and her vocal cords doing both. 'It's not like Max, is it Peter?' She twisted round to look down again at her husband.

He cowered back and shook his head.

She continued: 'Perhaps he's got laryngitis?'

Having examined the back of the cat's throat which was a little inflamed, and checked the glands in his neck which were a little enlarged, I took a deep breath and groaned. My head was still pounding.

Mrs Trilling misinterpreted my groan as one of dire foreboding; and it triggered from her an operatic rendition of anguish. A libretto of words poured from her with Wagnerian intensity. 'A friend of mine had a Persian that lost his voice. Turns out he had a lump in his throat.'

Mrs Trilling clearly had a lump in hers as her voice cracked. 'You don't think Max...'

'No... No... can't feel anything untoward,' I replied, before reaching for my stethoscope to block my ears to Mrs Trilling while I listened to Max's chest. His lungs were clear. All seemed fine. Not so Mrs Trilling. By now she'd worked herself up in to a real tizzy. An orchestrated aria. She'd obviously been reading up on cat diseases and a repertoire of medical conditions were spewed out, all uttered in a diva-style-soprano-pitched voice, eyes rolling, hands on heaving bosom. And all the while, Mr Trilling stood silently to one side, a world apart, looking as if he were on another planet, light-years away from his warbling wife.

I slid Max back into his basket where he silently curled up on his blanket.

'So what's your diagnosis?' Mrs Trilling's hail of words hit me like flak.

'Ah... well... I guess it's nothing too serious.'

'Guess?'

Oh dear. I'd struck the wrong note. 'As you say, a touch of laryngitis maybe.'

'Maybe?'

Whoops. Still way out of tune.

'We'll try... er... give Max a course of antibiotics. It might help.'

'Might?'

Oh dear. We were definitely not singing from the same song-sheet. Whatever, I persisted; antibiotics were dispensed and Mrs Trilling was instructed to bring Max back after a week's treatment.

When the cat basket grated on to the consulting table seven days later, Mrs Trilling took a step back, lined herself up next to her tiny husband and took a deep breath. I automatically flinched, ready for the expected outpouring of words. But she remained strangely silent. It was her husband who spoke.

'Max is fine now,' he whispered. 'It's just the wife.' He glanced briefly up at her before continuing. 'She's now got laryngitis. Can't speak a word.'

'Well that's a relief,' I said, referring to the cat's improvement.

But, from the blissful look on Mr Trilling's face, I'd a feeling he thought I was referring to his wife.

Then maybe I was.

I'd just finished the last of my blueberry muffin that morning, when Beryl reminded me about Bert's Bakery's kittens. 'They were also a good example of apt naming, if you remember.'

They were indeed. But more due to where they were found than anything to do with their character.

I'd discovered Bert's Bakery last summer and soon found myself popping across the Green to sample the range of baguettes and baps with their generous fillings for my lunch; and many times was tempted to buy one of their delicious rum babas for dessert. My sweet tooth was further encouraged when I discovered the delights of their muffins which I began having for my elevenses or at teatime in the afternoon. Through those frequent visits, I soon got to know Mrs Wainright, Bert's wife, who served in the bakery. A well-rounded lady (too many muffins perhaps?), always cheerful, always ready with a smile and a, 'What can we do for you, dear?' when you entered the shop.

One day, as she slid my bag of blueberry muffins across the counter, she mentioned, 'We've got some semi-wild kittens out in the old oven house. Any chance you could spare a moment or two to have a look at them?'

I promptly agreed. Who knows, there might have been a spare muffin or two for me afterwards.

'This is very kind of you,' said Mrs Wainright, as she led me out of the back and across a dark, cobbled yard flanked by a single-storey, red-bricked building.

'This used to be the old bakery,' she explained, putting her shoulder to the door, which juddered open on squealing, rusty hinges.

'As you can see, it's not used now,' she added. 'That's why we encourage the cats.' She flicked on a light that glowed feebly on flour-festooned cobwebs. 'To keep down the rats.'

As if to illustrate her point, something scurried behind a pile of sacks leaving a swirl of white dust. But my attention was diverted to the domed brick oven which dominated the end of the room. Its doors were missing and from the yawning black void echoed a series of pitiful weak miaows.

I peered in and as my eyes adjusted to the gloom, could just make out a bundle of smoky grey kittens at the back.

'No sign of mum then?' I asked, turning to Mrs Wainright.

She hunched her shoulders. 'Guess something must have happened to her. We think the kittens were born about a week ago. Up till then the mother was certainly around. We'd been feeding her.' She pointed to a dish, its contents now hard and stuck to the plate.

The kittens' plaintive cries were a clear indication of their hunger. Something needed to be done – and quickly.

'Looks as if we're in for a spot of hand rearing,' I said, reaching in to gently extract the limp kittens.

There were five in all, their grey fur damp and matted with flour. They all felt cold and the two smallest ones were almost lifeless.

Mrs Wainright sprang into action. She pulled down an old wicker basket from a shelf next to the oven and scooped the kittens into it. I hurried after her as she zipped across the yard and into her kitchen, where she pushed away the clothes-horse in front of the Aga and installed the basket in front of it.

Within minutes, a hot water bottle had been filled from a kettle singing on the stove, wrapped in a towel and placed under the kittens to provide additional warmth.

'Now for some food,' she declared, bustling across to the fridge and taking out a carton of milk.

I intervened at this point. 'Best to use a milk powder specially formulated for kittens,' I said.

She raised her eyebrows. 'Then what are we waiting for?'

She followed me back to Prospect House where Lucy fetched milk powder and a kitten fostering kit from the dispensary.

'Best use the smallest teat,' I advised Mrs Wainright, handing over the equipment, 'and fill the bottle with the milk-mix at blood temperature.'

'How often should I feed them?' she asked, raising her glasses to peer at the label on the tin.

'Ideally, every four hours if possible.'

'No problem,' she assured me.

There was a small cough from Lucy.

I turned to her. 'Anything to add?' I asked, encouragingly.

'Well, if Mrs Wainright could make the last feed as near to midnight as possible, and the first morning feed at about seven.'

'We can do better than that,' said Mrs Wainright. 'Bert's up at five to bake the first batch of bread, so the kits can have a feed then.'

'Oh... There is just one other thing,' said Lucy, hesitantly. 'Make sure the equipment's kept in sterilising solution between feeds.'

Mrs Wainright's face split into a broad grin. 'Brings back memories of my own brood,' she chuckled.

'Let's hope it all goes well,' I said, as she was ushered out.

'Should be okay,' she answered. 'Providing I use my loaf.'

Rather apt, I thought. Coming from a baker's wife. I was tempted to add, 'I'm sure you'll rise to the occasion,' but thought it better not to. Puns of that sort were best left to Finley O'Connor when he ran the story in the *Westcott Gazette* as I was sure he would. Readers of his local paper loved animal features.

In the event, Mrs Wainright was unable to save the two tiniest kittens, but the other three picked up a treat and she kept me informed of their progress whenever I called in for my baps and rum babas.

Two months later, Mrs Wainright was levering a wicker basket on to my consulting table and whisking off the chequered cover.

Three pairs of blue eyes blinked up at me. One by one, noses twitching, the plump kittens jumped out and cautiously sniffed the table, their tails erect like quivering flag poles.

With the kittens injected, I began to fill out their vaccination cards.

'Have you decided on names for them yet?' I asked, pen poised.

'Yes... It was easy,' beamed Mrs Wainwright. 'What else but Bap, Baba and Muffin?'

Obviously a piece of cake, I thought.

Sorry Finley... couldn't resist that one.

I dread to think what headlines he might have come up with had he chosen to report on what happened to me a few days after I'd had that chat in the back garden with Beryl.

An occasion when I rather disgraced myself.

I still shudder at the memory.

It was so... so... embarrassing.

7

All In A Daze's Work

I had a premonition that all would not be well one Thursday, even though it was going to be my half-day off and I usually looked forward to it. Gazing into the mirror first thing, I said to my reflection, 'It's going to be one of those days.' Don't ask me why I knew. I just did.

The drive over the Downs from Willow Wren was uneventful. The usual wait to get out of the lane from the cottage on to the main road that was always busy with commuters heading over to Westcott at that time of the morning. People who preferred to live out in the countryside the other side of the Downs rather than along the coast in the ribbon development which made up Westcott and its environs. And there was the usual traffic snarl–up on hitting the outskirts of town – always a bottle-neck during the rush hour. 'Rush' hour? – that's a joke, I thought as I stop-started my way along the final stretch of road to the hospital. Not that I was in a rush to get there as it was going to be one of those days, wasn't it?

'Good morning, Paul,' said Beryl perkily, while applying another thick layer of crimson lipstick to her already thickly crimsoned lips, before opening her powder pack and applying another thick layer of dark beige powder to her already dark beige-powdered cheeks. All this via a small mirror which she kept next to her computer for two reasons – one, to touch up her make-up and two, to keep a check on who might be coming up the corridor from the office behind her. Still in a bright and breezy manner, she added, 'How are you today?'

Mmm... Beryl wasn't usually this bright and breezy first thing. Wonder what had got into her? Then I remembered the *Karma Sutra*-inspired painting that now hung over her bed. Ah...

My response was civil if not effusive.

Then Eric breezed in. Ever effervescent. Like a dose of salts. Fizzing with energy. 'Hi folks,' he declared, rubbing his hands together. He looked at my po-face and immediately turned to Beryl's smiling one, declaring, 'Why, Beryl, you look as pretty as a picture.'

Like the one above her bed no doubt.

Crystal was in similar good mood when she arrived, flashing the three of us a gracious smile. Her appearance, as ever, was smart and business-like. The blue suit. The neat white blouse. The set of her copper curls. And the light, sweet scent of honeysuckle. Usually seeing her was enough to raise my spirits if ever they were flagging. Perhaps I ought to have a photo of her above my bed? Good Lord. Just what am I thinking of? Very disturbing.

I heard the chatter of voices from down in the ward followed by peals of laughter. Mandy and Lucy sharing a joke? Wow.

Wish I could have shared the joke. Or at least shared the mood in which it was made. Everyone seemed to be in such good spirits. Except me. But then I still had this premonition that things were going to take a turn for the worse.

And they did. Just after eleven o'clock when the phone call came through.

The morning's appointments had been routine. Nothing too challenging. And the ops list that followed had been light with just a couple of cat spays, one dog castrate and a dental on a dachshund. No sweat. But the phone call did that to me – made me break out in a cold sweat.

'Paul,' said Beryl, 'I've just had a call from Mr Nunn. He was in quite a state, asking if you'd come out and put Coco to sleep.'

Ah... There we had it. The unease I'd been feeling. Decision time for poor old Coco had been reached.

He was a medium-sized mongrel owned by an elderly couple, Arthur and Ethyl Nunn. As Coco's name suggested, he was a bit of a clown – in fact he was one of the soppiest, most endearing dogs I'd ever encountered. And there was an element of the clown about his looks. White furred, except for a large patch of black on his rump, he had over-sized paws and a wide mane of white like a clown's ruff. One black ear erect, one white ear floppy, and big black bulbous eyes and nose completed the comical look. And what a fun dog he was, always playing up to his name. He had his own special toy – a rubber ring which he'd bring in hanging from his jaws whenever he was booked in to be seen. Say, 'Hello Coco,' and he'd somehow twist the ring in his teeth and let go of it so that it sprung up over his muzzle and landed as a crown on his head, wedged between his ears. That trick made everyone laugh. And it pleased him as well, to judge from the big grin that would then engulf his face.

I began seeing him after he'd started a course of long term treatment for congestive heart failure. The signs were already there. Getting out of breath

113

after short walks. A non-productive cough. A heart murmur easily detected when listening to his chest. But with digoxin therapy and diuretics to prevent too much fluid build-up in the body, Coco kept going. But as I'd warned Arthur and Ethyl, there would come a time when Coco's heart would give out, the drugs he was on unable to support him. Seems that time had come. Hence the request for me to put him to sleep. But to be done at home, in familiar surroundings.

Thus, just before mid-day, I found myself driving east from Westcott towards Brigstock and then cutting across the Downs before I reached the Ouze estuary to head for the small town of Hamfield. The Nunns lived in one of a small cluster of terraced Victorian cottages on the main road a couple of miles before you reached the town centre. Theirs was the middle of a row of five, the front door reached up a flight of brick steps from the pavement below. I'd barely rung the bell before Arthur answered it.

Of slight build, with thinning grey hair, and normally ruddy-cheeked, he was ashen faced and agitated.

'Do come through, Mr Mitchell,' he said in a hoarse whisper, and led me down a narrow, dark hallway into a lounge which opened up through French windows on to a lawned area in the near corner of which, in a patch of sunshine, lay Coco stretched out on his side, barely conscious. Next to him, gently stroking his head, was Ethyl. She was usually a bright, bustling little lady with a mass of springy grey curls and luminous grey eyes. Today she was slumped on the lawn, those curls lank, those eyes glistening with tears.

She looked up as I approached. 'Coco crept out here earlier this morning and collapsed,' she wept.

'And he hasn't moved since,' said Arthur, his voice catching in his throat.

I knelt down next to Coco and opened my black bag I'd brought with me, removed my stethoscope and listened to Coco's heart and lungs. I checked his colour, felt his pulse. Tested his reflexes. Went through the motions of a clinical examination. Though it wasn't really necessary. Coco had suffered a massive stroke. But I did it to smooth the way to what had to be done next.

'I think the time has come,' I said as quietly and as gently as possible, running a hand down Coco's inert back.

Arthur pulled Ethyl to her feet and they clasped one another tightly, both now in floods of tears.

'If you think it's best,' sobbed Arthur.

'And Mr Mitchell,' faltered Ethyl, 'could you do it out here? It's Coco's favourite sunbathing spot. He's been using it all summer.' She took a shuddering breath. 'And can we stay with him?'

'No question,' I murmured, trying to hold back the tears that were fast beginning to well up in me.

'Thank you,' said Arthur as he and Ethyl lowered themselves next to their beloved dog while I drew up the syringeful of lethal barbiturate.

'Okay, Coco, my old friend,' I said lifting up his front leg and clipping away some hair. 'This isn't going to hurt.' I turned to the Nunns. 'He's too far gone to feel anything,' I reassured them. And then using my right thumb to raise the vein, I slipped in the needle attached to the syringe; and once, having drawn back on the plunger to see some blood seep in, I released my thumb, and gradually, cautiously, injected the lethal dose. A tense moment. A moment of raw emotion. The rise and fall of Coco's chest slowing down. A final shuddering breath. Then nothing. Just a tremor of muscles, before they too ceased moving. Eyes that once had been so bright, so full of fun and mischief, glazed over as Coco's life slipped away. Came to an end in a warm pool of sunshine that September afternoon, next to the two people with whom he had shared a life full of fun and frolics – their loyal and trusting companion for over fourteen years. The Nunns. Now bereft at his parting and who, at that moment, were too grief-stricken to speak.

I packed up my things and slowly walked across to the French windows and waited in the lounge until Arthur had recovered sufficiently to come over, leaving Ethyl on the lawn, still in tears, her arms wrapped round Coco's body.

Once inside, Arthur pointed to a photograph of Coco on their mantelpiece. Coco the clown. Coco with his rubber ring balanced on his head, that broad soppy grin on his face. The ring lay on the table. Arthur picked it up. 'We'll bury him with this,' he said, twisting the ring in his hand, more tears beginning to trickle down his cheeks.

So that was it. That was the premonition that had been hovering in my mind since the moment I'd woken up that morning.

It left me feeling emotionally drained and rather depressed as it brought back memories of the loss of my dear little Nelson. The void it had left. One that had still not been filled.

As I drove away I tried to gee myself up a bit. After all, it was a bright, beautiful clear September afternoon, and I did have the rest of the day off. My intention had been to return to Willow Wren but on second thoughts, decided that while I was over this way it might be pleasant to spend the afternoon doing a spot of sightseeing. It was ages since I'd been round these parts. In fact well over ten years. Then I had visited the area with my parents.

As a youngster in my early teens, I used to organise day trips out from our home in Bournemouth. Oh, those were the days. Remembered in the warm glow of nostalgia. The folding picnic chairs. The tartan blanket. A Thermos of tea. Three types of sandwich – one of which always had chunky brown pickle in it. There was something almost military in the way I'd study potential places to invade (visit) in the previous week, plotting the routes there – working out how far away they were, the best scenic ways to get there, how long to stay at one particular beauty spot before moving on. I'd work out the specific points of interest at the chosen destination that could be fitted into the scheduled time I'd planned on staying there, before returning by a different route. Never ever would I contemplate returning the same way as we'd come. Heaven help it if we were forced to. I considered that a dismal failure of my mission.

Part and parcel of that mission – in fact the most important part as far as my parents were concerned – was to ensure that the stop we made for lunch was done at a pub. From my point of view, to justify spending time sitting in one when that time could have been better spent visiting the nearby Victorian school to see where some local dignitary had carved his initials on a wooden desk as an eight-year-old, it was essential the pub chosen had some character. The heavy-oaked-beamed-roaring-fire-in-inglenook variety was my mum's particular favourite. But she would happily tolerate the artex-ceiling–popping-gas-fire sort so long as it stocked Barley wine – her favourite tipple.

I seemed to remember there was a pub in Hamfield where the above criteria for choosing it, fell between two stools. Certainly my mum did on the occasion we visited it, having had one too many Barley wines. She slept all the way back to Bournemouth, only briefly opening her eyes and murmuring, 'Nice,' whenever I nudged her awake to view one of my carefully chosen places of interest we were passing en-route along the A27. The only time she showed real interest was when we stopped at a block of public lavatories on the outskirts of Chichester. Then both she and Dad shot out with indecent haste to use them.

So it was to this pub in Hamfield that I decided to head. Not only for old time's sake but for the fact that I was feeling rather peckish despite the emotional turmoil just experienced.

In its heyday, Hamfield had been a coaching stop on the toll road between London and Brighton. It had boasted three inns. The Prince Regent at the bottom end of the High Street was once visited by the carrier of that name on his way down to dip his oar in the sea. It was now a Chinese takeaway. Its rival, at the top end of the same street, always attempting to go one better, changed its name from The Ploughman to the King George on the latter's accession to the throne and a brief stop-over for a royal pee; it was now a sushi bar with fourteen mews-style houses in the former coach yard. This just left the third inn, The Crown, never knowingly visited by any Head of State and now marooned on the outskirts of Hamfield by a new by-pass with its tentacles of spur roads to new housing estates. I suspected the jaws of bulldozers were just waiting for the owner to cave in so they could do the same to his pub.

I drove round Hamfield's by-pass – new since the visit with my parents – trying to determine which of the numerous slip roads I was passing would give me access to what I thought was The Crown, spotted over to my right. Having completed three circuits of the by-pass, I managed to track down the right one, thundered through an under-pass and ground to a halt in a shower of gravel in the pub's car park lurking in deep shadow below the by-pass's parapet which surrounded the building on three sides, effectively engulfing it in a concrete abyss.

So despite it being a bright sunny September day, not one shaft of light playing on the road above, was able to percolate down to the pub below, so making a mockery of the collection of wooden benches and tables set out in the front – designed to encourage people to sit outside on a warm summer's evening with their drinks. The thick layers of green mould with which the garden furniture was coated were a clear indication that no one had attempted to do so for a very long time.

As to the pub itself, the inn sign creaking in the breeze proclaimed 'The Buccaneer'. Not 'The Crown'. Why 'The Buccaneer' was beyond me. Though Hamfield had once been a port, that was three hundred years ago: and since then, the sea had retreated and was now a good three miles away. This building, though somewhat dilapidated was never three centuries old. And it was never the pub I'd visited with my parents. Surely not? My memory must have been playing tricks on me. No doubt aided by the confusion of the new by–pass and numerous slip roads leading off of it. The Crown we'd visited had had pristine, white-washed walls, hanging baskets overflowing with cascades of purple petunias and a neatly manicured front lawn.

Whereas this 'Buccaneer' was a sickly shade of sea-green, moss-stained pebble dash, with four huge balls of green plastic imitation box bushes hanging from hooks along its front, and a weed-dotted gravel car park deserted save for one solitary car. All very uninviting.

Oh well, I thought. Now I'm here, I might as well give it a go.

The entrance lobby felt dank and cold, and smelt faintly of rotten eggs. For once, a squirt of Beryl's Summer Bouquet wouldn't have gone amiss.

The only occupants of the lounge were a middle-aged couple sitting in the gloomy bay window. The only sound was the drone of traffic hurtling past at ceiling height. Smoke lazed up from the embers of a fire smouldering in the hearth in front of which a small brown and black haired terrier lay tightly curled in a ball, shivering slightly.

As I walked in, the dog sat up, emitted a short, sharp yap and then proceeded to give itself a vigorous scratch. Head to one side, its back leg frantically pumped up and down, its claws digging into the side of its neck, the name tag on its collar rattling furiously. Then as quickly as it had started, it stopped and retreated into its ball again.

At the same time, the man reached down to his ankle, where he pushed up his trouser leg to vigorously scratch the skin exposed above his sock. He was joined by the woman sitting next to him, who started scratching the inside of her calf just below the hem of the navy blue skirt she was wearing.

Both quickly stopped when they saw me looking at them and slumped back in their armchairs. The man took a sip of his lager and the woman drew her coat over her shoulders and took a sip of her wine.

I approached the bar above which was draped a series of fishing nets through which gawped some brown plastic trout and in which hung clusters of pink plastic starfishes. I stood at the bar waiting for someone to appear – a mein host to give me a cheery welcome and ask what he could get me.

No one did.

'Try pressing the bell,' suggested the man with the lager, now scratching the inside of his wrist while the woman was now scratching a spot just below the collar of her blouse.

I walked the length of the bar to where he'd indicated, read the card 'Press for attention' I found there, and then pressed the bell next to it.

A rattling ring rang out akin to a locust being eviscerated.

Clickerty click.

I tried again.

Another clickerty click.

At the third click, a tall, loose-limbed man swayed into view and loped behind the bar; gold-rimmed spectacles attached to a length of string dangled from his neck. I sensed he was well oiled with drink. Verified when the smell of whisky and rotten teeth wafted over me.

'Sorry to have kept you,' said the man, 'I was trying to unblock one of the gents' toilets. You'd be surprised what gets stuck round their S bends.'

My mood, not being that good anyway, sank to greater depths on receiving such news. No way did I want to know what got jammed round gents' S bends, but feeling that this man was about to tell me, I took a deep breath and opened my mouth to speak. But the man jumped in first.

'Mind you, I can't always hear the bell. It's my ears.' He leaned forward assailing me with another waft of bad teeth and whisky fumes. 'Wax you know. Should get them syringed.'

As if to demonstrate the point, he held up a little finger and rammed it into his right ear, where he waggled it around emitting little grunts of pleasure. When eventually it plopped out with a blob of brown wax on it, he sighed with satisfaction, wiped the finger on his cardigan and then asked me what I'd like to drink.

'A scotch and dry,' I replied.

'Double?'

'No... No... I'm driving.'

Though his wax probing had curbed my appetite somewhat, I thought it prudent to have some sort of snack as my stomach was rumbling and I didn't want my whisky to go straight to my head. I eyed the chalky menu blackboard behind the bar. Whatever had been on it had been rubbed out. Just white smears remained. 'Have you anything to eat?' I asked.

The landlord had been reaching up to pour my shot of whisky and appeared not to have heard me. No doubt his ear canals, like the S bend in the gents' loo, needed further unblocking.

When he had slid my tumbler of scotch over to me, I tried again.

'Any food?' I enquired, in the vain hope that in a kitchen out the back somewhere sizzled a lasagne or mushroom bake.

The landlord raised profuse ginger eyebrows that would have fitted a bigger forehead and scratched a wiry tangle of matching coloured beard.

'The missus usually organises the catering,' he said, knocking back half the whisky he'd just poured himself. 'But she's in bed with a migraine, drugged up to the eyeballs.

'So no hot meals today I'm afraid. But we've got crisps, nuts. Or you could try one of the wife's specials here.'

He pushed a tall jar across to me.

'Her pickled eggs slide down a treat.'

I stared at the smooth grey ovals bobbing in front of me like the balls I'd removed from the dog that morning and suddenly lost my appetite.

'Pork scratchings then?' suggested the landlord, waving a packet at me.

I nodded. 'Might as well go the whole hog and make it two,' I said.

'Hey, funny guy,' snorted the landlord, downing the rest of his whisky and pouring himself another. 'Whole hog... I like it. Here have one on the house.' He grabbed my glass and before I could stop him had poured another shot of whisky into it.

'Well, that's kind of you sir... but I really don't think...'

'Nonsense...' interrupted the landlord. 'A wee dram or two won't do you any harm. The name's Gordon by the way. And yours?'

'Er... well... Paul.'

'So, Paul. Cheers.' Gordon raised his tumbler. 'To your good health.' He nodded encouragingly at me. 'Well go on then...'

Hesitantly, I put my hand round the full glass in front of me. Oh what the hell. One wouldn't harm, surely? I raised the glass. 'Cheers,' I said and took a cautious sip.

Ten or so sips later with caution blown to the wind, my tumbler had been drained and refilled.

'Just one for the road eh Paul?' Gordon had said, filling both our glasses, two shots in each.

Which road? I thought, my mind filling with by-passes and slip roads that would have to be negotiated before too long. Certainly before I got too pissed to drive.

'Bye... Bye,' Gordon called out, with an exaggerated wave to the couple who had been sitting huddled by the embers of the fire, scratching themselves on and off for the past ten minutes or so. Seems they'd been itching to leave, for they'd suddenly sprung to their feet.

'Do pop in again when you're passing,' he added with another wave as they crossed the room. The woman gave a small wave in return – a nervous tweak of her fingers – the man a more forceful one – two fingers up – and then scratched his neck with them.

'Oh, well,' exclaimed Gordon with a shrug. 'Guess that's the last we'll see of them.' He took another swig of his whisky. 'Don't get much passing trade these days. Most of it passes over.' He pointed upwards. 'Across the flyover.' He sniggered. 'Passes over... flyover... get it?'

I got it – and another tot of whisky at the same time.

'Really... No... I shouldn't,' I protested putting my hand across the top of my glass. But it was already full. Now how had that happened? I could have sworn it had been empty. Or had it been already full? Maybe it was just my mind. A bit befuddled after the trauma of dealing with poor Coco.

'Cheers,' said Gordon. Here's to you.' He tossed back the dregs in his glass. 'Same again?'

Before I could answer, my glass was full. But maybe it had never been empty. Oh what the heck. I took another swallow.

'Good to have some company,' Gordon said topping up my glass as soon as I put it down. 'Can get a bit lonely here sometimes. No one to talk to.'

'But you did mention a wife earlier on. You told me she did those.' I pointed to the jar of pickled eggs.

'Oh, yes... those. Sonya's a dab hand doing those all right.' Gordon drew the jar over, unscrewed the lid and fished two eggs out, cupping them in his hands. 'See these laddie. If they were your balls, she'd do this to them.' He crushed the eggs together.

Tears welled up in my eyes. I was unsure if it was due to the acrid smell of the vinegar or the uncomfortable thought of being balled by the likes of Gordon's wife. I hastily drained my glass and changed the subject. 'Well at least you've got the dog to keep you company.'

'Oh, Dorrie's a help for sure.' Gordon swilled a mouthful of whisky before swallowing it. 'Least she doesn't answer back.' He tapped the jar of pickled eggs thoughtfully and quickly took another swig of whisky.

'Too true,' I said. 'Our dogs love us to bits. Who else could be waiting for you when you get home, always glad to see you, always full of trust, tails wagging, eh?'

I leaned towards Gordon.

He leaned towards me. Our noses almost touched.

'Have you got one?' he asked.

'One what?'

'A dog.'

'Not at the moment... no...' My eyes began filling with tears as memories of dear Nelson came flooding back. Between sobs, I told Gordon what had happened. How Lucy had run him over. Killed him.

'There... there... matey,' said Gordon, reaching over to grasp my wrist. 'Don't get so upset. Have another on the house.'

I wiped back my tears and lifted my refilled glass and turned to gaze at the terrier who was sitting up, her head to one side, a paw digging into her left ear.

'Ears to you, little doggy,' I called over, before turning back to Gordon. 'And ears to you too, Gordon me old mate. Guess you've both had...' I paused. 'Can you guess?'

'No... tell me...' Gordon was leering at me, his face an oily crimson. 'What have we had?'

'An ear full.' I collapsed in tears again. This time tears of laughter. I felt them stream down my face. My fist pounded the counter. 'Get it? An ear FULL.' I stuck my left forefinger in my left ear and levered it up and down, simultaneously throwing my elbow up and down to exaggerate the effect.

A loud guffaw erupted from Gordon. 'I get it... I get it.'

Mimicking me, he too stuck a finger in his left ear and jerked it up and down. 'In out, in out, and shake it all about,' he sang before pulling out a mound of brown wax moulded to his finger tip.

'Let me take a look,' I said.

Gordon thrust his waxy fingertip in my face. 'Whatever turns you on,' he smirked.

'No... No...' I exclaimed leaning back violently, almost toppling off my stool. 'I mean let me take a look at your dog's ear... I'm a vet and might be able to help her.'

'Oh, in that case...' Gordon staggered out from behind the bar singing, 'Ear we go... ear we go... ear we go... oh,' his spectacles swinging wildly from side to side as he weaved through the stools lined up at the bar.

'How long hash... hash... whash 'er name?' I slurred, standing up to join him.

'Dorrie.'

'Ah, yes. How long hash Derek...'

'Dorrie.'

'Shorry. How long hash Dorrie been shcratshing?' I asked, as we weaved across to the hearth where the terrier took one look at us and bolted round the back of a settee.

Gordon came to a halt and stood there swaying like an unpegged tent pole. I, having dropped to my knees, was crawling round the back of the settee, wedged up against the wall, uttering a slurred, 'Coochie... Coochie... Coochie... Here Dorriekins... come to your nice Uncle Paul,' in the hope it would encourage Dorrie to appear and make friends with me. Instead, my inane utterances had the opposite effect. She shot out the other end and, scooting over to the matching settee on the far side of the hearth, vanished behind it.

Crammed behind that settee, my bum stuck out of its end, I was in no position to greet the person whose voice suddenly resonated across the room with a, 'What the bloody hell's going on 'ere for Christ's sake?'

'Ah, Sonya, my dear,' I heard Gordon say. 'You're feeling better then.'

'Who's that arsehole behind the settee?' queried the voice.

'A vet, my precious.'

Conscious the arsehole in question was mine sticking out of the rear of the settee, I shunted in reverse, until I was free and able to pull myself up. Only to find I was confronted by a woman, the like of which could have had me bolting back behind the settee.

'Meet the wife,' said Gordon, still swaying gently.

Sonya stood in the doorway to the bar, with all the charisma of a dead trout left too long in the sun.

She was a short, stocky lady, with a pink complexion and attired in a dated tight, pink trouser suit. Two gold loops swung heavily from her earlobes. A heavy gold chain hung from her thick neck. And a heavy gold belt bit into her rotund belly. The overall effect was that of a bling-laden blancmange about to burst.

She glowered at me as if I was something she'd trodden in on the way into surgery.

'Paul's offered to take a look at Dorrie's ears,' explained Gordon, fumbling with the chain on his glasses. 'Well, she has been scratching them rather a lot recently.'

Sonya spoke again. Did I detect something of the cockney in her voice? A touch of the Bow Bells ringing out in her syllables? Or was it just me? My consumption of whisky finally taking its toll.

'What? 'im take a butcher's at Dorrie? No, he bleeding well ain't. Just look at the state of 'im.'

'Whatever you say, my sweetheart,' said Gordon.

'He's as pissed as a coot.'

'Er... newt actually,' I corrected her.

'What?'

'He said, "He's as pissed as a newt",' said Gordon.

'Don't 'ave to tell me that,' said Sonya. 'It's bleedin' obvious.' She glared at her husband.

'Of course, dearest,' replied Gordon.

Her voice was resonating in my brain. All mixed up. A jumble of cockney rhyming slang. What was it she was saying?

'Can't see 'im hitting the Frog and Toad.'

'I'll be all right,' I croaked, my voice distant. Detached. 'Just need a Jimmy Riddle,' I sighed, feeling myself slipping into a stupor. 'Then I'll hit the road.' But it was the floor I actually hit. Zapped. Out of it.

'What a load of pony and trap,' I thought I heard Sonya say as I fell. 'You're in no state to go anywhere.'

'No honestly, it's not a load of crap. I can manage,' I moaned, writhing on the floor.

'Orchestra stalls!' Sonya retorted.

Balls? A picture of her pickled eggs floated into view. My stomach gave a lurch and turning my head to one side, I heaved up a pile of semi-digested pork scratchings.

I came to surrounded by an ocean of ultramarine wallpaper depicting a turbulent wash of waves over which wheeled hundreds of seagulls. It did nothing to quell my nausea. I felt as if I was on a heaving boat, about to do the same again. Heave-ho. The boat I was on was actually a sagging bunk bed with a headboard of rope rigging, adjacent to which, perched on a bedside barrel, was a plastic skull with a white lampshade sticking out of its cranium. Above the ropes hung a badly executed attempt to represent a pirate, ginger-bearded, scarlet-faced, with one oily green eye larger than the other, both seeming to look in opposite directions. It vaguely resembled that chap I had been drinking with. What was his name? It gradually came back to me. Gordon. That was it. There was also a Dorrie scratching its ears. And a Trouble and Strife. Eh? Oh yes, a wife – Sonya. I shivered as the events started to play back in my mind. But when did they all happen?

I fiddled with the neck of the skull and switched it on. A dull glow filtered through its cranium – enough light by which I could see the time on my watch. 7.00. Hells bells, had I really been zonked all afternoon? I got to my feet decidedly groggy and paddled across a flecked green carpet, past an antiquated TV stand on which perched a stuffed green parrot, half its feathers lying in a pool of down beneath it.

The bathroom echoed the seafaring theme – only fish replaced the gulls. There were shoals of them on every wall and gaping from every tile. I lifted the lavatory seat half-expecting a crab to wave a claw up at me. The cistern emptied at the third pull, the refill sounding like the tide grating up a shingle bank. I washed my hands in the trickle of cold water that burped out of the hot tap and dried them on a towel inscribed 'The Buccaneer Hotel'.

I hardly dared look at myself in the bathroom mirror but I risked a quick peep and promptly wished I hadn't. I had the frazzled look of someone who'd just been Jolly Rogered against their will. With a tongue the colour and smell of a buccaneer's backside, eyes that felt they had been marinated in wet sand, and hair plastered to my head like a dried-out pile of bladder-rack stranded on a rock, I felt an absolute wreck. So befitting the theme of this room – which I assumed was one of the pub's, and into which I must have been jettisoned by Gordon and Sonya like an unwanted lump of flotsam.

Time to set sail out of here, Paul, I thought. So I steered myself across to the door, conscious of the flocks of gulls reeling round the walls making my spinning head spin even faster.

I crept down the dimly lit stairs and into the foyer, meeting no one on the flight down. I peeped into the bar half expecting Gordon to be in there. But no. It was deserted.

I jumped when Sonya's voice boomed behind me as she emerged from a room on the other side of the foyer. 'Good morning,' she said, all bright and breezy. 'Got some sleep then?'

Morning? What? I glanced out through the glass panel on the front door. Outside, a glimmer of daylight showed between the concrete arms of the flyover. Only then did it dawn on me. I'd slept the sleep of the dead. Out of it for over twelve hours. And had woken up feeling like a zombie.

'Perhaps some breakfast would help yer?' suggested Sonya, hustling me through into the room she'd just left.

In it, there were a dozen or so tables, chair backs tilted against them. Only one was laid. On an off-white tablecloth, there was a mat depicting a pod of porpoises, a set of yellow cutlery, with barnacle encrusted handles, a crab and lobster cruet and a clam-shaped sugar bowl with a scalloped lid.

'You're to 'elp yourself,' said Sonya. 'Continental only, I'm afraid.' She indicated the nearby sideboard on which were displayed a jug of milk, orange juice, some mini-packs of cereals, three croissants, a small bunch of bananas and a large jar of pickled eggs. 'And would you like tea or coffee?'

'Er... coffee. Very strong if possible,' I replied. Anything to keep my throbbing head under control.

When she returned, I learnt that Gordon was still 'flat out' as she put it.

'And Dorrie?'

'In the kitchen 'aving her brekkie.' She smiled. The smile transformed her. She became far less intimidating. 'Could yer give 'er a quick butchers before yer go? 'er scratching's driving us round the bleedin' bend. And it's not only 'er ears. She's itchy all over.'

With a couple of cups of coffee and a croissant inside of me, I felt less zombie-like. A bit more human. And so was able to follow Sonya into the bar in a relatively straight line to where Dorrie was now sitting on the settee in front of which I'd collapsed the previous afternoon. I saw her tense herself, ready to spring off and visualised another dash behind the settee – only Sonya had anticipated that.

'Oh... no... me sweetie... you ain't going nowhere,' she said, holding out a lump of cheese, as she sat down next to Dorrie, swinging the terrier on to her lap as the titbit was wolfed down.

'Can yer manage like this?' she asked me, patting the space next to her.

'Let's try,' I answered, plonking myself down alongside her.

It wasn't ideal as I hadn't an auriscope to look down Dorrie's ear canals, but by lifting her ear flaps and squinting down each of them, noting the brown debris and reddening of the outer ear canal in each of them, it was obvious she was suffering from excessive build up of ear wax à la Gordon. I told Sonya that I had some ear drops out in the car which would dissolve the wax and ease the inflammation; the drops also included something to kill off any ear mites should they be present.

'And what-er-bout the itchiness that's getting on our tits?' queried Sonya.

I eased Dorrie round so her back-end faced me and ran my hands down her flanks and over the base of her spine. Her right hind instantly came up in a strong scratch reflex. And the reason? Fleas. I spotted one run through her hair. And there was plenty of evidence that they were around – lots of black flea dirts, especially over the base of her tail.

'Thought as much,' Sonya remarked. 'We've bin scratchin' ourselves silly recently.'

Likewise your customers, I thought, remembering the itchy couple yesterday. God. That seemed a lifetime away. Having fetched my black bag from the car, I gave Dorrie an anti-inflammatory injection, worked some of the drops in each ear canal and left the rest for Sonya to massage in twice a day.

'Could I use 'em on Gordon?' she asked.

Then seeing my dubious look, added, 'Only kiddin' yer.'

Flea control was discussed. The use of a spray to kill off fleas on the carpets and settees while anti-flea drops could be purchased on line and be applied to Dorrie's skin, where they'd be absorbed and so kill off any fleas that hopped on her to feed.

As I explained all of this, I did notice Sonya flinch away from me a couple of times. Had I bad breath? Still reeking of booze?

'Yer going straight into work?' she queried, when I'd finished.

'Yep. No time to get home first,' I replied.

'Then a couple of these might be of use to yer.' She handed me a packet of strong mints she'd pulled out of her pocket.

But I knew it wouldn't fool Beryl.

As I dragged myself into reception, there was a tut. A phss. And Summer Bouquet filled the air.

But what followed the next day filled the air with a different sort of phss. A hissing sound that had Beryl leaping on to her stool, frightened out of her wits.

8

What A Load Of Cobras

That morning, I strode into reception and found Beryl not perched on her office stool but standing on it, one foot raised in the air, her left arm stretched straight out, a finger pointing. I did for a brief second wonder whether she was attempting to practise a bit of Iyengar yoga – seeking to calm her mind, seeking to bring light to darkness and achieve samadhi. After all she was a long-time advocate of yoga. But wobbling about on a stool in such an ungainly posture just before morning surgery was about to start? Surely not?

I followed the direction in which she was pointing and realised that there was more on her mind than achieving a blissful state of super consciousness: she was trying to make me aware of what was wriggling around on the other side of her desk, in the middle of the reception's floor.

It was a pillowcase. Quite an attractive one with a modern design of dark blue stripes zig-zagging across a background of light blue. Perhaps not to Beryl's taste. I reckon her pillows would have had pink roses, or the like, scattered across them. But even if not to her liking, there was no reason why she should have taken such a warrior-pose stance to that zig-zag pattern had it not been for the fact those zig-zags were at that moment zig-zagging across the floor towards her desk, with the contents of the case hissing loudly. It suddenly stopped, deflated slightly, then reared up, one corner of the case flicking from side to side before it executed a perfect back flip, landing with a thump to continue its slide towards Beryl.

Beryl, on the point of flipping herself, hissed, 'Do something.' With her left arm twisted up behind her back, she raised her right hand as if about to attempt a gomukhasana – a move which had her fingers clip the edge of the lampshade above them. She ducked. The lampshade swung. The bulb in it flashed and popped. Out went the light.

'Do something,' she repeated, just as Eric bounced up from the office and caught sight of her. 'Hey, Beryl, no problem,' he said. 'I'll go and get you a bulb.' With that he disappeared.

Meanwhile the pillowcase continued wriggling across the floor, disappeared under the desk to reappear the other side under Beryl's stool, where it ground to a halt with another hiss. This generated a further wave of wobbles in Beryl, just as Crystal breezed in from the car park.

'Can someone please help me,' implored Beryl.

'Of course, of course, I'll get you a bulb,' said Crystal before she too nipped out.

Mandy and Lucy followed, Beryl's implorations the spur for them both to dash out for replacement bulbs.

'What's wrong with them all,' spluttered Beryl, slumping into a Baddha Konasana – seated, feet together, knees bent to the sides and heels drawn close to the body, with her hands clasped round her toes.

Quite supple-jointed for a sixty-four-year-old, I thought.

In that pose, she rocked back and forth.

'Can't they see what's going on?' she moaned.

Probably not, I thought. Hence the need for the bulbs.

Even though a 100 watt energy saving tungsten bulb might have thrown light on her Bahhda Konasana, it wasn't the answer to Beryl's predicament. My removal of the pillowcase from under her stool and examination of its contents in the prep room would be. To judge from all the hissing, those contents, when turned out, would turn out to be a snake.

Beryl didn't like snakes. In fact they really scared her.

Her Yama was shot to pieces and her Dharana ripped to shreds when she once found one in the fridge – she'd been intent on taking out the skimmed milk for tea that afternoon, only to discover an anaconda draped round the carton. The snake had been admitted having swallowed a heating pad, and I wanted to take an X-ray. As it had been a bit lively, I decided to cool the snake down first by coiling it up in the fridge. Only I forgot to inform Beryl that I'd done so. You could tell by the look in her eye when she charged into the office and collapsed in a chair just how scared she was. Very wild–eyed. Possibly more pronounced in her case than in someone else since her right eye – that glass one of hers – had swivelled round so that only the white was showing.

This morning, her false eye remained in situ. It was just her stool that was swivelling round. And her mind. That was in a whirl, very restless, which no number of Eagle or Tree poses would have helped to ease.

I don't get wound up about snakes. They don't bother me unduly. So I don't need any Pratyahara to unwind me. I put that down to the fact that, when growing up in Nigeria as an eight-year-old, there had been many encounters, many occasions, in which to test my nerves, see if I could really come to accept such creatures. Okay, admittedly, there were some heart-stopping, bum-clenching moments. Understandable when you think the snakes out there were mostly venomous – one bite or spit and you could be dead within minutes. There was the time a long – a very long – cobra slithered into the bathroom of our bungalow while I was sitting on the loo. I evacuated my bowels immediately. No fear of constipation. Just a passing fear of that snake as it passed my knocking knees – sufficient for me to pass wind. I produced a very loud fart. It had a startling effect on the cobra.

I've learnt since that snakes can't hear in the same way that we do. But nevertheless can detect very loud airborne sounds. I'm not sure what decibel level my fart achieved but as I let rip, I felt I had achieved something at the higher end of the scale. Seems snakes detect these sounds as vibrations transmitted through the ground. So perhaps it was the reverberations of my fart echoing yodel-like round the toilet bowl to be picked up through the bathroom floor that caused the cobra to bolt, since with a sudden whiplash action, it shot out through the soak-away hole in the wall and disappeared. Much to my relief.

But not to Mother's. It so happens she was desperate for a pee. But not so desperate as to risk lifting her skirt and pulling down her knickers just for a cobra to pop up and take it all in.

She stood in the shade of the frangipani trees next to the soak-away down which the cobra had slithered, her arms resolutely crossed – as indeed were her legs – she was now even more desperate for a pee. It was Father who came to her relief. Being an army officer, he planned a military-style attack on the soak-away.

The houseboys were lined up, two to each side, with spade, knobkerry, machete and broom at the ready. Father lit a smoke bomb and tossed it down the hole.

'Stand back,' he ordered.

But the command was unnecessary. Thick black smoke billowed out of the hole, forcing us all to retreat, coughing, eyes streaming, Father, Mother and I as black as the boys.

'Masa... Masa...' they chorused, doing a nervous war-dance on the spot. They pointed to the hole. The smoky entrance framed a large, whiskery snout. With a shrill squeak, out shot an enormous rat, equal in size to our cat. There was a swish and a glint of steel, and the rat was despatched only teeth-gnashing inches from my feet.

The cobra appeared next. Foot after foot of it whipped out of the hole to weave swiftly across the path. The boys went in for the attack. The snake reared up, inflated its hood, and swung round on them. The machete-carrier lost his nerve and leapt back as the cobra lashed out. It turned and struck the spade with a loud *ping.* The broom-carrier wisely swept himself out of sight. It was left to the knob-kerry man to end the battle with a head-crunching blow.

Father posed for a picture with his spoils of war; rat by the tail in one hand, arm held high to dangle the six foot cobra in the other.

Even with my experiences of snakes, I still felt some unease, staring at the bulging pillowcase that was now sitting silently on the prep room work top.

'Right,' I said, glancing across at Lucy, who was keeping her distance. 'We'd better open up and see what we've got, uh?'

The pillowcase suddenly hissed.

'Doors all closed?' I added.

Lucy nodded reluctantly. The bag gave another hiss.

Clenching my jaw and buttocks simultaneously, I cautiously cut the twine that had been tied round the opening of the case and allowed the end to fall open. The sides rippled as did my insides, when a triangular head, with an arrow-shaped cap of chestnut scales, highlighted by a yellow stripe to either side, squeezed out of the gap, a forked tongue flickering. Then, like a gigantic tube of toothpaste that had been violently trodden on, out shot a python. Its chestnut-blotched coils whipped across the work surface, weaving deftly through the bottles of hand-scrub and antiseptic until it hit the stainless steel instrument cabinet. There its head reared half-way up the side, pushed by the coils heaped behind it. This caused it to topple sideways, where the sheer weight of its body pushed it over the edge of the work surface to spiral rapidly down on to the floor, collapsing in a gleaming pile of coils. The force of those coils against the prep room door made it spring open. The snake rapidly untangled itself and shot through into the corridor at a rate of knots, just as Eric was passing, clutching a light bulb.

'What the blazes...?' he bellowed. The bulb spun out of his hand as the python zig-zagged between his legs, weaved up the steps and slithered rapidly on through into the waiting room. From here a cacophony of screams erupted and, a flood of clients poured out into reception, hauling dogs, clutching cats and swinging budgie cages. They surged round Beryl who was once more atop her stool, rapidly executing a series of wobbly yoga positions that would have done a Hari Krishna devotee proud.

To add to this electrifying scene, in stepped Crystal, Mandy and Lucy, each carrying a light bulb.

I squirmed my way through the melee and managed to catch up with the python under a chair in the waiting room, where I executed my own pose – a two-arms-forward, spine-curved, knees-bent, pull-back-python-to-prep-room pose by which means I dragged the python out. This caused a mass exodus of clients back into the waiting room and left three shattered light bulbs on the reception floor.

Once Beryl was persuaded to climb down from her stool, she was able to give me some information. But not much. A chap had roared in on a motorbike, looking rather menacing in black leathers, stomped into reception and flung the wriggling pillowcase on to the floor exclaiming, 'All yours,' before roaring off.

'All yours,' turned out to be this python. Later, a quick flick through images on Google identified it as a rock python. Those pictures showed multi-patched snakes, their olive, brown or chestnut ribbons of colour set against a background of yellow-white scales, all in polished, gleaming hues. Not so this specimen. Though spritely in its efforts to escape, there was no life in its scales. Even to my unpractised eye, I could see they were dull, dingy and dry, hanging loosely from its trunk which, when I plucked up courage to run my hand down it, felt thin and gaunt.

The exertion required to make its escape had left it exhausted. It lay in loose coils on the prep room counter, motionless.

'Wonder when you last ate anything,' I said to myself. 'Indeed, I wonder if you can eat?' I cautiously stuck my forefinger out and touched its nose. No reaction. I ran my finger over its head. Still nothing. Feeling a bit braver, I slid forefinger and thumb along the sides of its jaw, squeezing slightly until its mouth opened. Using the forefinger of my right hand, I opened its mouth, the jaws widening and dislocating. That dislocation, aided by backward-pointing teeth – which in this python's case looked in perfect nick – would have enabled the snake to swallow a rat with ease.

Just hope you won't have a go at devouring my hand, I thought.

But I needn't have worried. It was too far gone.

Not so the snake my mother once encountered. She had been weeding the rockery adjacent to our bungalow in Nigeria and had just pulled up a clump of wayward lemon grass. In doing so, she also pulled up a black mamba, tightly coiled in the grassy roots. Black mambas are vicious snakes known to attack and strike out rather than slither away. This one didn't attack. Only because its dislocated jaws and teeth were locked round a large toad in the process of being swallowed.

'Ugh! A snake,' shrieked Mum, and in a display worthy of a mountain goat, sprang from rock to verandah in one flying leap. There she collapsed, quaking in a chair. I hurried past, more concerned to see the snake before it slithered away.

I checked this python's mucous membranes. No sign of the deadly mouth rot – cheesy yellow, necrotic plaques layered in strands of ropey saliva and reeking of decay – often seen in reptiles and often the cause of appetite loss. Nope. Its membranes were fine.

'So Paul,' muttered Eric, striding in, bulb-less, his white coat flapping round his ankles. 'What's all this about a pillowcase stuffed with a python? Ah...' He ground to halt next to me. 'Guess this is the culprit.' He peered down at the coiled up snake. 'Looks a bit clapped out to me,' he said, adding, 'So what next?'

I shrugged. In the absence of any past history, it was all going to be a bit hit or miss. Or in the case of this python, a bit hiss or miss.

'I was thinking of attempting to rehydrate it with some subcutaneous fluid and orally administer some more by stomach tube,' I said in a rather authoritative tone of voice.

'Worth bunging some fluids in, I suppose,' Eric mused. 'Shove 'em under the skin and down the hatch.'

Precisely. Thanks Eric.

Having re-examined the limp python, I decided against trying to give any fluids subcutaneously. The skin just felt too fragile, the scales too puckered.

'Down the hatch then,' said Eric.

'Stomach tubing, yes,' I replied.

'I'll grab its head and hold it for you if you like.'

'That would be extremely helpful. Thanks.'

'No problem.'

But there was a problem. No head.

'Where's the blighter gone?' said Eric, briefly scratching his own bald pate, as he peered down at the coils stacked like a pile of tyres, and into the middle of which the python's head had sunk from view, tucked under one of those coils.

'Er... Eric... I shouldn't if I were you,' I warned, as Eric slid his right arm down through the middle of the pile spreading his fingers out to slide them over the snake's head and grasp it round its neck.

'Got you, you little devil,' he declared triumphantly, giving me a broad smile. 'Easy when you know how.' He yanked his elbow up, his hand still holding the python's head. Only it wasn't the head that lifted up. It was the whole python, now coiled tightly round his forearm.

'Oh sodding hell,' said Eric rapidly turning puce. Momentarily he managed to lever his arm into the air, biceps bulging like a weight-lifter, only for it to fall back on to the counter under the python's weight. 'Seems I've got myself in a bit of a jam here,' he confessed, his arm locked in the folds of the snake. 'Come on, Paul... quick... What do you reckon I should do?'

'Let go of its head.'

'Already done that.'

'Well... Er...' I was lost for words.

'Think of something for God's sake. I can't have this bugger squeezing me, thinking I might make a tasty meal.'

I did have a thought. How very disarming this was all becoming. Ouch.

Eventually, the python flagged again, went limp, its coils lessening their grip sufficiently for Eric to slip his arm out. As he did so, he snatched the snake's head again. This time, he managed to extract it from the coils and stretch it high enough up to hang level with his shoulder, while I hastily lubricated a rubber stomach tube and slid it down over the entrance to its windpipe and down into its stomach. Using a sixty millilitre syringe, I then squirted in some glucose saline – a temporary solution until a specific reptile concentrate mix could be obtained.

Now the question of where to house it.

'Certainly not here,' declared Mandy, who marched in just as I finished.

'No?' I queried gruffly, ready to challenge her.

'No way, Paul,' declared Crystal who had appeared in the doorway. 'We've already seen what an escape artist it is. What if it got out and went for one of the in-patients? As you know, we've got a couple of cats in. The last thing we want is for it to go for one of those. It could happen you know.' She leaned in from the doorway and gave me one of her hard blue-eyed stares. 'I wouldn't like to chance my arm, would you?'

'Eric?' I turned to him hoping for some support. But with Crystal's unfortunate choice of words ringing in my ears and him rubbing his arm, I knew I didn't have a chance in hell.

So that's how I came to be driving back to Willow Wren with a dark blue zig-zagged striped pillowcase wriggling in the boot of my car.

During the fifteen minute journey across the Downs to Ashton, I'd worked out where I'd put the python. I dismissed any of the outbuildings as not being secure enough. The last thing I needed was for it to escape and slither round into Eleanor's cottage. She'd gone berserk the time her tortoiseshell, Tammy, had brought home one of the many 'trophies' she liked to present to Eleanor. On that occasion, it had been a young grass snake which Tammy deposited up in Eleanor's bedroom, where it had slithered under her chest of drawers and remained coiled up there until I was called in to pull it out and take it down to the village pond. A python of this size in a similar situation just didn't bear thinking about. No way. Eleanor would simply go out of her mind. So no, this python would have to be housed safely indoors.

I'd already thought where. My tiny bathroom would be ideal providing I didn't mind sharing it with a python. The partition wall dividing it from a similar bathroom on Eleanor's side was original. Timber-framed with laths and plaster to each side. But in good repair.

The window overlooking the back garden was also secure; and the wood-panelled door into the bathroom could only be opened with difficulty as it dragged over a fitted carpet. There was an electric heater over the wash basin which I could leave switched on all night. The smallness of the room ensured it would soon heat up making it feel as snug as a bug (or in this case – a python) in a rug. No. I could see no reason not to use it to house the snake – temporarily at least until a reptile enthusiast could be found to take it on. I did have one slight niggle of concern. What if I needed to have a pee in the night? It did happen on occasion. The thought of me staggering through to point Percy at the porcelain only to have a bigger snake point back, sizing mine up for a possible snack, was not worth contemplating. So I slid a washing-up bowl under my bed, mentally reminding myself that, if used, I'd need to rinse it out thoroughly the next day before washing my plates.

So with the python's lodgings sorted out, I yanked the pillowcase out of the car boot once I'd arrived at Willow Wren and carried it upstairs to the bathroom, untied the case and watched as the python slid round the side of the bath panel and coiled itself up in the corner next to the toilet pan. Job done. I just prayed I wouldn't need to do likewise before the morning.

I was up early, anxious to see to the python – stomach tube it again if possible – before leaving for the hospital. I gingerly pushed open the bathroom door and stared round it. No sign of the snake. Nothing. I could feel my heart start to beat a little faster. I craned my neck behind the door in the hope it was coiled up there. Nope. No snake. My heart was definitely beginning to pound now. I could hear it in my ears, feel it thumping in my chest. Where was the wretched python?

I stepped in nervously, scouring every nook and cranny. The dividing wall between the bathroom and small second bedroom through, which you had to walk to access the former, had been stripped of its plaster and laths to reveal the original timber frame work, allowing the cross beams to be used for toiletries – shower gel, shaving cream, deodorant stick, the usual paraphernalia required for daily ablutions. I half hoped to see the python draped between it all, head resting on my expensive bottle of 007 cologne. But no such luck.

I lifted the lid of the toilet seat. Maybe it was coiled up in there? Nope. With the 'call of nature' getting the better of me I slumped down for a slash. It was a rule of mine never to pee first thing in the morning standing up. Being sleepy then meant there was always a risk of missing the pan, overshooting it. As I waited for my bladder to contract, I was suddenly aware, sitting there, that the bath panel didn't look straight. It was tilted. Out of vertical. And at the end nearest to me there was a gap. Not large. Maybe a couple of inches or so. But plenty big enough... yes... more than big enough... for that bloody python to have slipped through.

I pulled my boxer shorts up with a sigh of relief. Relief for having an empty bladder. And relief at now knowing where the snake had disappeared to. Hidden under the bath, behind the panel. It required a screwdriver to unscrew the four screws holding the lower edge of the panel in place. I was removing the third when I heard Eleanor enter her bathroom. The sound of water moved from water trickling into the pan to water flushing from the cistern to water pouring from taps. She was running a bath. A bath that ran parallel to mine – just the thin partition wall separated the two. Really too close for comfort. I always felt uneasy playing with my rubber duck knowing Eleanor could be inches away, playing with hers.

As I was about to remove the last screw, I heard a splosh and a sigh. Then a voice burst out in song. The melody, the words, floated through the wall. Oh no, it couldn't be? Surely not him again? But yes it was. Bloody Max Bygraves. I recognised it as part of a Singalongmax compilation CD that my gran also owned. Eleanor had switched it on and was joining in. She actually had a pleasant voice. She had joined the local church choir, Reverend James was overjoyed at having a new member of his ever dwindling group – several recently having sung for their last supper before joining the great sing-a-long in the sky.

Max's *You need hands* percolated through the wall, accompanied by Eleanor no doubt using hers to soap herself down and get in a lather, while I used mine to get out the final loose screw.

'*When you feel*
Nobody wants to know you
You need hands
To brush away your tear.'
... burbled Max.

I don't know about brushing away a tear, I felt a bucket-load of them about to sweep out of my eyes when I pulled away the bath panel and discovered there was no blasted snake behind it. And with a gap in the laths and plaster going through to

Eleanor's bathroom and the increasing suspicion that I knew exactly where the python had headed, the *You need hands to hold someone you care for* were rapidly changed to the need for hands to wrap round a ruddy snake's neck.

Max was now cheerfully singing:

'There's a tiny house
By a tiny stream
Where a lovely lass
Had a lovely dream.'

Only when he got to the word dream it was drowned by an almighty scream – Eleanor had hit a high note far beyond the normal range of a mezzo-soprano.

'And the dream came true
Quite unexpectedly.'

As did another scream piercing the wall.

'In Gilly-gilly-Ossenfeffer-Katzenellen-Bogen-by-the-sea.'

... chortled Max.

'Eleanor, it's me Paul,' I shouted through the wall. 'Don't panic.'

Another scream.

Max started a new song.

'When you come to the end of a lollipop.'

'Eleanor, just stay where you are.'

'To the end to the end of a lollipop.'

'Don't move.'

'When you come to the end of a lollipop.'

'I'll be right round. Okay?'

'Plop goes your heart.'

Mine already had. And to judge from Eleanor's screams, hers had as well.

Meanwhile Max Bygraves was now merrily warbling on about *Tulips from Amsterdam*. Thanks a bunch, mate.

I dashed round, taking Eleanor's stairs three at a time and burst into her bathroom as Max finished *Tip Toeing Through the Tulips* and was now *Forever Blowing Bubbles*.

So was Eleanor – blowing bubbles that is. Positively foaming at the mouth. I averted my eyes from her bubble covered breasts floating just below the surface of the water like two pink pods. She pulled a hand out of the sea of foam to curve a finger over the edge of the bath.

'What is it?' she croaked, head to one side, eyes averted.

'I'm a pink toothbrush,' sang Max.

'Oh for Christ's sake,' I said, switching him off.

I looked down to where she was pointing.

'There, under the bath, wrapped round the claw feet,' she said, waving her hand from side to side. 'Some sort of snake. Huge.'

'Not any more.'

'What?'

'It's not there now.'

'What?' she repeated.

'It's gone. Must have slipped back underneath.'

'What?' Eleanor was clearly lost for words. But not for action. There was a sudden surge of water. The goddess Venus (Eleanor) rose from a sea (bathwater) bedecked with rosebuds (soapsuds), her hands covering her private parts (naughty bits), while a gorgeous, mulberry-coloured drapery (pink towel) was handed to her by a nymph (me). Then with an exaggerated step, she was out of the bath and staggering across the room, shell-shocked, buttocks wobbling, before you could say 'Botticelli.'

I watched her rear retreat on to the landing. 'It was a python. They're perfectly harmless,' I said in what I hoped was a convincing tone of voice.

'Don't care if was a teacher's pet, get the confounded thing out of here, will you?'

I bobbed down and peered under the bath. Seems the python had done that for itself. There was no sign of it. Must have slithered back into my side. Beat a retreat.

I grabbed another towel and rammed it into the hole, trusting it would keep the python at bay.

Back in Willow Wren, I began the hunt for the python, convinced it would be easy to find. Two metres of snake couldn't just disappear surely? But as I scoured the house from top to bottom and found no trace of it, I began to feel distinctly uneasy.

Eleanor eventually ventured round with a hopeful, 'You've found it then?' My shake of the head induced her to rapidly skedaddle back to her cottage, where doors could be heard slamming shut.

Half an hour spent traipsing round the back garden poking through the shrubs and parting clump after clump of border plants was a complete waste of time – much as I suspected it would be. In the end I had to give up, as I would have been late for work.

'No python then?' commented Beryl on my arrival. I suspect she was ready to leap on to her stool had I been carrying the pillowcase. I explained what had happened.

'Poor thing,' she remarked, scratching at her wart.

'Yes, it was quite a shock for Eleanor.'

'No, I meant the snake. Must be getting hungry by now.'

Beryl went on: 'Good job you haven't any cats.'

True. I didn't have any cats now. But 'Good job'?

Beryl reminded me why. 'Look what happened to that one over in Brigstock last year.'

Yes, of course. It was all over the front page of the *Westcott Gazette*. A python escaped and ate a neighbour's cat called Tinklebell. No punning headlines on that occasion. Far too serious. The vet practice over there X-rayed the python. The radiograph showed a cluster of skeletal remains and attached to it a collar with a bell that would no longer tinkle. Poor Tinklebell.

'Argg... I've just had a horrible thought,' I spluttered. 'Tammy.'

Beryl raised her eyebrows.

'Eleanor's tortoiseshell.'

'Oh I'm sure she can fend for herself,' said Beryl, reassuringly. Then spoilt it all by adding, 'Mind you, if the python's very hungry...'

You can imagine my feelings when I got back to Willow Wren that evening. A big 'What if?' persistently flashed in my brain. I went round and knocked on Eleanor's door. There was much sliding back of bolts, the rattling of a chain and the turning of locks before she opened it a fraction, one eye peering out through the slit, her voice hopeful when she said, 'Found it?'

'Not as yet,' I said as cheerfully as I could. 'But I'm sure it will turn up soon. Perhaps Tammy will bring it home as a trophy,' I joked, trying to ease the tension. 'She's good at doing that sort of thing isn't she?'

Eleanor's eye closed briefly. 'Tammy's gone missing. Haven't seen her all day.'

I gulped. In much the same way I imagined the python may have gulped – Tammy being at the receiving end of that gulp. This wasn't good news. Eleanor sensed my unease. The door flew open, I was pulled in, the door slammed shut behind me –

the result of a deft kick from one of Eleanor's shoes – a patent leather not python one.

She grabbed both my lapels. 'You're not suggesting...' Her voice trailed off. She let go, visibly crumpling in front of me. 'It's unlikely, surely?'

I nodded, the reassurances spilling out, while Tinklebell's bell rang in my ears, making them burn.

EastEnders had just started when the screaming started. I threw down my chicken madras ready–meal and tore out into the garden, now getting dark. And leapt on to the small pile of bricks stacked against the fence that separated our gardens. A useful way to pop my head over and see what was going on whenever the occasion arose. Like now.

'Eleanor? What is it? Have you found the snake?'

Clutching a black bag, she was backing away from her recycle bin, its lid open, 'It's in there,' she said, in between sobs. I saw it move.'

I lost no time in shooting round. Peering into the bin I could just make out the coiled-up snake in the semi-darkness. But something wasn't quite right. I leaned in a little closer and my heart jumped into my mouth. There was a bulge a third of the way down the python. Its body at that point was definitely enlarged. An enlargement big enough to be that of a cat. My sharp intake of breath was instantly picked up by Eleanor.

'Wha... What's wrong?' she faltered, cautiously creeping up to peer in herself, while holding on to my sleeve for reassurance.

'No, I shouldn't, Eleanor,' I said, attempting to pull her away.

Too late. She'd spotted the bulge. 'Oh my God... you don't think...'

'Listen... We mustn't jump to conclusions. I'll drag your bin round to my place and tape the lid down.' I took a deep breath. 'Then let's review the situation in the morning. Who knows, Tammy may have turned up by then.'

'And what if she hasn't?'

'Just let's wait and see,' I said, gripping her shoulder with my hand, desperately trying to stop the tremor in it. All I could see was an X-ray of Tammy's mortal remains floating inside the python.

'Well there's certainly something there,' said Mandy the next day, studying the radiograph she'd clipped up on the viewing screen once we'd managed to X-ray the snake – not an easy task, the snake being rather lively – but all credit to Mandy and Lucy for pinning it down on the X-ray plate, holding the bulging section between them as if they were about to pull a cracker. But no Christmas hat, gift and joke here. Just a jumble of bones. Animal bones for sure. But feline bones? Tammy's?

The elongated skull with its curved incisors gave the answer. A rat.

'Phew. Thank God for that,' I exclaimed, wiping away the beads of sweat on my upper lip. Wherever Tammy was, it wasn't inside the python. It turned out she was inside a shed. Its door, rather than the python's teeth, clamming shut to lock her in. Reverend James discovered her that afternoon when he prised open the door.

As he later explained in his customary long drawn out manner: 'I had ventured down the garden, my intention to procure a rake and hoe for weeding purposes from my potting shed where all my tools are kept. I found that much to my surprise the door to that shed was firmly closed when I recollect having left it open earlier in the day. So I can only assume a gust of wind caused the door to shut in the intervening time and during that time Tammy must have ventured herself inside prior to that said gust of wind.'

This was one of Reverend James's typical diatribes. As long winded as his sermons. It was another reason church numbers at St Mary's were falling off or at least nodding off amongst those stalwarts who sat his sermons out.

Having listened patiently, I nodded. 'In other words, Tammy got trapped inside your shed.'

He nodded back a little impatiently. 'That's precisely what I've just said.'

Precisely? I thought to myself. Really? But didn't say a word in case I got a bucket-load back.

With Tammy sorted, I still had the problem of what to do with the python.

It was Beryl who came up with the solution.

'What about Mr Hargreaves?' she suggested.

I looked at her, puzzled for a moment. 'Hargreaves?'

'Yes, you know. That chap who owns all those creepy crawlies. He might relish having a python to add to his collection.'

I remembered then who she was talking about. Yes, Mr Hargreaves – he was an avid collector of geckos, skinks and the like. It was his hobby. Having initially expressed interest in such creatures, I then found myself being presented with them on a regular basis. A whole succession hopped, slithered or hissed their way through my consulting room. Each time, Mr Hargreaves insisted on referring to whatever plopped out by its Latin name. Fine if it had been their 'pet' Latin names – a Romulus, Remus or Nero. I could even have coped with a Tiberius or two. Though an Elagabalus might have been a bit of a challenge. But it was his use of their scientific names that flummoxed me. His *Trituris vulgaris* had me floundering as much as the newt I was trying to pick out amongst a tangle of weeds. While his *Trachysaurus rugosus* left me cold – in much the same way as the stump-tailed skink was when I operated on him to replace a prolapsed rectum.

So I wondered what Mr Hargreaves' reaction would be to being presented with a python. I might have guessed.

'Oh... A *molurus bivittatus*.' Mr Hargreaves craned his stick-like body over the consulting table and scrutinized the python at close quarters, apparently unfazed by the snake's head resting on top of its coiled body only inches from his own. 'Thought I might strike lucky and find it was a *morelia spilota variegate*. But this will do me fine.'

I thought, if you get any closer mate it will be the python getting the lucky strike and you'll be the one doing it fine – straight down its throat. But that was just me thinking 'ahead' – in particular, Mr Hargreaves' head – wedged in the python's throat. But that was between him and the snake – well him and the snake's dislocated jaws if it ever got that far. Enough, Paul.

I tried to disengage myself from the disturbing image it conjured up, as I wished Mr Hargreaves well and watched him scurry across the car park clutching his new acquisition in its pillowcase.

I turned back into reception to find Beryl standing precariously on her stool beneath the lampshade.

'No need to panic, Beryl,' I said calmly, walking across to her. 'You can get down. The snake's gone.'

'Paul, it's not that,' she snapped, flapping one hand at me and gesticulating with the other up at the lampshade. 'I need a new bulb.'

9

When Everything Makes Sense

Whenever the smell of Summer Bouquet pervaded the hospital, it was like some mobile lavatory block was stalking the corridors, smothering us with its cloying scent. Only it was Beryl who was doing the stalking, scuttling round, a red-clawed finger on the trigger of her can of air freshener. A quick phss here. A quick phss there. A longer phss... phss if she deemed a particular odour required complete annihilation. And it was often the case that something was afoot – or more likely underfoot. Something nasty trodden into reception by an unsuspecting client or a nervous discharge deposited on the reception floor by a client's dog.

It seems Beryl had a particularly strong sense of smell. Not that she could match that of a dog. Though she might have the six million olfactory receptors we humans have up our noses, dogs have 300 million making their sense of smell up to 100,000 times as acute as ours. While we might detect the smell of a teaspoonful of sugar in a mug of coffee, a dog could detect that teaspoonful in two Olympic-sized pools of water.

Even so, Beryl could impress with her ability to sniff out odours – especially a whiff of alcohol on someone's breath.

Eric had fallen foul of her on several occasions, having returned from The Woolpack after a liquid lunch. Poor chap.

He'd be met with a very pronounced sniff from Beryl. A waving of her scarlet talons across her face and some withering comment along the lines of: 'God Eric, you could anaesthetise a poodle at twenty paces.' If he had imbibed more, she had an uncanny way of detecting it – as if she had a breath analyser implanted amongst the olfactory receptors up her nose. The poodle would be replaced by a Great Dane or similar sized dog and the twenty paces increased to fifty or more – the size of dog and the distance from Eric proportional to the number of units of alcohol she suspected he'd drunk. It pissed him off no end.

'Forewarned is forearmed,' said Eric, offering me a mint on the way back from The Woolpack one lunchtime, where we'd enjoyed a ploughman's with pickle, and just the one pint of beer each.

'Bloody woman. She's costing me a fortune in peppermints,' he moaned, stuffing three in his mouth.

But it didn't fool Beryl. Her nose started to twitch as soon as we stepped into reception. But she didn't say a word. Just reached down for her can of spray and gave us a blast of Summer Bouquet.

There was one client who didn't need the likes of Summer Bouquet.

Whenever Rosie Bloome turned up for an appointment with one of her cats, it was like a breath of fresh air sweeping through the hospital. Even her name conjured up an image of bowers of

158

sweet scented roses, which meeting her in the flesh did nothing to dispel. No thorn in our side was our Rosie. Mind you, you'd pass her in the street and not give her a second glance. She was of medium height and build, medium length ginger-brown hair, medium-brown eyes; but with round, full cheeks, apple red in colour, and full red lips, ready to smile, her face would light up with genuine pleasure, her eyes dancing with delight as soon as she saw someone she knew. And her laugh, high pitched, joyous, was like a stream tinkling through an alpine meadow. In addition, there was a freshness about her – a touch of white cotton sheets drying on the line, the gleam of a polished table, a posy of freshly picked sweet peas, their petals still moist with the dew of a summer's dawn. This aura of hers never failed to invoke a sense of well being in you. Distilled in a bottle, it would have been worth a fortune.

Rosie owned four cats, each from an animal shelter over near Brigstock, each acquired during my first year at the practice, and each brought in for a full check-up, one by one, as each settled into a new life with her.

The first to come in for its MOT looked part Balinese with a silky ivory coat, small white goatee, ears, gloves and socks a deep brown; and a tail that blossomed into a magnificent dark plume. Rosie had christened him Rowan – in a nudge to the then current Archbishop of Canterbury, Rowan Williams; though her Rowan had more of a cross to bear – in fact could have used a cross as a crutch – since he had a deformed left foreleg, shaped like a seal's flipper with no paw. That marred Rowan's good looks. As did one other thing – well, two other things to be precise. Somewhere in his ancestry, a family had branched out and acquired an unfortunate gene, which had been passed down through the generations and which Rowan had now inherited; and that was two outsized ears. They were big. Huge. At the slightest sound, they swivelled and whirled into action like two giant radio-wave dishes.

'It just seemed to fit,' said Rosie when I referred to his name. 'Rowan's got a very composed manner about him. One you could put your faith in.'

Only if you were C of E, I thought. But I knew what she meant.

I watched Rowan sit in quiet contemplation on my consulting table, the picture of ecclesiastical reverence. I could imagine him conducting courteous courtships beneath the shadows of cathedrals or on the back walls of bishops' palaces. Not that I was suggesting the present incumbent of Canterbury conducted himself in such a way. Nor was the manner in which Rowan then raised his left hind leg, to hold it rigidly in the air while he bent his head down to lick his penis – not an act any self-respecting archbishop would contemplate doing unless he was double jointed and it was performed in the cathedral's closet or behind the closed doors of the vestry.

'How does he manage with that leg?' I asked, referring to the deformed one rather than the rigid rod that was still stretched heavenwards, while Rowan continued to nuzzle his nuts.

'Amazingly well,' said Rosie. 'He hobbles round the garden and scents what he considers his territory. His favourite spot is in a corner under one of the climbing roses. A real suntrap. He loves it there.'

'And how does he get on with this new addition?' It was two months on and I was examining Blossom, a spayed female, a hodgepodge of greys and black with piercing yellow eyes.

'Oh Rowan's definitely the boss.'

'And no problem with that flipper leg of his?'

Rosie shook her head and gave me one of her radiant smiles. 'To the contrary.'

'In what way?'

'He uses it to thwack Blossom across the nose if he thinks she's stepped out of line – especially if she tries to join him under the climbing roses. That's a no-go area. His only.'

Rowan, it seemed, practised a baptism of fire – full of the holy spirit, no doubt. Especially if a cat ever dared to encroach on his diocese.

Within six months, Petal and Willow had joined the 'gang' as Rosie called her quartet of cats. A brother and sister, a touch of Burmese in them, both blue-grey in colour, Petal having three white socks, Willow two.

I wasn't to hear from Rosie throughout last winter but I did learn about her gang's exploits. It was Beryl who alerted me to them.

It was one of those Thursday afternoon tea-breaks when she had her head buried in that week's edition of the *Westcott Gazette*.

I could see the front page as I sat opposite her. Leaning forward I skimmed through the main story. It was about a local man, Kevin Foster, who was crossing the Channel on an inflatable tomato as part of a flotilla of fruits including a banana and several apples. The tomato had been lagging behind but as the *Gazette* went to press, Kevin's tomato was now neck and neck with the banana as they approached the French coast. So the headlines – in typical Finley O'Connor's punning style – read *Kevin Manages to Ketch Up!*

Lucky Kevin hadn't been sailing on a bunch of grapes2 I mused. I could picture the headlines then, *Kevin Battles with Strong Currants*. Or maybe, *Kevin is Grapeful to be Rescued*. Well, something along those lines.

But it was some lines inside the paper that had caught Beryl's eye.

'Remember Rosie Bloome?' she said, from behind the paper.

'Yes of course.' How could I forget that fragrant rose, her petal-soft freshness, a welcome contrast to the many thorns in my life?

Beryl gave me one of her barbed looks over the top of the paper. Was she reading my mind?

'What about her?' I stammered, knowing I'd gone as red as Kevin's tomato.

'Well, she's started a weekly column in the Life section of the paper. It's called *Rowan's Ramblings*. All about what her cat's been up to.' She folded the paper at the relevant page and handed it to me. 'That's something you could do, Paul. You'd have plenty of material with all the cranky people you get in here.'

Too true, Beryl. Too true.

'What's this about cranky people?' Eric had just bounced in, rubbing his hands together, declaring he was dying for a cuppa.

'I was just saying Paul would have plenty to write about with the eccentric clients we have to deal with,' explained Beryl.

'Yes indeed,' replied Eric, mashing a teabag in his mug. 'He wouldn't have to step out of the door.'

Careful Eric, I thought. You're getting yourself into water that's hotter than what's going into your mug.

'What are you insinuating, Eric?' said Beryl, focussing her eye on him, getting him in her sights, ready for a bit of archery practice. Her arrow was poised.

'It's just that... Well...' Eric tailed off lamely and gulped down a mouthful of tea.

'I might be a bit of an old bat as far as you're concerned,' said Beryl, clearly in a huff. 'But you need someone to keep order round here otherwise the place would go to the dogs. Which reminds me, Eric. You've an appointment at 4.00 to see Mrs Elstone's two Westies. They've had the squits ever since you put them on that new diet.'

I was trying to keep a straight face.

Beryl stood up. 'As for you, Paul. I've got Mrs Alsopp coming in to see you. That cat of hers you saw – the one that had been in a fight. Remember?'

I nodded meekly.

'Well, the antibiotics you gave her haven't done the slightest bit of good. The cat's now developed an abscess that needs lancing.'

Having put the two of us firmly in our place, Beryl smoothed down the wings (sleeves) of her ruffled feathers (black cardigan) and flew (walked) back up her perch (stool) in the Tower of London (reception).

'You're right about one thing,' I said, throwing Eric a rueful look. 'There's plenty of column inches to be had here.' In fact, with Beryl about, there were yards of them – if not miles.

I became a firm follower of Rosie's column in the *Westcott Gazette*, enjoying Rowan's adventures. And there were many. Several struck a chord with the antics I'd experienced with Queenie, Push-in and Garfield when they had been in residence at Willow Wren during the time Lucy also lived there.

One article in particular stood out as it involved me. An abridged version of what actually happened.

Beryl had waved her vermillion claws at me and summoned me to her desk.

'Guess who's coming in this afternoon,' she'd said, hunching forward, her head sticking out at an angle so that her good eye peered up at me, giving her the overall appearance of a boss-eyed crow with a crick in its neck.

'Who?' I replied, controlling the slight irritation I felt bubbling up. Much as I admired Beryl, I was never fond of her when she was in guess-what-I've-got-for-you mode.

'It's one of your favourite pets.' Her good eye continued to give me the glad-eye, the finely pencilled eyebrow above it arched, questioningly.

Another bubble of irritation rose. 'Yes?'

'A cat.'

More bubbles.

Beryl cupped her hands behind her ears and wiggled them. 'Guess... Ears... Big ears...' She continued wiggling hers.

A whole stream of bubbles.

'Rowan with the bat ears,' she hissed. 'You know, Rosie Bloome's cat. Her husband's bringing him in for his stitches.'

The bubbles finally burst when she mentioned Rowan.

Of course I knew him. Who didn't? He'd become something of a celebrity now with his weekly ramblings in the *Westcott Gazette*. Besides I'd just operated on one of Rowan's ears. One of those gigantic radio receivers of his.

Toby and Rosie had first presented him a couple of weeks back.

Once on my consulting table, Rowan proceeded to give himself a full whisker and paw wash, looking up at me just once, as if to say, 'If you dare interrupt, come the Revolution, your head will be the first in the basket.'

One of his enormous ears – the right one – had blown up to twice its normal size.

I found it difficult to concentrate on the cat's ears because I kept seeing those of Toby's. He also sported ears that out-spanned those of Noddy's companion. A real live Big Ears. Like Rowan's, they seemed to flap and stretch with every nod of his head. They were so fascinating to watch that I could barely take my eyes off them and when I first met him – he'd come along with Rosie when they'd brought in Petal and Willow for their initial check-ups – I found myself framing questions just to see those auricular appendages spring into action. Naughty Paul. Naughty.

I later remarked to Beryl about them during a coffee break, as I stood with her outside the door to the back garden, while she had her customary fag. She'd drawn heavily on her ciggie and declared that she was very familiar with them. I'd reacted with surprise and even more so, went she went on to explain that last autumn she'd taken up evening classes in life drawing at the local college and Toby Bloome happened to be the model at the time. *So I've seen him naked*, Beryl had said matter-of-factly. And yes, they were enormous.

So with a view to seeing them swing – the ears that is – I'd innocently asked, when examining the two tabbies that Rosie and Toby had brought in, how Rowan was getting on, hoping it would be Toby who'd reply. He did.

'Well... thank you. Well,' he said, rewarding me with a nod... nod... flap... flap of those enormous ears of his.

'He's still boss man?'

It was Rosie who answered this time. Shame.

'Oh definitely.'

She turned to Toby. 'Wouldn't you agree?'

He nodded.

And did he? Oh yes he did.

Wiggle... Wiggle... went his ears.

Lovely stuff.

But two weeks ago, it had been Rowan's ears that were the more active – in full swing, twitching and quivering, way out-of-control; and the right one was swollen and puffy.

'Been shaking his head a lot?' I asked and was rewarded with a flick... flick of Toby's ears as he nodded.

'Just a little to start with,' he replied.

'So we weren't too concerned,' Rosie butted in.

'We didn't want to get in a flap about it.' This was Toby.

Yes... well... I thought. You're not doing too badly now. Flap. Flap. Wiggle. Wiggle.

Toby went on, 'But when his right ear started to swell up we thought it best to bring him in and have him checked over.'

'Quite right,' I agreed, picking up my auriscope from the surgical trolley. 'We'll just take a look down and see what's going on. That's if Rowan will oblige.'

The cat, as usual, was nonchalantly sitting in the middle of the table, giving himself another rear-end clean – left hind in the air, head buried in his privates. He looked up from his ablutions as I spoke and gave me a piercing, rather unchristian, yellow-eyed look.

Oh ye of little faith, Paul.

'Oh I'm sure he will,' said Rosie, with more confidence than I felt; and encircling Rowan with one arm, she levered the cat towards her. 'Now you be a good boy,' she commanded, sliding her free hand around and up the side of Rowan's chest, pinning him gently to her bosom, his head pinned between her breasts. God Almighty.

'There. Will that do?' she said.

'Perfect,' I replied. But the gospel truth was that Rowan's close proximity to Rosie's bosom made it awkward for me. Nevertheless, I managed to peer down through the illuminated cone of the auriscope into Rowan's left ear canal; and then, with Rosie having turned the cat round and restrained him as before, I took a peep down the right one. Each was a seething mass of ear mites – packed in like commuters on the Tube – crawling through a viscous sea of brown smelly wax. When I told Rosie and Toby what I could see, they both asked how on earth he could have picked them up.

'One of the hazards of having so many lady friends,' I suggested. I was including Blossom and Petal in that number.

'And is the swollen ear the result of one of his lady friends biffing him?' asked Toby.

My turn to shake my head, though with no wiggle of the ears.

'No. No. I would imagine it's due to the irritation caused by the ear mites,' I said. Then wickedly added, 'Don't you think?'

I was rewarded by another synchronized wiggle of Toby's.

Excellent. I went on to explain that the head shaking caused by the irritation had resulted in the rupturing of a small blood vessel, which had allowed blood to seep out between the skin and cartilage of the ear, leading to the swelling. 'It's called a haematoma,' I informed them.

'Sounds serious,' said Rosie.

'Not that bad,' I reassured her. 'And we could leave it. The blood clot would gradually be reabsorbed. But there is the danger that the scar tissue left could twist Rowan's ear out of shape.'

Was it my imagination or did Toby's ears buckle in slightly on learning that? I half expected them to turn into cauliflowers. No. That was definitely my imagination. I continued to say that it would be a shame to let that happen; and so it would be better to operate and drain the fluid off. Which is what I did the next day.

Once Rowan was anaesthetised, with the help of Lucy to hold his good leg up while supporting his deformed one with her other hand, it was a simple task to incise and drain the swelling. Stitches right through the ear's pinna ensured the area was sufficiently compressed to prevent any reoccurrence. While he was still unconscious, I took the opportunity to clean out each ear canal and instil some drops to kill off any remaining mites; Rosie and Toby were to continue with the medication for the next fortnight. 'And do your other cats as well,' I instructed.

Rowan was now in my consulting room ready to have his sutures removed.

'Did you manage to keep him in all the time?' I asked Toby.

'All bar last Saturday night,' he confessed, his ears giving an apologetic wiggle.

I was to discover the outcome of that night on the tiles, several months later when a Mrs Mason who lived a few houses down from the Bloomes came in with five beautiful fluffy grey-ivory-coated kittens for vaccination.

'Aren't they gorgeous,' she cooed. 'I'd love to know who their father is.'

'I could hazard a guess,' I said as five sets of out-sized ears swivelled in my direction and went flap... flap... wiggle... wiggle...

I wasn't to meet up with Rowan again until the end of June. This time on his own patch. In that favourite corner of his. Under the magnificent bower of climbing roses – the spot mentioned by Rosie. His spot only. Any interloper got a wallop from his flipper. Not that it included me. Nor any other of the visitors that afternoon. And there was quite a trail through the Bloomes' garden. It was one of six in Hamfield open for just that one afternoon as part of the National Gardens' Scheme. And their garden was certainly worthy of inclusion. A mass of roses at their peak, a riot of colour, a heady mix of perfume that filled their tiny garden, their flint-stone and brick cottage a splendid backcloth, the walls splashed with the creams of *Madame Alfred Carriere* and the pale pinks of the heavily perfumed *Malmaison.*

As I breathed in the scented air my mind went spinning back to my gran's garden, not too dissimilar to this one.

She adored roses, her garden a cascade of blooms; the creamy-white heads of *Moonlight*; the heavy fragrance of *Old Pink Moss*; and the rich clove scent of *Blush Noisette* with its delicate clusters of small lilac-pink flowers. Here, as a boy, I would lie on the sun-scorched lawn of her garden on a hot June day, eyes closed to the bleached blue sky, ears filled with the hum of bees, and breathe deep of the heady scents that surrounded me.

Her garden was certainly magic. And I tried to weave a similar spell in the back garden of Willow Wren. But there was no magic there despite my many attempts to emulate Gran and cultivate my own roses. A way to distract me from feeling sorry for myself. For not having the likes of Lucy to share the pleasure. But it didn't work.

Many times I've stared glumly at my dripping rose gazebo, built using a ready pack from B&Q, the wrought–iron pillars covered in a thin layer of leaves – leaves covered in a thick layer of Blackspot. The buds of my soaked *Malmaison* roses failed to open and looked like sodden cream tennis balls rotting on their stems.

They say 'roses grow on you' but not on me they didn't. The ramblers I planted – three for two from B&Q – failed to ramble; climbers failed to climb despite being shown the way – carefully trained to trellis – another self-assembly unit from B&Q – I should have shares in the store. But those climbers failed to grasp it.

'You're not having much luck are you?' commented Eleanor, popping her head over the garden fence to inspect my flopping floribundas. As for my China roses – they looked as if they were on a slow boat back to where they came from.

I bet Gertrude Jekyll didn't have such a problem. She recognised the full potential of roses and combined them with other plants while giving them architectural roles on buildings and garden statuary.

I did try her approach. I purchased a grey, concrete aggregate statue of a well-endowed lady holding a bunch of grapes above her left ear. I got her cheap as her breasts were chipped. In Jekyll mode, I intended smothering the statue with a mass of *Golden Showers*, picturing the sprays of canary yellow blooms cascading over her shoulders, covering her nicked nipples. Alas, no. My *Golden Showers* turned into a drizzle of blooms that hung feebly round her feet.

Eleanor was rather po-faced at the appearance of Gloria – the name I gave to the statue. Distinctly sniffy. Possibly it was the exposed chipped nipples pointing up at her bedroom window – reminding her perhaps of her own imperfections – that failed to impress.

Reverend James was a little more circumspect. He circum-inspected the statue in silence (a first surely?), studying her contours in minute detail, lingering a little on her chipped nipples, his tongue hanging out slightly.

Despite my own lack of success, there was always the memory of Gran's garden with its profusion of roses to fall back on.

Only recently, Mum let me into a secret.

It was in Gran's garden, on a tranquil summer's evening, the sun just having set in a molten halo of orange, fingers of warm air sifting through the roses, their fragrance heavy in the air as described by her – very poetically put (but then she was on her third Barley wine) – that Dad went down on bended knee and asked her to be his wife. She said, 'Yes.' And I was born nine months later. The dirty buggers.

Two more Barley wines later and I learnt that Mum had been expecting a girl.

'Really?' I exclaimed, somewhat put out.

'Yes,' she admitted. 'Just had this feeling. You know.'

I didn't know, not ever having been pregnant.

Seems Mum had been so certain she'd already made a short list of names. Rose had topped it. Followed by a Daisy and Lily.

'So what happened when I popped out?'

'We picked a name out of a hat.'

Charming.

Perhaps that's why I've got this thing about roses. Deep in my psyche there's a Rose lying dormant, awaiting its chance to blossom. Can't say I've felt any compulsion to start wearing women's clothing and have my breasts enhanced. If I do, I guess it would be best to nip it in the bud straightaway. Otherwise, the sight of silky satin panties and bras *hanging in the breeze to dry* (oh, no, not Max again), would really freak Eleanor out and start tongues wagging – especially Reverend James' – heaven forbid.

That may also be the reason I've got this thing about scents in general. I'm subjugating any liking for girlie perfumes for fear it might bring out the girlie in me. Either that or it's the thought of Beryl gunning me down with lashings of Summer Bouquet.

Certainly of late, I've been looking at, and experimenting with, various products on the market designed to bring the man out in me, so keeping my Rose under wraps.

I dabbled briefly with an eau de cologne called *L'Homme Libre*, hoping, as the name suggested, it would make me a free man, uninhibited, untainted by any whiff of a rose. Will and Kevin, the two gay hairdressers, seemed to sense my liberated body and asked me over for dinner and stay for a ménage a trois. I declined. Colognes called *Happy For Men* and *Men's Kiss* I thought best to avoid if I didn't want more dinner invites coming my way. As for *Eau de cologne du Coq*... That would have got me a long weekend if applied in the right place. Enough said.

The one fragrance that I did give serious consideration to was one called *007*. Maybe I was hoping an element of Bond would rub off on me. Certainly the marketing blurb suggested it could.

It promised to give me mesmerising confidence, unfailing composure and the ability to keep cool under pressure. All useful attributes to have when tackling one's fifth cat castrate, with two dog debollockings to follow. A man needs balls to do that. *007* promised to deliver. As to its intensely masculine fragrance enhancing my body and mind to enable me to complete daredevil activities, I wondered whether activities such as the expression of anal glands' contents into a wodge of cotton wool would fall into that remit.

Nevertheless, unlike Bond's martini, I felt the need to have my body bits shaken AND stirred, so I bought a bottle. It's now perched on the timber-frame shelf above my bath. Called a Flacon, it has an intricate metallic meshing texture on its robust gloss-finish silver glass. Very flash. It sits alongside my box of corn plasters, a bottle of ear wax remover, a tube of athlete's foot cream, dental gel, throat lozenges and mouth wash. Eat your heart out, James.

Having liberally splashed my chin and wrists with *007*, I felt full of confidence as I drove my gleaming XJ6 (battered Vauxhall Cavalier) over to MI5 (Prospect House) to plan my latest mission (morning surgery) with M (Beryl).

I strode manfully into reception.

Beryl looked up, wrinkled her nose and said, 'God, you stink Paul,' and reached down for her can of Summer Bouquet.

Scent played its part in another encounter with a client.

This time involving a parrot.

He was a smart green-plumaged bird with lighter under-parts, and a grey forehead matched by a similarly coloured breast. I didn't have a clue what he was. The same could have applied to his owner.

He was tall, heavy framed, late forties, with a halo of shimmering blonde hair, shoulder-length, slightly askew, the hint of a dark hairline showing;

173

smartly dressed in white blouse, fitted blue jacket matching mascara-encircled, cornflower blue eyes set in a full face, with a strong jaw line and heavily painted lips in deep crimson.

An almost pitch-perfect picture of how a woman should look apart from the dark five o'clock shadow and deep vocal response to my question as to the parrot's identity.

Beryl, in a conspiratorial whisper, had told me the gentleman was called Julian Wellbeloved, but preferred to be known as Miss Julianne.

'He's a Quaker parakeet,' said Miss Julianne in a bass-baritone voice, fluttering her eyelashes at me.

A broad stubby nail was thrust into the parrot's cage and the parakeet given a tickle of its back. True to his name he quaked with pleasure while I quaked with nerves. Who on earth was I dealing with here?

'That's my lovely,' growled Miss Julianne.

'He'll roll over in my hands and let me tickle his tummy,' she added. 'He simply adores it. Don't you Jimmy?' Miss Julianne grinned, her glossy, crimson lips parting to reveal a row of uneven tobacco-stained teeth.

'It was love at first sight,' she went on.

Must have been very confusing for the bird I thought.

'I saw him in the local pet shop, hunched over his feed bowl, looking thoroughly miserable.'

I momentarily thought of me hunched over my bowl of cereal each morning. Yes. I could sympathise.

'My heart went out to him, the dear little chap,' Miss Julianne was saying, her crimson lips all of a tremble, fingers momentarily playing with the string of pearls she had strung round her neck. 'He seemed to be saying, "Please rescue me", so rescue him I did.'

A very lucky bird then, I thought. To have such a considerate owner whatever his/her gender was. Out loud I asked, 'What's the problem with Jimmy?'

'It's his eye.' Miss Julianne leaned across the table. 'Can you see? The right one.'

As I looked, the parakeet fixed me with a dark, beady eye. But just the one eye – his left one. The other was a dull, opaque disc.

'I can get him out for you if you like,' Miss Julianne said.

'No, no, that won't be necessary. I can manage.' And without further ado, I winkled Jimmy out of the cage, his wings held firmly in the clasp of my right hand.

'I'm impressed,' said Miss Julianne, edging up to me. 'You're obviously an expert at handling birds.'

I was enveloped in her perfume – rich, musky and sensuous. Quite alluring. I recognised it as *Mystique* – a perfume Lucy used to use. It unsettled me. I attempted to focus on Jimmy's damaged eye, squinting down through an opthalmoscope, now very conscious of Miss Julianne standing in close proximity to me.

'What seems to be the problem?' she asked, her platform heels clonked on the vinyl as she took a heavy step nearer.

'The cornea's scarred. Probably an old injury.'

'Can he see through it?'

'Very much doubt it.'

'Oh well, at least he's got the one good eye,' said Miss Julianne. 'So he can still see what's what.'

More than I can sir/madam, I thought, her perfume arousing all sorts of mixed emotions, making me tremble slightly.

'You all right?' Miss Julianne suddenly enquired, reaching across the table to touch my elbow.

'Yes... Yes... I'm fine,' I spluttered, flinching from her and flinching from Jimmy as he hissed at me and gave me the eye. His good one.

'Now, now, Jimmy,' growled Miss Julianne, turning to the parakeet. 'You mustn't get so het up. The good doctor's only trying to do what's best for you.'

What a sweet gentleman/lady.

Beryl later told me he only liked to be called Julianne when he was off duty and out of uniform.

'Out of uniform?'

She cupped her hand to her mouth and whispered, 'He's a fire officer.'

I often found myself thinking about Julian Wellbeloved over the ensuing months. He started to crop up in my dreams. There was a recurring one of me slung over his manly shoulders, being hauled out of a burning tower block, shinning down a ladder, my pyjamas smouldering, his tights laddered. All very confusing. It set alarm bells ringing in my mind every time.

So it was with some trepidation that I found myself having to make a home visit to see Jimmy one bright and breezy October afternoon. Miss Julianne answered the door, suffused in *Mystique*, impeccably dressed in a lilac tweed skirt and similarly coloured cotton blouse. I was led into a lounge where Jimmy's cage was mounted on a stand next to a heavily bolstered settee covered in heather hued Dralon. Obviously these were Julian/Julianne's favourite colours.

Miss Julianne first enquired after my health.

I hastily assured her all was well. But what about Jimmy?

The parakeet looked warily at me as I approached.

'He's actually become rather possessive to tell you the truth,' replied Miss Julianne. 'I still adore him of course. But it's all a bit worrying for my brother.'

'That's me,' said a deep voice over my shoulder.

I swung round and took a double take at the man who had walked in from the next room.

'My twin brother, Des,' said Miss Julianne, by way of introduction. The likeness was striking even down to the five o'clock shadow. Only Des wasn't sporting a blonde wig and had no lipstick or mascara on.

And striking was clearly Jimmy's intention. He leapt off his perch and flung himself up against the bars of the cage, one leg pushed through, claws opening and closing with impotent rage.

'See what I mean?' said Miss Julianne. 'Whenever Des is around Jimmy goes into an absolute tizzy. He gets so jealous.'

'I've tried to make friends with him,' said Des. 'But it hasn't worked.' He pulled up the sleeve of his shirt and held up his right arm, the side of which was badly scratched. Three long welds. Very angry looking. Clearly he and Jimmy weren't the best of friends.

'Is there anything we can do to make him less jealous?' asked Miss Julianne. 'We've scoured the Internet for suggestions. We've tried a few but nothing seems to have worked.'

I looked pensively at the two of them. If they'd been wearing identical outfits I couldn't have told them apart. And I was sure it could have fooled Jimmy had they done so.

'Well,' I said hesitantly, 'there is something we could try. But there's no guarantee it will work.'

A week later, I was in Tesco's when the fragrance of *Mystique* suddenly filled my nostrils. As I was at the fish counter it could only have been... I turned expecting to see Miss Julianne. But no, it was Des, a basket of groceries under his arm.

I enquired after Jimmy.

'Oh, he's fine... Much, much calmer. We did what you suggested. And it seems to have worked.'

'So Jimmy's made friends with you now? No biting?'

There was the guffaw of a laugh. 'Not a nibble. And all thanks to the *Mystique* perfume you suggested I tried using. Like Julian does when he's dressed up as Miss Julianne.

'No doubt you can smell it on me now. Draws some funny looks I admit.' Des shrugged. 'But better than dressing up as Julianne, eh? Somehow I don't think a blonde wig would suit me.

'Besides the scent has foxed Jimmy into thinking I might be Julianne. Just as you thought. And Julian doesn't change into Julianne when he's around Jimmy. But still wears the fragrance. And so do I. It gets Jimmy utterly confused.'

He's not the only one, I thought.

But providing *someone* was making scents what did it matter?

10

Going To The Dogs

When the Welsh Springer scooted across the carpet on her bum, a back leg stuck straight out either side of her, Eleanor didn't turn a hair, didn't bat an eyelid, didn't say a word. Which I thought showed remarkable composure for a lady who wore Marigold gloves just to fill her bird feeder. Only when Emily turned and scooted back past her in the same position, rear still firmly in contact with the carpet, did she comment. 'Seems your new dog has got an itchy bottom,' she ventured to say, as Emily turned once more and did a final arse-lap past her, while she calmly took another sip of her coffee.

I nodded, a little embarrassed.

'Mind you,' Eleanor went on, 'I know just how she feels.'

Really? The image conjured up of my next-door neighbour bum-sliding across her carpet was instantly dismissed with a shudder. Like her carpet, she might have piles, but there was no need to go into details.

Eleanor shifted in her seat. Was I about to get the full works?

'It's allergy, you know,' she said. 'I get itchy as well.' There was another shift of her seat. 'It can get quite uncomfortable when you're desperate to have a good old scratch. Not knowing where to put yourself.' She eased herself forward and looked across at Emily who had now stopped scooting and had padded under my refectory table to lever herself under the cross bar like she was attempting a limbo dance. She stopped half-way, with the bar wedged across her back and proceeded to sway from side to side with grunts of pleasure, her head raised, her lips curled back.

Another image of Eleanor doing likewise under her own dining table sprang to mind and lingered a little longer than was necessary.

Fortunately Eleanor spared me the details of her allergy and what she did when she felt in need of a good scratch. 'Hope you manage to sort Emily out,' she said at the front door, side-stepping round the spaniel that was now sprawled across the coir hall mat rubbing her belly against it. Didn't Eleanor have a similar mat in her hall? Enough, Paul. Enough.

But it highlighted the problem I had. Besides one of having too vivid an imagination, I had a Welsh Springer spaniel with an allergic dermatitis proving difficult to treat. And that ongoing skin problem was the reason Emily had ended up here with me.

She was a lively youngster, eighteen months of age, typical of her breed, brown and white, with freckles on her face, floppy brown ears, a brown white-tipped stump of a tail forever wagging, and eager to be friends with everyone.

It was Eric who had first seen her as a puppy – given her her vaccinations, worming and health check. It mentioned on her records then that the owners were a bit concerned about her scratching.

Fleas had been mentioned as a possible cause. But nothing it seems had been done about it.

When the spaniel was booked in to see me, Beryl warned that the young owners, a Mr and Mrs Fitch-Williams, were a bit on the fussy side.

'I tried booking them in with Eric again,' she said, 'but they refused, insisting they wanted someone who knew what he was talking about.'

Oh dear. Poor old Eric. He obviously hadn't impressed them. Yet I couldn't see myself doing any better. How true that turned out to be.

When they strode in with Emily that Wednesday afternoon, they gave the impression of having just stepped in from the Chelsea Road. Their manner and dress screamed 'Sloaney'.

But this was Westcott-on-Sea – where the majority of the population was elderly – retirees wishing to enjoy a slower pace of life with salt-laden airings along the promenade. There was, of course, a younger element of which Mr and Mrs Fitch-Williams were clearly part. But I couldn't visualise them ever sitting on Westcott's seafront in wind-rippled macs, staring out to sea with a polystyrene cup of chips. They were far too full of self-importance, and would have been more at home amongst the antique emporiums and chic designer clothes boutiques of Fulham than Westcott's shopping precinct with its Help the Aged and Pound shops. Yet here they were, standing in my consulting room, their spaniel, her tail wagging, tongue lolling out, standing between them.

'So you're to have a look at our Ems, yah?' said the girl in a voice that sounded as if she had a plum lodged in her throat. She was in her early twenties, blonde with darker highlights in which were tucked an over-sized pair of sunglasses, her face spray-tanned to a mahogany hue. She was wearing skinny jeans tucked into suede Ugg boots with white fur trim. Draped round her shoulders over a blue gilet was a pastel pink pashmina. And from her neck, hung a huge faux-pearl necklace.

'Our Ems has been having a bit of a problem, hasn't she, Rupert?' She turned to her husband, a young man of similar age, sporting a Ralph Lauren rugby shirt with its collar turned up, a lemon coloured sweatshirt strung over his shoulders, knee-length cargo shorts and blue deck shoes.

'Yah, she certainly has,' he replied, in an equally plummy voice, pushing his slim-line shades further back into his thatch of fair hair. 'A problem we hope you can sort out for us, yah?'

'Well, let's see what we can do, shall we?'

'Yah,' they both chorused.

I instructed them to lift Emily on to the table which they did with a string of 'There babes,' 'It's all right babes,' and 'Mumsie and Pops are with you babes,' being cooed as they did so.

On questioning them, I was told between 'Yahs' that Emily was constantly scratching and nibbling herself.

'Just doesn't stop does she, Charlotte?' drawled Rupert.

His wife shook her head. 'It's perfectly frightful,' she drawled back.

With Emily sitting, and Charlotte holding on to her collar, I ran my hands down her back and parted some of the hairs on her rump on the lookout for tell-tell signs of fleas – the black flea dirts like those I'd found on Dorrie. But the spaniel's skin was clear.

'It's not fleas,' sniffed Rupert. 'The other guy suggested it might have been. But no way Jose. Not our Ems.' He gave a snort of disgust.

I could have pointed out that it didn't need an abundance of fleas to get an allergic reaction. Just one flea bite could do that. And so lead to the itchiness we were seeing in Emily.

But I decided to hold my counsel until I'd finished examining her, and had extracted as much information from the Fitch-Williams as I could before reaching a diagnosis. It must have been at that point in the consultation that things began to unravel. Like pulling out the end of a piece of wool buried in a ball of the stuff, the unravelling process then slowly gathered momentum with each subsequent consultation over the ensuing months: finally, when things didn't knit together, a crisis point was reached which definitely left me needled and very crotchety.

We'd turned Emily on her side and she was obligingly staying still with Charlotte's restraining hand on her neck. There were a few tiny red wheals on the dog's flank where her claws had dug in during her scratching sessions; and the hairless areas of her groin were slightly pink. When I ran a finger along her side, her skin twitched strongly. All symptomatic of an allergic reaction. But a reaction to what?

It wasn't quite typical of a flea dermatitis – I would have expected some inflammation and soreness along her back – but knowing it was the commonest cause of such itchiness I decided to plump for that as the cause of Emily's problem.

I could see it didn't go down at all well with the Fitch-Williams. There were a lot of Haws and Harrs, shades removed, their ends chewed, hands on hips, as my advice on flea treatment was listened to, while the looks on their faces clearly showed they were unconvinced.

'Well, darls, maybe we should try out what this guy's suggesting,' Rupert finally said to his wife. 'But we'll be back tout suite if it doesn't work, eh babe?'

'Yah, tout suite,' she replied.

They were back not exactly 'tout suite' but within the month.

They admitted there had been some improvement in the first couple of weeks but I knew that was going to happen since I'd given Emily an anti-inflammatory injection and a prescription of similar in tablet form to give on a reducing dosage. That would have provided her with some relief but not solved the underlying problem which I hoped would have been fleas.

Not so it seemed.

'She's started up again, hasn't she, darls? said Rupert his voice less of a drawl, more of a grate. Slightly on edge.

Charlotte nodded, pulling her mouth to one side and smoothing down her pashmina at the same time. I sensed a little tension between them, a little unease.

Emily, though, was her usual bouncy, friendly self. Pulling forward to greet me with her tail all of its customary wag.

I'd been doing a bit of reading since I'd last seen them. Going through my university notes, refreshing my memory on allergic dermatitis – its symptoms and causes – especially the causes. And there was quite a list. Food. Contact with bedding and carpets. House dust mites. Feathers. Mixed moulds.

And during the next few consultations, I worked through that list with the Fitch-Williams. But with each appointment, their keenness to help Emily seemed to diminish, while the friction between the two of them intensified. Then came the day when I was presented with a shattering resolution to the spaniel's condition.

'It's like this,' drawled Rupert Fitch-Williams, pulling off his shades and swinging them in one hand. 'We feel enough is enough, don't we, darls?' He turned to his wife.

She tugged at the end of her pashmina with one hand, her other hand holding Emily's lead. The spaniel sat patiently between them, looking from one to the other, her tongue lolling out, her liquid brown eyes full of trust. 'Yah, it's not fair on the dog.'

'Difficult decision and all that,' Rupert was saying, Emily gazing up at him, tail wagging. 'But we want her put down.' Emily's tail still wagged.

'It might seem a bit harsh, but it's for her own good,' said Charlotte, Emily now having switched her attention to her, head cocked to one side. The tail still wagged. The tongue still lolled. The eyes still full of trust, as her owners requested her execution.

I was completely floored. Absolutely dumbstruck. My mind reeling from what they were suggesting. Okay, we had here a dog with a skin problem that was irritating for all concerned. But to have the spaniel put down? No way. Far too drastic.

But the Fitch-Williams had clearly talked it through with each other and had reached their decision. Nothing was going to dissuade them. I reasoned. I pleaded. I got dangerously near the point of rudeness. But not a word I said made any difference.

My suggestion of re-homing was greeted with vigorous shakes of the head. Referral to a skin specialist likewise.

'Ems has been through so much already,' drawled Rupert. 'It's not fair on her.'

With a heavy heart, I slid a consent form across the table. Rupert signed it with a flourish. 'There, that's done then,' he said, stepping back. 'We won't stay.' He turned to his wife. Give the guy Em's lead.'

Charlotte hesitated. Rupert pulled it from her and handed it to me. 'There we go. Now babes, we'll make tracks, yah?' He grabbed his wife's hand and yanked her towards the door without a backward glance. I was left holding on to Emily who was straining at her lead, tail wagging furiously, trying to follow them.

I waited until I was sure they'd left the hospital and then led Emily down to the prep room. She trotted eagerly by my side, poking her head into reception as we passed.

'Hi Emily, sweetie-pie,' said Beryl. 'In for some more tests are we?' She glanced at me. 'Still not got her sorted yet then?'

I was still seething with rage. Silently fuming. With a curt shake of my head, not trusting myself to speak, I yanked Emily back into the corridor and marched her on down to the prep room.

Lucy looked up from where she was sorting out some instruments ready to be autoclaved for tomorrow's list of ops.

'Oh hello, poppet,' she exclaimed reaching down to stroke Emily's head. The spaniel responded with a grizzle of greeting, her back end thumping against the side of the counter. 'What's the nasty man going to do to you today?' Over the previous few months, Lucy had assisted in getting blood samples from Emily, and helped to restrain her when I set up allergen skin tests. By now, they were old pals.

'Why, Paul, whatever's the matter?' she exclaimed. 'You've gone as white as a sheet.'

'I... er... uhm...' I couldn't bring myself to say it, especially with Emily now looking up at me with those big brown eyes of her, brimming with trust. 'It's Emily,' I finally choked. 'I've got to put her down.'

Lucy took a sharp intake of breath. 'Paul. You're joking. You couldn't possibly...' Her voice trailed off. She bent down and put her arm round the spaniel's neck. Emily turned and licked her face. 'Don't you listen to that nasty man,' Lucy murmured. 'We can't let him do that to you.'

'But Lucy,' I hissed. 'Her owners have insisted. And they've signed the consent form.'

Lucy shrugged. 'So what? It's only a bit of paper.' She stood up and stared at me, her hazel eyes ablaze, as they bore into me. 'I can't believe you'll go through with this. It's just not you. Why not find a new home for her?'

'I suggested that. The Fitch-Williams were adamant that she was to be put down.'

Lucy shrugged. 'So what. They needn't know.'

'What do you mean, "They needn't know"?' I gave her a quizzical look. 'Hey, you're not suggesting... Think where that would leave me.'

'Paul. Don't be so selfish. Just think where it would leave poor Emily if you put her to sleep. Shoved in a black plastic body bag. Sorry, sweetie, you're not hearing any of this.' Lucy reached down and pressed her hands over the spaniel's ears.

'But a new owner might ask questions. It could get back to the Fitch-Williams. Then I'd really be in for the high jump.' I shook my head sadly. 'Nice idea, but I don't think it's really on.'

Lucy was still giving me her icy look. 'It could work, you know.'

'How?'

'If you took her on.'

'Me?'

'Yes, you. You've always said how much you like Springers. So here's your chance to own one.'

I suddenly felt conscious of another set of eyes on me. Those big brown eyes of Emily's. With her head cocked to one side, they were asking, 'Well, what about it?'

So that's how I came to have a Welsh Springer spaniel scooting her butt across my living room carpet.

But apart from that, she really was adorable. So friendly. So willing to please. A pleasure to be with – providing you didn't let her bum-scooting, her under-the-table back scratching and her belly weaving on the hall rug get under your skin – like whatever had been getting under hers. But surprisingly, that itchiness slowly subsided. Much to my relief and certainly to Emily's. And within three months it had gone completely. I can only assume she'd been allergic to something in the Fitch-Williams' environment. Yah?

Having a dog around made me realise how empty life had been without one. That and not having the likes of Lucy to keep me company. Having her around as well would have been even better. I certainly missed dear little Nelson, the Jack Russell who had been accidently run over and killed by Lucy – a catalyst to us finally splitting up. A painting of him hung over the fireplace – it pictured him sitting in the nearby bluebell woods. That was a 'thank you' present for saving the life of Henry the boxer, owned by Sandra and John Coles, who lived at Ashton Manor, across the field adjacent to Willow Wren. Nelson and I spent many a happy hour wandering though those woods, with me watching him scampering down the narrow paths created by deer, badgers and rabbits, his rudder tail swishing from side to side through the bluebells as he picked up a fresh scent. As my relationship with Lucy became more untenable I'd often find myself chatting to Nelson as we walked down those paths, unleashing my troubles on him even though I knew he wasn't taking it all in – more interested in attempting to catch a rabbit. Besides which, the poor little chap was stone deaf. But nevertheless, I felt better for doing it. I'll always remember one particular summer's evening. One of those glorious evenings when the sun caught ribbons of cloud on the horizon, turning them into fingers of gold. I was sitting with my back resting against the bole of an oak tree, feeling at peace with the world. Nelson was by my side, the customary broad grin on his face as I tickled his ears. The setting sun reflected in his milky eyes. Reflected the bond that tied us together. A bond that was broken when two days later he was crushed under the wheels of Lucy's car.

Now with Emily, I looked forward to venturing back into those woods again to revive the pleasures to be found there. The rustling leaves of the beech trees. The dappled shade they provided. The petals of Hawthorn blossom now falling like showers of confetti to sprinkle the pathways in white. Those tracks edged with towering columns of foxgloves, their purple bells alive with the drone of bees.

But it wasn't to be. Not least for a while.

The reason? I crashed out with cellulitis – a condition which could so easily have killed me.

11

Not Having A Leg To Stand On

I woke up one morning feeling decidedly groggy. Not one-of-those-days-down-in-the-dumps sort of grogginess. More like the 'hung over' feeling I'd experienced after that evening over at The Buccaneer. The recollection of that afternoon still sent shivers down me timbers. Yet I'd had an early night. No drinking. The onset of flu, maybe? Certainly I felt shivery as if running a temperature. So I took mine using a thermometer from my black bag. Conscious of the many times that thermometer had been stuck up a cat or dog's bum, I'd made sure it had been fastidiously washed and rinsed several times before I stuck it under my tongue. A 39.8 °C reading verified I was running a bit of a temperature. Okay not the end of the world. I could still make it into work. Just. In the short time I'd had her, Emily had taken to the practice car like a duck to water, sitting in the front passenger seat, quite happy to jump out when we got to Prospect House and dash in to greet everyone. Today was no different for her. But quite different for me. Beryl sensed something was amiss as soon as I got into reception and was quick to say so.

'Paul. You look dreadful.'

191

'Blimey Paul, had a late night?' was Eric's comment.

'Fighting something off, are you?' came from Crystal.

'Hope it's nothing infectious,' was Mandy's reaction.

Thanks guys. You certainly know how to make a guy feel worse.

Only Lucy showed any sympathy with a look of concern and the offer of some Paracetamol tablets should I require them.

I managed to struggle through my morning appointments. Fortunately there was nothing too taxing. A couple of cat boosters. A bitch spay's stitches to take out. And an overweight pug with a fatty lump on her flank, which I booked in to have removed. Though one case did prove a little bit more tricky to deal with. It really needed a clear head to ascertain exactly what was going on. Something I hadn't got. Which only made matters worse.

Beryl was usually able to give me some idea of what I was to expect with each appointment. But with this one, all I got from her was, 'They wish to discuss something rather delicate.'

That usually denoted something of a sexual nature. Fluffy had a discharge from her you-know-what. Or Fido's whatsits needed removing.

Despite my muzziness, I picked up on Mr and Mrs Tomkins' embarrassment as soon as they entered my consulting room with Bertie, their Westie. It wasn't hard to do.

Mrs Tomkins, a tiny wisp of a woman in her late forties, with mousy brown hair, constantly fiddled with her handbag, opening and closing the clutch; while Mr Tomkins, of equally short stature, with whiskery jowls, was carrying Bertie, constantly reassuring the dog all was well and not to be afraid. Which a timid Mr Tomkins clearly was.

My standard, 'What can I do for you?' elicited an anxious exchange of twitchy looks between the couple as the Westie was cautiously lowered on to the consulting table. As soon as his front paws touched the surface, he started to whine and scrabble like a drunken penguin on ice.

'Now Bertie, don't get in such a tizz wazz,' said Mr Tomkins lifting the dog back up into his arms and apologising about his behaviour. 'He's a bag of nerves.'

Not the only one I surmised.

Click... click... click... went Mrs Tomkin's bag.

I still had no clue as to why they were here. And with the pounding in my head steadily getting worse, I felt my concentration slipping away.

It was Mrs Tomkins who next spoke. 'Bertie keeps having a go at my husband's slippers.'

'Well, he is still a youngster. What... five months old now?' I said. 'You'd expect it in a dog of his age. Just make sure you give him plenty of toys. Chew bones. Squeaky balls. Tug-of-war ropes. That sort of thing. It will take his mind off your husband's slippers.

'And of course,' I paused not wishing to state the obvious, 'you should keep the slippers out of reach of Bertie.'

'But he does it when my husband's wearing them.'

In my befuddled state, I didn't comprehend straightaway.

'And with his trousers,' continued Mrs Tomkins. 'He's always hanging on to his legs.'

Her face went red.

Her handbag went click... click... click...

I too then clicked. It was an open and shut case. Bertie was beginning to feel his oats. Developing a sexual appetite for all things humpable. Which – as Mr Tomkins told me with much clearing of his throat and reddening of his face – included the postman's leg, a furry handbag alongside a table in a cafe, and three of their neighbour's pet rabbits. With his face now puce, he went on to say that they'd been innocently nibbling their morning lettuce leaves with their backs to Bertie, when he slipped through a hole in the fence and jumped them (an action I suspect my Uncle Peter had in mind for me when he sat on the edge of my bed and read me stories about what Benjamin Bunny got up to).

I explained that Bertie was still a bit too young to have his bits removed.

Click... click... click... went the handbag.

But I reassured them they wouldn't have to put up with it for much longer. Maybe a month or so.

Click... click...

And once he'd had the operation, the problem would be sorted.

Click...

He'd quieten down.

The handbag went silent.

I wished my head could have gone silent. But there were hammers in it which persisted in bashing against my cranium throughout the rest of the morning, so that by lunchtime, I felt completely knocked out.

Everyone was now sympathetic. Get yourself home was the order of the day – well of the afternoon at any rate. Where she could, Beryl rearranged any appointments that had been booked for me and transferred those she couldn't over to Eric. He'd come bouncing up to reception stating, 'I'll be happy to double up on some of my appointments if that's of any help.'

'No need,' replied Beryl in a matter-of-fact voice. 'You've got plenty of spare slots as it is.'

A reply that had Eric, who was standing behind her, raise his hands over the back of her head and squeeze them together, while pulling his tongue out to one side in an exaggerated grimace.

'I saw that,' retorted Beryl, swinging round to give him one of her Cyclops specials.

An eye in the back of her head? No. It was via that small compact mirror next to her computer used for touching up the crimson lipstick with which her lips were always smeared.

I returned to Willow Wren, fed Emily, and then went straight to bed. Despite it only being 3 o'clock in the afternoon, I was out like a light as soon as my head hit the pillow. I woke briefly in the early evening. Staggered down to the kitchen. Let Emily out into the back garden for a final pee. Poured myself some iced water. Then it was back to bed where I tossed and turned, unable to get comfortable. Duvet was thrown to one side when I got too hot. Yanked back when I got too cold. Pillow thumped down when it felt too high. Plumped up when it felt too low. And the dreams. Oh the dreams. I found myself vividly re-enacting Bertie's movements. First with a cushion. Then a slipper. Moving on to mount a handbag. Click... click... click... And finally three rabbits' bottoms bobbed into view – their cute little scuts beckoning. I woke hot and sweaty, feeling flopsie.

I lay there for what seemed like hours, slipping in and out of sleep until the dawn chorus – that of Eleanor's cockatiel, Wilfred, screeching through the partition wall – finally managed to rouse me.

As I shuffled through the spare bedroom to the bathroom, I felt a twinge in my right ankle, a small area on the medial side, just as if I'd sprained it. Nothing too painful. When I prodded the spot, I could feel some puffiness. By the time I'd let Emily out and had forced down some cornflakes, the puffiness had spread and the area had become red and more painful. By the time I'd shaved, washed and dressed – all done with great effort – the puffiness had spread half way up my lower leg, the foot was swollen, and angry red spots had appeared across the arch. Each spot felt like a needle had been driven in.

'Time I saw a doctor,' I muttered to Emily.

I was lucky when I phoned the surgery.

The receptionist said, 'Dr Merriweather has one appointment left at 12.30. Would that do?'

It did. I was there on the dot.

Besides being my doctor, Graham Merriweather was also a client of the practice. A jovial sort, always full of beans – and with a rounded tummy that would have made his Body Mass Index a little on the high side.

He lived in Grand Avenue, a leafy-lined road of Edwardian red brick-built villas, most of which had been converted into flats, though Graham's remained one of the few that hadn't – Number 28 – Crompton Towers – a reference to the twin turrets that abutted the front corners of the villa. It provided a spacious residence for Graham, his wife Annabel, their three children, four cats, a Cavalier King Charles spaniel and two castrated, dehorned pygmy goats called Mac and Tosh – in naming them, our Dr Merriweather had a sense of humour it seems.

The pygmy goats had been my introduction to the family, a visit required to check their feet. They were brother and sister, black with white muzzles and white capped heads. Graham had sectioned off the back garden to make them a small paddock, secured with wire fencing, in which there were benches and tables for them to climb, sit and sunbathe on; and an old scooter, tyres and footballs for them to butt and play with. For shelter, he'd provided them with a waterproof shed that had a half door which could be opened or closed via a bolt. The shed had more than just straw bedding in it. Graham had installed internal lighting and a goat-proof, weather-proof speaker cable to a stereo system in the house.

I was waiting for Graham to tell me they loved listening to Max Bygraves. But thank goodness, it seemed they had better taste and preferred classical and jazz.

Though having the tables and benches to climb on, it wasn't the rugged terrain they'd have had in the wild. As a consequence, their claws had nothing to keep them worn down. Hence they required trimming every two months or so.

Graham had become adept at doing this himself. But noticed during a recent trimming, there seemed to be some infection between Tosh's back claws.

Having herded the two goats into a corner, it was easy enough to restrain Tosh and turn her up, rump on the ground, back against Graham's legs, with him holding her in that position, while I checked her feet.

'You're right, there's a bit of scald between her back claws here,' I said, noting the inflamed and swollen skin between the claws and the foul smell issuing from them.

'Fusobacterium necrophorum?' said Graham.

Ah. He'd been googling the condition. And knew what treatment was required. An antibiotic aerosol spray.

'Thought it might be the beginnings of foot rot,' Graham went on.

'No sign of Dichelobacter nodosus having got in there yet,' I replied. My turn to show off my knowledge – also gleaned off the Internet the night before. If it had been that bug, then if would have been a far more serious condition – very painful, undermining the horn, often causing it to completely slough off. And if left, the whole foot could have swollen up.

'Just make sure you keep both goats' feet as dry as possible,' I added. 'Then all should be well.'

Not like me, now. When all was certainly not well.

I hadn't got Dichelobacter nodosus, but whatever bug or bugs had got into my ankle it was causing me considerable grief.

While sitting in the waiting room, waiting to see Graham, I couldn't help but compare it to the one at Prospect House.

Both rooms had a rack of pamphlets advising on the various medical conditions one could encounter and how they could be prevented. Ours focussed more on worming and fleas as opposed to prostate enlargement and breast screening that headed the list of medical problems we humans might encounter. A list that you could work through in the wait to see a doctor and end up feeling worse than when you arrived; so that by the time you eventually staggered in to see the GP your list of ailments had doubled.

Having been freaked out by the medical pamphlets and finished flicking through a dog-eared magazine expounding the virtues of making your own Christmas log and plum pudding now the festive season was fast approaching – that being last year – I turned my attention to surmising why others sitting in the chairs around me were here. I gave a calculated guess for the eight-year-old with his right forearm in plaster. Likewise, I was pretty certain the young woman sitting opposite me with the grossly swollen abdomen, hadn't got ascites or an enlarged liver. The blue bootie she was knitting rather gave it away. Not so certain though about the gentleman with the large pustular patches on his face and hands. Some sort of skin disease which I thought looked rather contagious. Evidently everyone else thought the same as they were all packed at one end of the room, he conspicuously on his own, surrounded by empty seats at the other.

'So, Paul, what seems to be the problem?' Graham asked when I eventually got in to see him.

I described my symptoms, concluding by saying, 'I think I've gone down with cellulitis.'

'You're right,' said Graham, when I prised my shoe and sock off to show him the swollen ankle and spreading red rash. 'It is cellulitis. I'll put you on a double mix of antibiotics to be taken four times a day for the next two weeks. But if there's no improvement in twenty-four hours or meanwhile, if you start to feel nauseous or have difficulty in breathing get back to me straightaway, or get yourself over to A&E at Westcott General.' He paused while the computer printed off my prescription – to be twelve tablets a day – strewth, I was going to rattle. 'You know this could get serious.'

I did know. I'd googled the condition before setting out to see him. Septicaemia could set in. Damage vital organs. Kill me within twenty-four hours if not checked in time. I nearly died on the spot.

I was knocking back the first set of tablets within the hour. The third by that evening. And feeling no worse.

Having phoned the practice earlier to let them know I'd be laid up for a least a couple of days – here at home and not in some hospital bed hooked up to an IV drip – or so I hoped – I organised downstairs for a lie-in. The settee was cushioned with pillows and blankets piled to hand; while a foot stool was stacked on a chair so that I could keep my leg raised. I now prepared myself for a marathon session of daytime TV, box sets of my favourite Westerns and a copy of Hardy's *Far from the Madding Crowd* which I'd done for O level English, had thoroughly enjoyed, and intended to re-read sometime. That time was now – nine years on – with a copy I'd bought on the spur of the moment from Help the Aged only last month. As for food, there were loads of ready meals in the freezer – the result of several 'buy three for two' deals resulting in a surfeit of tandoori chicken dishes and a load of boil-in-the-bag cod. And Emily was catered for – there was a tray of tinned complete dog food only just opened. We'd manage between us for a few days – that is, if my condition improved and didn't take a turn for the worse.

Seemed the antibiotics kicked in quickly, as by the next day I was beginning to feel a bit better. My temperature had come down and the agonising pain had diminished. I was still unable to walk at more than a snail's pace – a pickled mollusc's pace even then – but at least it was an improvement. And having Emily around to talk to did help to pass the time in-between watching Wyatt Earp slug it out at the OK Corral and reading how Sergeant Troy wooed Bathsheba with his sword play.

Add to that, a few visitors.

Eleanor popped round at least twice a day, and fussed about like a mother hen, bringing me a dozen eggs after she'd rummaged in my fridge and spotted I was down to my last one; and she made sure I didn't run out of milk by presenting me with a two litre carton – enough to last until the cows came home. Bread too. Which meant I didn't have to use my loaf – the one I kept in the freezer in case I ran out.

Reverend James also popped over from the vicarage.

I hobbled to the front door to meet him, bracing myself to be flooded in a torrent of words. I wasn't disappointed.

'Sorry to be informed that you have been unable to partake of the normal activities associated with the ability to walk due to the advent of a condition that prevents you from doing so,' he gushed. 'So I just popped over to give you this.' He thrust the cake he'd been holding into my hands. 'A little something Marjorie knocked up for you.' He gave an embarrassed little smile.

His wife was well known in the village for the soggy offerings she 'knocked up' in the way of cakes for the annual Ashton fete. Here, for £1.50, villagers could buy a cup of tea and a slice of cake and then spend the next thirty minutes sliding her currant creation around their plates, before seeking somewhere in the vicar's shrubbery to discretely dispose of it.

I found myself clutching a large wafer-thin plateful of sponge, the middle of which dipped deeply; in the centre of the crater, a loose pile of chocolate chips had been dumped as if a mouse had suddenly been caught short there.

'Oh, before I forget, Marjorie also asked me to give you this.' He swung the carrier bag he'd been holding in his other hand over to me. 'Some eggs, milk and bread in case you're running low.'

Once I'd thanked him for his offerings, he stepped back, wished me a speedy recovery and hurried away.

My third visitor that week was a surprise one. And received with mixed emotions. I heard the car draw up on the hard standing to the front of Willow Wren and, looking out, saw a blue Fiesta. Could it be? Yes. The fair-haired girl who slipped out from behind the steering wheel was Lucy.

She was about to step into a home she had shared with me for seven months and this would be her first visit back since leaving... how long ago was that? Must have been four months or thereabouts. Actually it was four months, three days and two hours to be precise. I'd worked it out as I was laying, with my leg up, watching Randolph Scott in the 1962 film *Ride the High Country* for the third time.

I wasn't too sure how to greet her when she made that brave step inside. A handshake seemed silly. Too formal. A kiss then? The brushing-of-cheeks-lips-kissing-the-air sort. Possibly. But Emily, rushing up to greet her with a frenzied bark of welcome, was sufficient. The awkward moment passed as Lucy bent down and stroked the spaniel's ears and said, 'Hello sweetie pie.' That stroke and endearment wouldn't have gone amiss had she applied it to me. 'How's your master then?'

'Master's on the mend, thank you,' I said taking the carrier bag she was proffering.

'Some eggs, milk and bread in case you're running low,' she said.

Over coffee, Lucy enquired about my cellulitis while Emily sat by her side, eyeing the plate of Marjorie's cake, uneaten on her lap. Lucy dropped the spaniel a large morsel which she took one sniff at, curled up her lip and then turned away.

'So any idea how you caught this bug?'

'Er... yes... I think so.'

Lucy played around with a crumb of her cake. I did likewise with a crumb of mine.

Crumbs. This wasn't the way I'd hoped the conversation would go. I somehow imagined it would have centred on her concerns for me. Indicating a softening of her attitude towards me. Maybe a hint that she might consider us getting together again. Allow love to blossom once more. To which I'd respond with endearments whispered in her ear.

Instead, all she got from me was, 'I've got onychomycosis of my toes.' Hardly the basis for love to regenerate unless done with a tube of antifungal cream applied twice daily. But having now set out on this path I had to continue down it and explain, awkward though it was to do so.

'I've got rather thick and scabby toe nails.'

Another portion of Majorie's sponge was shunted round.

'The one on the big toe broke off leaving a jagged edge which dug into the skin.'

I bit into a piece of my cake and swallowed hard before I resumed.

'That allowed the Staphs and Streps normally found on the skin's surface to get in and set off the cellulitis.'

'All down to crabby feet then,' Lucy mused as I felt mine curl up with embarrassment. 'You should have got them seen to sooner.' That was said in her strict no-nonsense-vet-nurse voice. 'But least you're on the mend now by the looks of things.' She hadn't actually looked at any of my things, as I'd resisted the urge to whip off my sock and wave my mangy fungal-toed phalanges in her face for fear that the sight of them would have killed off any last chance of our relationship being rekindled – however remote that chance already was.

Instead, I steered the conversation to the practice, asking how they were coping without me. I wish I hadn't.

'Fine actually,' Lucy told me. 'Crystal decided to get someone in from the locum agency they use. Until such time as you're back on your feet that is.' She played around with another crumb, moulding it thoughtfully between her fingers and, still looking down at her plate, said, 'Nice guy actually. Australian. Beryl's taken quite a shine to him.'

I began to feel a niggle of irritation creep in. Perhaps it was the tone of Lucy's voice. Her manner of speaking. Had she also taken a 'shine' to this locum? I was being irrational surely? The result of being cooped up here – the cellulitis affected my brain as well as my ankle. Nevertheless, I couldn't suppress that irritation and it spilt over into what I said next, 'You too?'

Lucy looked up sharply. 'For Christ's sake Paul, do grow up.' That blaze was in her hazel eyes again. With a final pat of Emily's head, she jumped to her feet. 'Besides, if I did fancy the guy, what's it to you?'

What indeed? I wondered. I was hardly in a position to do anything about it – especially in my current position with my leg up over a stool rather than up over her. In my dreams, Paul. Get real. It's not going to happen.

'Greg happens to be a quiet, unassuming guy. And he's a competent vet.'

Greg, eh? I thought. I was already beginning to create a mental image of this 'Greg' – a muscular, well-honed Aussie, with tanned pecs and rugged outback charm. 'Got a good bedside manner, has he?' I said, unable to keep the sarcasm out of my voice. It was totally uncalled for. And I could have kicked myself for saying it. Not that I could have done in the physical sense of the word, with my ankle so swollen.

Lucy was right to ignore such a trite comment. She merely shook her head sadly and said, 'I hope you'll feel better soon,' adding, 'I'd better go. Mandy wants me back to help Crystal with her afternoon appointments.'

'But Mandy always does that.'

Lucy hesitated a moment. 'Not today. She's helping Greg with a bone pinning.'

Like that bone, something snapped inside me. Since when had anyone been allowed to do their own orthopaedic surgery? It had always been the prerogative of Crystal's. Always assisted by Mandy. No one else had a look in. Until now it seemed. Until this Aussie bloke, Greg, had appeared on the scene and got his foot in the door in a manner that was too damned quick for my liking. Thank goodness he'd be leaving once my feet were firmly back in the hospital.

But I was wrong in that assumption.

Lucy enlightened me. 'Crystal said to let you know they're employing Greg for the two weeks they're away. So you'll be able to meet him in person and see what he's like for yourself.'

Oh dear. This could be a case of how much can a koala bear.

Already, I felt he would tread on my toes. And what with their crabby nails, that would hurt in more ways than one.

Which proved to be the case.

When I eventually met Greg, I found myself on an emotional rollercoaster beyond my wildest dreams. And it proved to be a very bumpy ride.

12

What Does Your Didgeri Doo?

When I first saw the guy standing in reception, I thought perhaps he'd strayed up from the beach. Beryl had just popped out to get the lunchtime baguettes and Mandy, covering for her, had gone to the loo, so the reception desk was momentarily unmanned.

I was passing the inner door on my way down to the office, saw him standing there, and poked my head in just to say, 'Someone will be with you in a minute.'

He turned, and a broad smile spread across his rugged, tanned face. 'G'day mate,' he said, levering himself round the reception desk, his hand stretched out. 'You must be Paul. Pleased to make your acquaintance.' His eyes were deep set, and dark – eyes that could have inspired sonnets – Romeo come hither eyes that could have made an army of Juliets lose their cool and plunge from their balconies providing his muscular arms were waiting below to catch them. They gazed at me with such smouldering passion that I too felt like taking the plunge. Crikey, he was turning my knees to jelly; and there's me, thinking I wasn't of that mould unless dreaming of being swept on to the shoulder of a fireman had more significance than I realised. I gazed back, my eyes no match for his – watery grey with a sty in the bottom lid of the right one – enough to make a girl plummet from a high rise flat in despair.

'I recall you had a humdinger of a problem with your leg,' he continued. 'Hope it's sorted now.'

He pumped my hand. The bronzed bare biceps below his short sleeves, rippled while my puny muscles, hidden under my long ones, tweaked feebly in return. I was wearing a casual shirt with a understated criss-cross of stitching over the chest, and with cream chinos to match – an outfit I considered gave me a reasonably cool image, compatible with that required for a young professional. Apart from the gold studs in my ears, the one note of rebellion I'd clung on to since leaving university – and perhaps the tinted blonde hair as well – it was an image that most residents of Westcott could find acceptable. But this guy? Well this guy – and I'd twigged by now who he was – that locum, Greg – looked super-cool, charged with potent charisma. He had a deep weathered tan and sun-bleached hair, moussed into spikes. An out-door look enhanced by a navy sweatshirt, blue knee-length cargo pants above deep caramel calves and open-toed sandals.

With my hand still being pumped with a fireman's grip – I couldn't let go or he wouldn't let me – I managed to blurt out a, 'Pleased to meet you.'

'Me too,' he said, finally releasing me. Phew.

I had to admit, begrudgingly, he was a handsome guy. Even features. Even teeth. Even tempered, no doubt. Even in bed? The fire smouldering in those sensual eyes suggested not. No wonder he attracted attention. Such as the attention he got when Mandy burst back into reception.

'Thought I recognised the voice,' she declared in a high giggly squeak, rushing across to throw her arms round him in a fireman's hug. To which he responded with a hug of his own and a solid kiss on her cheek. Boy... oh boy... and there was me with only a handshake. Paul, what on earth...?

It was Beryl's turn when she arrived back. The baguettes got tossed on to the desk and she was embraced, grinning like a Cheshire cat that had just been rescued from up a tree by a burly fireman. Paul... for goodness sake.

Crystal was a little more restrained in her greeting but was unable to stop the guilty flush of pleasure that spread up her cheeks as Greg kissed her on both of them. Mmm... No smoke without firemen I thought. Paul... do stop it.

Whereas, when Eric breezed in, it was all hands back to the pump. All desire quenched. I felt quite relieved.

As for Lucy. Well it was her afternoon off, so the pleasure of seeing her reaction to the arrival of Greg had yet to come.

When I discovered his surname – Beryl told me in between bites of her tuna and mayonnaise baguette that lunchtime, after all the fuss of Greg's arrival had calmed down – Pullman – I felt certain Lucy would think the same as everyone else. If any man could be on the pull that athletic young Aussie could – and pull it off with ease. Curse the guy.

The plan was for this Greg Pullman to cover for Crystal and Eric as of that coming Saturday. They were off on a fly-cruise to Venice and the Dalmatian coast, returning in two weeks' time. As I knew only too well, the Aussie had stepped in when

I was off sick and seemed to have done a good job. Hence his return for this two week stint. Accommodation was no problem. Like before, he was staying with Cynthia Paget, the lady who had put me up when I first started at Prospect House. I wasn't surprised to learn from Beryl that she'd been thrilled to have another young vet staying under her roof. Especially when it turned out to be such a handsome young man as our Greg Pullman. When I lodged there, I'd been subjected to many a wistful stare from her as I often had to get out of bed when on night duty, dressed only in my boxer shorts, and answer my mobile in her hallway, as it was the only place where the reception was any good. She would suddenly appear at the top of the stairs, fag in mouth, clutching her beloved Chihuahua, Chico, to her bosom, and offer to give me a hand should I need it. Chico had since died – killed in a road accident – but no doubt Cynthia would still be keen to give Greg a good reception even when not on his mobile.

The first week with our hot hunk, went smoothly enough. I missed Lucy's initial meeting with Greg which was a shame. But she didn't seem to be fazed by having him saunter round the hospital looking sexy, stethoscope draped round his neck, feet casual in flip flops, his scrubs defining the contours of his well-honed pecs and six pack. My stethoscope was forever slipping off when I tried the same. Flip flops were of course a no-no with my fungal feet; and as for my scrubs, they made me look like a scuffed shoe bag being dragged down the corridor. Grr...

Mandy and Beryl were like two adolescent school girls with a crush on their favourite pop star. No doubt back in their teenage days they'd had pin-ups of their favourites. Mandy perhaps with some posters of Coolio or Shaggy, Beryl with pictures of Perry Como or Frankie Laine. To judge by the way they were conducting themselves now – all giggles and coyness – I could image them wishing their respective bedroom walls were smothered with pictures of Greg Pullman in various poses and outfits. Him in full fireman's gear, a thick hosepipe between his legs, flared up in my mind. I quickly extinguished it.

On the Thursday morning of that week, I found him in reception, leaning casually against the wall in smouldering James Dean pose, chatting to Beryl. I stopped just outside and listened in.

'Have you got any exciting things for me to do today, Beryl?' he was asking her.

'Not yet. But I'm sure something will crop up. And when it does I'll make sure you're the first to know.'

'You're a good sport, Beryl.'

'Well I do try my best,' she simpered.

Yuck.

She was right in thinking 'something' would crop up. It did. Later that morning. But in her wildest dreams, I couldn't imagine her ever having guessed what that 'something' was. Nor was Greg the first to know. We were both told at the same time.

Beryl was at her desk, me and Greg standing next to her, checking on the remaining appointments we each had yet to see. The phone rang. Beryl answered it. Having listened, she said, 'Hang on Kevin, I'll see if that's okay.' She cupped her hand over the mouthpiece, and looked up at the two of us.

'Well boys, guess what I've got coming in for you two.'

'Tell us, we can't wait, eh Paul?' said Greg, digging his elbow in my ribs and giving me one of his heart–stopping looks.

'It's an injured wallaby,' said Beryl. 'Kevin's asking if he could bring it over rather than one of you visit the park, as he thinks it will need surgery.'

'Sounds the best option, especially as we're short staffed,' I said.

While Beryl got back to Kevin, I explained to Greg who he was. The Head Keeper at Westcott's Wildlife Park.

Greg's ears pricked up at the mention of a wildlife park.

'Hey. That sounds a fun place to visit. Maybe you and I could go over there sometime, eh?' He gave me one of his dazzling smiles, his eyes searching mine.

I quickly put him straight. It was actually a rather run down motley collection of animals – a couple of gazelles, a mangy, bad tempered camel called Chloe, whose foot I had to treat last year, a small troupe of macaque monkeys, and a collection of moth-eaten budgerigars and cockatiels. Greg asked if there were any endangered species being bred and I told him the only successful breeding was in the guinea pigs' pen – that was stuffed full with randy rodents. So much so that, whenever a car backfired on the nearby main road, the sudden panic induced in their pen had the teeming masses emit a barrage of terrified squeaks, and then surge from one side of the pen to the other, throwing themselves over their feed and water troughs like migrating wildebeests in the Serengeti. I concluded by saying they now had three wallabies – latest additions which I had yet to see.

Seems it was one of this trio we'd be seeing now.

Kevin was in quite a state when he arrived. Quite the wild man of Borneo. But then he always tended to give that impression with his shaggy mane of black and grey hair, and the nervous energy that seemed to pulsate through him. There was much letting off steam, much whistling through the gap in his front teeth as he spoke – like a boiling kettle that couldn't be switched off.

'I've got Cindy-Roo in the back of the van,' he gasped, bursting into reception just as I was showing out my last appointment of the morning – Major Fitzherbert with his latest acquisition, an over-sexed Cairn called Caruthers. Greg was still in the other consulting room, with two appointments yet to be seen.

'Ha... Ha...' harrumphed the Major. 'Got an emergency on your hands have you, laddie?' His white caterpillar eyebrows shot up with anticipation. 'Never a dull moment here, what?' Major Fitzherbert had been here – rooted to the spot he was now standing on – when earlier in the year a fox had escaped into the hospital and torn past him, evoking a series of 'tally-hos' from the Major and the waving of his stick at the disappearing 'varmint' as he called it. 'What's it this time, laddie?' he asked, peering out of the door at the van with its Westcott Wildlife Park logo on its side. 'Something exotic I bet, eh?'

I ignored him and rushed down the steps to where Kevin had flung open the rear doors of the van and was leaning into the back, gently easing a blanket towards him, on which another blanket was piled. Sandwiched between the two was a body, only its head showing. A brown head. Black-eared. Black-nosed. A white stripe on its upper lip. The head of a wallaby. What sort I didn't know. But this one that looked lifeless. Eyes wide open, unblinking. No twitch of the whiskers. Nothing.

'Let's give you a hand,' I said and helped ease the wallaby out between us, her weight supported by the blanket ends we were each holding. Swiftly we hoisted her up the steps into reception. In my haste, I skidded on the vinyl, twisting over on my right ankle – the one that had been weakened by the cellulitis. With an explosive, 'Look out. Drat!' I managed to right myself and carry on past an ogling Major who had been joined by a lady clutching a toy poodle, whose top knot was tied with pink ribbon. She, on enquiring what was being carried through, was told by the Major, having misheard me, that it was a rat, a bloody big one by the look of it, so probably an African Bush rat. He'd come up against many in his time in Kenya. They were savage beasts that could kill a poodle like hers with a single bite.

At which point the lady fainted.

Kevin and I continued down the corridor into the theatre, leaving Beryl to pick up the pieces in reception – the broken remains of Major Fitzherbert's walking stick, snapped into pieces by the lady who'd fallen on it, while the Major helped the lady to her feet and Caruthers tried to mount her poodle. As Beryl was to tell me in every juicy detail later, Major Fitzherbert and the lady then dusted each other down with utter decorum. They said to each other that it was neither of their faults and to make amends, they'd go and have a spot of lunch together. So with a final 'tally-ho' from the Major, they left. The Major followed the lady, his hand under her elbow. Caruthers followed the poodle, his nose under her tail.

Mandy, in her usual efficient manner, had everything ready in the theatre, anaesthetic machine on stand-by, connected to a face mask on the table, an autoclaved set of surgical instruments adjacent on the ops tray should they be required. She stood waiting, Lucy hovering by the door in case extra help was required, while Kevin and I slid the wallaby on to the operating table and peeled off the blankets covering her. Only then could I see the real state of her. And she didn't look good.

'Got spooked by the guinea pigs going on one of their rampages,' explained Kevin. 'All three wallabies started careering round their pen, Cindy-Roo here suddenly made a bee-line for the fencing and crashed straight into it. Face-on. I saw it happen.' Kevin gave a low whistle and shook his head sadly. 'She just slumped to the ground like a pack of cards. Unable to move. And hasn't done since. As you can see.'

I could see. And what I saw I didn't like.

Cindy-Roo lay there, motionless, save for the rise and fall of her chest and a slight twitch of her deer-like ears. Her dark eyes were wide open, pupils dilated, full of fear. But she did blink when I tapped the medial edge of her lower eyelid. So at least that reflex was still intact. I lifted one of her front legs and then let go. It flopped back. Likewise, one of her thickly muscled hind legs when I lifted that. The wallaby appeared still dazed. Out of it. In a state of shock. And as a result, unresponsive. That was my initial thought.

But something didn't seem quite right. Her colour, when I raised her lip and pressed her gums, wasn't too bad. Certainly nowhere near as bad as Fredric's – Lady Derwent's elkhound – had been. And the wallaby's breathing wasn't as laboured as his. If Cindy-Roo had just been dazed by hitting the fence, surely she should have been recovering by now? Struggling to get up. Her legs moving in attempts to right herself. But they weren't. And that's what worried me.

A tic in my forehead started to throb. I chewed my lower lip. Tell-tale signs that I was beginning to panic a little. I'd never treated a marsupial before. So was I missing something specific to her species? Something that put her apart from a dog or cat? I could feel the eyes of Mandy, Kevin and Lucy on me. Waiting for me to make a diagnosis.

'Hey, so this is our patient then?' A voice over my shoulder. Greg's. He'd just sauntered in, having seen his last appointment.

'Ah, a red neck I see,' he said, approaching the table to stand next to me and peer down at Cindy-Roo. 'Bit far gone by the look of her.'

'She smashed into a chain-link fence,' said Kevin.

'Sorry, this is Kevin, the Head Keeper,' I said, introducing him to Greg.

'She got spooked by some guinea pigs,' said Kevin with a whistle.

'Not surprised there. One fart and they can be off,' said Greg. 'Seen it happen several times.'

I turned to him. 'You have?'

'Yeah, mate. Did a summer stint at Adelaide Zoo. There were plenty of old farts there to make the roos shift. One ended up breaking her bloody neck.'

Thanks Greg, I thought. That's it. That's what's probably happened here. It would explain the lack of muscle tone in Cindy-Roo's legs, the lack of movement in them. No wonder she looked so petrified, poor thing. She was paralysed.

'Any tone in her cloaca?' Greg said to me.

Cloaca? I didn't realise wallabies had cloacas like birds. But assuming it would be in the same place as a bird's I lifted Cindy-Roo's tail and there it was. 'Was just about to check,' I said, feeling my cheeks go red. 'Mandy, a needle please.'

Pricking the edge of the sphincter with the one she gave me, induced no reaction. No twitch. The only twitch produced was an extra tic in my forehead as I cursed myself for not having thought to check the cloacal reflex before – had I been aware she had one of course. That would have been a clue to her problem. The paralysis caused by crashing into the fence. A broken neck.

A radiograph of her neck, taken later when everyone had dispersed, confirmed it. Her second and third vertebrae were out of place. Dislodged. Pushing up into her spinal cord. There was nothing that could be done. Or so I thought.

'Wrong, mate,' said Greg, leaning over my shoulder to study her X-ray, his trouser scrubs briefly pressing against the back of mine. 'We could operate.'

I turned and gave him a sceptical look.

'Naw... Don't give me that look mate. I've done one.'

'Honestly?'

'Swear on a wombat's willy.'

'And did it work?'

'Nope.' Greg shrugged his broad shoulders. 'But what the heck. If we don't try, it's caput for Cindy-Roo and she'll end up as dog meat. So what say we give it a go?'

In the next twenty-four hours, it was the main topic of conversation – the impending operation on Cindy-Roo's neck – to be carried out by Greg. There were constant arguments between Mandy and Lucy as to who would assist to pass him a pair of artery forceps, a clamp, a swab, etc. whenever he looked over the top of his face mask with those bedroom eyes of his, and asked someone to give him one.

217

It was me that did in the end. Assist. At his specific request – much to the chagrin of the two nurses.

Greg oversaw the anaesthesia, checking it was balanced and suitably maintained by Mandy once Cindy-Roo had succumbed and been laid out belly down on the operating table, her chin resting on a plastic covered bolster, the back of her neck shaved of fur and disinfected, ready for Greg to incise the skin from the base of the wallaby's neck upwards. He seemed to know what he was doing as he deftly cut through the underlying thin white layer of connective tissue and traced the muscles below it. He carefully tracked the path of each one, before using clamps to pull the muscle fibres to one side. By this means, he ensured they wouldn't get damaged and be able to retain their function post-operatively. Even so, there were areas where the muscle strands were darkened and mottled purple – evidence of the trauma that had occurred when the wallaby smashed into the fence. And it took considerably skill and diligence for Greg to navigate these areas without causing further damage. As I watched, my admiration for the young guy increased by the minute. It was nearly twenty such minutes of painstaking dissection before Greg finally exposed the misaligned vertebrae – done with minimal bleeding – so the need to have me pass him swabs was hardly required.

'Okay, Paul, now for the risky bit,' he murmured, catching my eye briefly, his own totally fired up with the task in hand. 'Let's see if I can do it.'

'I'm sure you can, Greg,' I whispered, willing the guy on.

The two misplaced vertebrae were now to be pushed back into their original positions which would re-align the spinal cord. Once aligned, it would remove pressure and give the damaged nerves a chance to heal. A successful outcome. But the process itself could cause further damage and bleeding in the traumatised area. The outcome then would be failure.

Slowly... oh so slowly... with perspiration beading his forehead (I resisted the temptation to mop that handsome brow of his, much as he might have wanted me to), Greg skilfully eased the vertebrae back into their original positions. I heard a slight pop when he'd done so.

Now the vertebrae had to be stabilised to make sure they didn't pop out again. Fascinated, I watched Greg proceed. It was if he'd done it many times before such was the confidence he exuded. A confidence that was sensed both by Mandy and Lucy, their mouths ajar like gulping guppies, spellbound by the young Australian. As indeed I was.

Having instructed Mandy as to what would be required the day before, the sterilised instruments were laid out on the green drape next to Greg. I handed them to him whenever he instructed me to.

Small steel pins were drilled through the spinal processes of the second and third vertebra; and then wired to each other and over the top to form an H-shaped pattern.

Bone cement was used to strengthen and reinforce both pins and wire.

'It's a bit belt and braces,' admitted Greg. 'But when Cindy-Roo gets up... if she gets up – '

'She will Greg, I'm sure of it,' I interrupted.

'Well, if she does, then that first hop of hers will be a real test. It will jar all of this.' He nodded at the neck area he was now stitching up.

When Greg had finished, he removed his gloves and mask, and turned to me, fixing me with one of those knee-weakening looks of his, 'Thanks for your help, mate. Much appreciated,' he said, running his hand down my forearm.

'Well... I... er... uhm... No problem,' I stuttered, feeling myself blush.

'And you too, Mandy,' Greg said turning his dreamy-eyed gaze on her. 'You did a superb job with the anaesthetic.'

She too stuttered and went a lurid shade of beetroot.

On Greg's advice, the walls of one of the ward's pens had been lined with heavy recovery mattresses and the floor deep-littered with straw, to ensure that Cindy-Roo didn't hurt herself as she came round from the anaesthetic or subsequently, when she attempted to sit up or stand.

Greg and I were there the moment Cindy-Roo finally managed to stumble to her feet, swaying backwards and forwards, but staying upright. Just. I saw the expression on Greg's face as she looked round, puzzled. It was one of gentle, benevolent concern and relief. The empathy with that wallaby plain to see. His commitment. His passion. It was there in his eyes.

'Well?' he said, turning those eyes in a similar fashion on me.

Within three days, Cindy-Roo had recovered some movement in her legs and tail; and had started to eat. So a delighted Kevin was able to take her back to the Wildlife Park, to be housed in an indoor enclosure, where daily he helped her to her feet and grasped her tail – as instructed by Greg – while she hopped on the spot. Gradually she was able to stand for several minutes at a time on her own; and over the ensuing weeks got stronger and stronger until finally she gained complete control over her movements and was able to hop round as normal.

Before Greg's time with us came to an end, there was one more Antipodean-linked confrontation that involved him. And that was with a galah.

'Plenty of them back home,' he said, when Beryl told him she's booked one in for him to cut its claws. 'Fair dinkum. That's if Paul doesn't mind. I was told he's the bird man round here.'

I didn't mind. In fact, to be honest, I was rather relieved as it turned out Greg was to see a David Drummond, an obnoxious man whom I'd taken an instant dislike to when I first bumped into him at the reception desk earlier in the year.

He'd reminded me of a bulldog. All drooling jowls, rheumy eyes, head thrust out from a squat, barrel-chested body. And when he spoke, the words rasped from his throat sounding like a wad of coarse sandpaper going against the grain.

Straightaway, he rubbed me up the wrong way by barking, 'Are you much of a parrot man?' Before I could utter a word, he went on, 'And I'm not talking about your pretty-boy budgies.'

I opened my mouth.

'Need someone who knows their moluccans from their macaws. Well?'

'I have treated the odd parrot or two,' I managed to say, Beryl agog the other side of the desk, no doubt relishing this exchange, warming to every word as each one heated up.

'There's nothing odd about my galah cockatoo, I can tell you.' Mr Drummond's three chins quivered, saliva glistened on his lips. 'Though Aggie is proving to be a bit of a handful.' He raised his right hand. Two fingers had plasters on them. 'I realise galah cockatoos can be nippy of course. But then I didn't want some cuddly namby-pamby sort of parrot. All the same, I need someone to clip Aggie's claws.' He glared at me. 'I guess you'll have to do.'

The consultation that ensued was not a success. In fact, it was a howling failure, with Aggie screeching blue murder and David Drummond doing likewise as I tackled the task of clipping the parrot's claws. Eventually it was completed after many heated words had been exchanged. No wonder he didn't want to see me again. Hence the request to have Aggie's claws retrimmed by some other vet in the practice – 'Not that Mitchell man,' as he put it to Beryl, when he phoned through. He needed someone who understood galahs. Someone who could relate to them.

Beryl had suggested he might like to see Greg. He'd had many dealings with such birds.

'Too right, Beryl,' Greg told Beryl. 'Had flocks of the buggers back home in Melbourne. Bloody pests.'

It wasn't quite the relationship I suspect Mr Drummond had in mind.

I did warn Greg that Aggie was a bit of a blighter.

'Don't worry, mate,' he said, giving me a lingering pat on my shoulder. 'I'll use my charm offensive on her to win her over.' He gazed at me with his bedroom eyes and his hand continued to linger. 'Know what I mean?'

Beryl gave one of her 'excuse me' coughs and he quickly withdrew his hand from my shoulder.

Mr Drummond duly turned up with Aggie glowering in her cage, emitting the occasional growl. Would poor Greg manage to get her out of it in order to clip her nails, I wondered?

When he called Mr Drummond in, Beryl just happened to be passing the consulting room having been to the loo. Mandy and Lucy just happened to be in the dispensary opposite, making up prescriptions. I just happened to be hovering at the end of the corridor waiting for my next appointment. All of us on tenterhooks, straining our ears to hear what would happen.

We didn't have to wait long.

First, there was a muffled discussion, Greg's Aussie twang in his questions, easily distinguishable from the nasally notes of Mr Drummond's replies. Then there was a pause. A brief silence. The metallic rattle of a cage door being opened. There followed a tsunami of sound as a crescendo of shrieks, a cacophony of cries, rent the air and came pouring through the walls and door of the consulting room, to wash down the corridor and swirl into our ears. The voices carried on that wave were heightened, heated, clear to hear.

In between Aggie's piercing shrieks, there were:

'Careful now,' 'Watch it,' 'You're killing her,' from Mr Drummond.

'Bugger,' 'Sod it,' 'Fuck you, you little bastard,' from Greg.

We quickly ebbed away when the consulting room door finally flew open again and a ruffled, red-faced Mr Drummond emerged, with an equally bedraggled, pink-faced Aggie, followed by a white-faced Greg, clutching his left hand with his right, through the fingers of which dripped blood.

While Beryl sorted out the irate Mr Drummond up in reception, I found Greg down in the prep room carefully applying antiseptic to the deep bites on his hand inflicted by Aggie's beak.

I was surprised Mandy or Lucy weren't fussing around him, tending to him, and said so.

'It was clocking off time,' he replied when I asked him why one of the nurses wasn't helping him. 'So I told them I'd manage on my own. But actually...' He paused, glanced over my shoulder and pushed the door closed behind me. 'Perhaps you could dress it for me as I'm finding it a bit awkward.' His puppy-brown eyes searched mine, questioning. 'Would you mind?' he murmured, pulling up a nearby stool to perch on its edge, his legs stretched wide apart, one touching mine.

I felt my heart beat a little faster, my pulse quickening as he leaned towards me, his knee pressing into my thigh.

I inched away and said, 'Let's take a look then.'

The wounds were quite severe. Aggie's beak had gouged puncture wounds each side of Greg's forefinger, and one in the cushion of his palm, the edges of the wound there curled back to expose a thin line of flesh.

'Almost needs a stitch or two in that,' I murmured, running my finger lightly across it as, with my other hand, I gently dabbed it with antiseptic. Greg flinched, his hand curling up to catch mine.

'Hey, steady on mate. That hurts.'

His hand continued to squeeze mine for what seemed like an eternity. In reality must have been just a few seconds. 'Sorry mate,' he said, as I pulled my hand away. And went on, 'How about a couple of beers once we're done here? I feel I need some after the set-to with that bloody galah.'

Under the circumstances, it seemed churlish to say 'No'. Hence thirty minutes later saw us down at The Woolpack, Greg having phoned Lucy on the practice mobile – she was the duty nurse that evening – to tell her where he was in case any emergency calls came through.

The Woolpack was our local, run by Bernie and Brenda Adams, who owned a rather overweight Labrador called Peggy, with whom I'd battled to get her weight down. Not a successful exercise as it turned out, though in the process Brenda benefitted from losing a few pounds herself.

It seemed strange sitting in there with Greg rather than with Jodie, my recent ex-girlfriend. She and I had sat at the very same table, on the very same banquette, chatting to each other in much the same way Greg and I were. Finding out a bit more about each other – as I was now doing with this young Aussie. I remembered how animated my conversation with Jodie had become. How gradually it had been punctuated by pockets of flirtation. A shoe touched. A hand on the elbow. The brushing of knees together. The 'let's strip each other naked and go for it' slowly seeping into our eyes with each successive glance – until we could barely wait to do just that. And we did – on the walk back to Prospect House, half-way up the rhododendron tunnel – the darkest point at which we could satisfy our desire for each other.

'So, mate, what are you thinking of doing next?' Greg was asking.

'Sorry?' I said, startled out of my reverie.

'Well, I guess you'll not stay at Prospect House forever more.'

True. That wasn't likely. But I hadn't really thought that far ahead. So I turned the question round. 'What about you, Greg? Have you any plans?'

I'd already learnt that he'd qualified from the University of Melbourne in 2001, two years before me. He had an interest in orthopaedics – his father

225

was a surgeon at the Royal Melbourne Hospital, specialising in spinal surgery. That gave the clue to Greg's astonishing aptitude in dealing with Cindy-Roo's fractured neck. He told me he reckoned on doing a bit more locum work here before bumming off round Europe for a few months. Then head back to Oz. Find a good hospital. Specialise in orthopaedics. Settle down. That sort of thing.

'Marry and have kids?'

He looked across at me and grinned. 'Come off it mate, do I look the marrying kind?'

'Well, yes, actually you do, since you ask.'

He flashed me another of his radiant smiles. 'Kind of you to say so. But it's not for me, mate.'

I felt his shoe slide against mine. 'I'm not that sort of guy. But would still like to meet Mr Right. Guess I'll know when I meet him.' His knee touched my knee.

I swallowed the last of my beer.

'Think we should be getting back,' I remarked, getting up suddenly.

'Whatever you say, mate.' His bedroom eyes briefly locked on to mine. 'Anyway, it wouldn't be the done thing to get pissed as a pickled possum. Never know where it might have led.' He hunched his shoulders and added, 'Besides, I'm on duty anyway.'

Half-way up the rhododendron tunnel, at the spot where Jodie and I had set on each other, the practice mobile started ringing. Greg slowed the pace of his walk, thrust his hand in his pocket and took it out, 'Hi Lucy. What's up?' he said gruffly.

I saw him cock his head to one side as he listened. 'Really?' The tone of his voice changed. 'Okay. Tell him I'm just on my way back. Should only be a couple of minutes. Ciao.'

'Problems?'

'Er... No, mate. Just need to get back.' His voice had an edge to it. An urgency.

I hurried after him as he strode ahead, his pace quickening the nearer we got to the hospital. He took the steps two at a time and disappeared into reception way ahead of me.

I found him in animated conversation with a slim Mexican-looking youth, in his late teens or early twenties, dark complexion, black hair that sprung from his head in tight curls, wearing jeans and a grey hoodie.

Greg swivelled round as I entered.

'Hey, Paul, let me introduce you to my mate, Carlos.'

The youth stretched out a well-manicured hand, a friendship bracelet of red and blue strands at the wrist, similar to the one Greg wore. 'Pleased to meet you, Paul. I've heard a lot about you.' He flashed me a radiant smile, exposing gleaming white teeth.

'All of it good, I trust,' I said, kicking myself for coming out with such an inane reply.

'Nothing bad about our Paul. More's the pity,' sighed Greg, with a shrug. 'Carlos and I are off to Amsterdam tomorrow,' he continued. Take in a bit of culture and then hit the clubs. Fancy coming? You'd be more than welcome.'

He spun round as the inner door opened and Lucy appeared.

'Oh... hi Luce. It's not an emergency. Just a friend here turned up earlier than I'd expected. I was just saying to Paul, we're off to Amsterdam tomorrow.'

'I heard you,' said Lucy quietly. 'But Paul's needed here.' She cast an eye at me. 'Isn't that so?'

I nodded.

She was right of course. Crystal and Eric would have only just got back to the UK, so I needed to be here on their return to the hospital.

'We'll pop round to Cynthia's,' said Greg. 'Hopefully, she might be able to put Carlos up for the night.'

Lucy and I watched them leave.

As we turned back in to reception, she said quietly, 'I always suspected Greg was gay. I'm sure you did as well.'

I didn't need to reply. I could see she knew my answer by the way she looked at me. That made me wonder. Was there another need for me to be here? A need to show Lucy I did still care for her? A need to find a place once more in her heart and no one else's?

I was certain there was.

And I was soon proved to be right.

13

See You Hate... Er... Alligator

'**P**ity Greg's not still around,' mused Beryl the week after the young locum had left. 'This would have been just up his street.' She tapped the visits' book open at that day's date. 'Instead I've booked it in for you to do this afternoon.'

I leaned over, curious to read the entry. Mr Conway, thirty-three Drover's Drive. Nothing more. So what would I be visiting? Cat? Dog? Parrot?

'Guess,' said Beryl, looking up from her computer screen, a glint in her eye.

I groaned inwardly. Not another of Beryl's guessing games. I really wasn't in the mood.

'You tell me.'

'Go on, have a go.'

'Have a go at what?' asked Eric, who had just bounced into reception.

'Beryl's wanting me to guess what animal I'm seeing later.'

Eric glanced at the visits' book. 'Oh, Mr Conway. Yes... I remember. Doesn't he own that enormous...'

'Shh...' Beryl interrupted.

'An enormous what?' I said trying to keep the irritation out of my voice and control the hands I felt like throttling these two with.

'Didn't you read about him in the *Westcott Gazette?*' This was Beryl.

'Had a two page spread.' That was Eric.

'With a picture of Kaiser.' Beryl again.

'Looked a bit of a monster.' Eric.

'*Please.*' That was me.

Eric looked at Beryl. Beryl looked at Eric. Then they both looked at me. 'Crocodile,' they chorused

'What?'

'A crocodile,' said Eric, chuckling. 'You know... like those Steve Erwin programmes on TV where he wrestles with them.' He reached over and grabbed Beryl by her shoulders and shook her. 'Snap... snap... snap...' he snapped.

'That's enough, thank you, Eric,' Beryl snapped back, pushing him away.

I was not amused. 'You should have asked Mr Conway to bring it in.'

'I did, pointing out that we usually only see people by appointment.'

'And...?'

'He said Kaiser was too big to fit in his car. He only drives a Mini.'

Another 'What?' rang out from me as I gulped at the vision conjured up. Me wrestling with some eight-foot monster in the murky swamps of Broadwater, the residential estate where Mr Conway lived.

Beryl sat back on her stool. Lips gaping, head tilted forward – cocked to one side – good eye wide open, staring unblinking at me. It was her half-blind-bashed-with-a-brick owl look again.

I stared back with a similar look – but unabashed, seething.

'No need to look at me like that,' she retorted. 'If it worries you that much, I'm sure Eric here would be more than willing to do the visit. Wouldn't you Eric?' She looked questioningly at him.

'Er... well... It's not really my cup of tea,' he said.

Nor mine, I thought. It's more of a mug's game.

Two hours, later I was the mug who found himself tackling the intricate maze of roads that made up Broadwater Estate. Anyone unfamiliar with its lay-out could have driven into the estate one day and emerge days later completely disorientated and still not have located their intended address. Fortunately, I'd navigated the estate before in my search to track down Mrs Tidy and her cockatiel, Billy. So I knew my Lark Rises from my Shepherd's Closes – examples of the string of road names allocated to the estate in an attempt by the district council to evoke memories of by-gone days when sheep grazed meadows that were now the lawns of the bungalows crammed into it.

I found Drover's Drive without too much difficulty and came to a halt outside number thirty-three, full of apprehension as to what I would be encountering. Outwardly, the bungalow was no different to the others in that road. Red brick to windowsill level, white rendered above. Concrete tiled roof typical of a 50s build with a dormer in it and a garage with matching tiles and double wooden doors attached to the right-hand side. What did distinguish it from all the others in that road was its front garden. Whereas they had neat, well-tended pockets of lawn edged with roses or summer bedding plants, number thirty-three's garden was a rank wilderness which looked as if it hadn't been touched in years. It was dominated by an overgrown lilac tree which towered over the bungalow, its branches spreading out over the pavement, over the privet hedge adjoining number

231

thirty-five and over the concrete path leading up to thirty-three's front door. The path itself was only just visible, its sides overgrown with sickly yellow-green mats of ground elder, more of which had run riot through a square of lank grass – the remnant of what once must have been a lawn. This merged with a flower bed under the front window now choked with elder and couch grass through which poked a sparsely leaved hydrangea bush, bearing a few tiny blue flowering heads straining to seek the sun in the dense shade cast by the lilac tree. With overgrown privet hedges shoulder height to the front and sides, it felt like I was entering a cocooned emerald world – one akin to a pocket of equatorial rainforest. As I crept up the path I half-feared a monkey might swing down from the lilac tree and sink its teeth into my neck or a cobra to strike out from the couch grass before I could reach the front door. But I made it in one piece, thankful when Mr Conway opened the door and ushered me in. In the hallway, I found myself in more of a jungle than I'd experienced outside. It was packed with tree ferns and potted palms – some of the fronds touching the ceiling – with barely room to squeeze past them. With introductions made, I found myself suddenly assailed by three angry green parrots that had swooped out of the dense canopy of palms and were now flapping in my face and winging over my head with loud raucous squawks of alarm. I ducked down and beat the air with my hands. With further belligerent cries, they wheeled away to disappear through the fronds into a room on the left.

'Sorry about that,' apologised Mr Conway. 'They don't like visitors.'

He was a man of my height and build, though some twenty years older, with thinning grey hair, greasy strands of which were plastered across his forehead, and was wearing a sweaty armpit-stained, grey sweat shirt and grubby jeans.

'Just stay close to me,' he went on, 'then you shouldn't come to any harm.'

I quickly edged up to him. An unfortunate move as I was immediately engulfed by the smell of dead rats in a sewer that emanated from Mr Conway's armpits.

'We'll check out the front room first,' he said. 'Follow me. But remember, stay close.'

'Don't worry, I will,' I said, taking a deep breath. I found myself getting increasingly hot and sticky as we forced our way through the jungle of ferns and palms, parting their tightly packed fronds to squeeze through. It was only a few yards, but it felt as if I'd been up the Limpopo and back without a paddle, when dripping with perspiration, I finally lurched into the front room behind Mr Conway.

This room, too, had greenery but not nearly as much. The parrots had settled in some vines which hung across the pelmet of the front window. Liana trailed down from wall lights and from a central fixture. Heart-shaped leaves arched from the roots of Philodendrons that had climbed the walls and smothered them in glossy greenery. But the middle of the room was devoid of vegetation. Instead there was a small mountain of boulders with several larger ones stacked in the fireplace, and more piled under the window. Between these outcrops of rocks darted a variety of lizards skimming from one pile to another across a floor buried in a deep layer of sand. While on a large boulder in the central pile was coiled a rock python.

Mr Conway glanced round. 'Ah, Kaiser's not in here. Though you can see he has been.' He pointed to the wavy trail outlined in the sand that skirted round the central pile of boulders and headed back towards us and out through the door we had just entered.

I'd never been that clued up on the tracks and trails left by animals, but one didn't need much imagination or know-how to realise that some slithery, creepy creature of very large proportions had recently crawled round that room.

'Kaiser?' I said in a squeaky voice.

'Oh most definitely,' confirmed Mr Conway. 'I've only got the one. Just as well as he's grown into quite a monster.'

'He has?' I said in a more squeaky voice.

'Yes indeed. As you'll see when we catch up with him.'

'I will?' I said in a voice that was off the scale for squeaks.

'We just need to find where he's got to.'

I was left squeakless.

'I reckon he's probably wandered back to his pool out in the conservatory,' mused Mr Conway. 'So let's go and check that.' He turned and started to thrash his way back through the hallway's jungle, adding over his shoulder, 'Remember, keep close. But if you get lost, just follow your nose.'

You don't have to tell me, mate, I thought, taking a deep breath before plunging after him.

As we journeyed down the hallway, Mr Conway filled me in with Kaiser's details. The more I heard the more I felt I could be heading for a sticky end up ahead. In the conservatory. In Kaiser's jaws.

Apparently he was a caiman, not a crocodile.

'But everyone keeps calling him a croc,' said Mr Conway, pushing back the thick aerial roots of some tropical flowering plant hanging from the ceiling, holding them to one side while I edged by.

'Not that I mind. But there is a difference, you know.'

'There is?'

'Oh, yes. Caimans are much smaller.'

Hearing that, I breathed a sigh of relief. Then wished I hadn't as more dead rat wafted up my nostrils.

'But they can still reach quite a size.'

'They can?'

'Oh yes.' Mr Conway stopped to look up at a humming bird dipping its beak into the creamy throat of an exotic flower head. 'Conjures up quite a picture eh?' He nodded up at the bird. It was indeed exotic. Very tropical. Made more so, when an African Grey parrot suddenly poked its head out of a clump of vines and twisted its neck to look down at me.

'Ah, there's George,' declared Mr Conway. 'Come to see who you are.' He peered up at the parrot. 'So what do you say, George?'

George bobbed his head up and down and then squawked, 'Look out... Look out... There's a croc about,' before disappearing back into the vines with a loud cackle of laughter.

Mr Conway chuckled as well. 'Don't take any notice of George. He's a bit of a show-off. Always teasing Kaiser, pecking his tail, making him lash out, getting him really riled. It's one of his party tricks whenever I have visitors.'

Great. I now had a mental image of a pesky, pecking parrot turning a caiman completely crazy. Just what I wanted.

'He was only a foot long when I got him,' Mr Conway went on.

'Eh?'

'Kaiser. He was barely twelve inches long when I bought him.'

Ah, not so big as I feared, then. Maybe I was worrying about nothing.

'But that was nearly eight years ago. He's grown quite a bit since.'

Bugger. That was more of a worry.

'He's well over seven feet now.'

Shit. That was a bloody big worry.

With the journey down the hallway completed, I was led into what once must have been the kitchen, though now stripped out.

'In case you were wondering,' Mr Conway informed me, 'I've converted the loft space and now live up there. It's allowed Kaiser and his chums to have free range down here.'

And where was Kaiser ranging now? I thought, nervously looking around, George's warning echoing in my mind.

The kitchen, though stripped, was not bare. It was south facing and so was able to sustain the vibrant kaleidoscope of tropical plants with which Mr Conway had filled it. I was greeted by a raft of crimson canna lilies and bowers of orange, white and purple bougainvillea, through which fluttered a host of butterflies – large swallowtails, yellow and black winged, others orange and black. Several I didn't recognise, but they were striking to see – especially one which glided past me, each wing bigger than my hand, a dazzling mix of green and black. So awestruck was I that for a moment Kaiser was forgotten.

Until Mr Conway said, 'Kaiser hasn't had his dinner yet. So I guess he must be getting hungry.' My attention was immediately re-focussed. Razor-sharp.

'I usually give him any raw meat I can get my hands on.'

I quickly folded mine behind my back.

Mr Conway had stopped and was looking down at the central aisle – a sandy throughway ridged with Kaiser's comings and goings. 'He's certainly been very active this morning,' he said, lifting his arm to scratch his head – an action which sent another fetid puff of dead rat in my direction. 'So he maybe still on the hunt and not have gone back to his pool. Don't hold your breath in case he hasn't.'

But I did hold mine – partly to avoid a dead rat intake – and partly in the hope that Kaiser had returned to his pool.

Most conservatories are traditionally fitted out with cane furniture on tiled floors with a pot or two of tastefully positioned tropical plants in ceramic planters made in China. Not so Mr Conway's conservatory, as I found out when I cautiously stepped into it.

Most of its floor space had given way to the excavation of a shallow, blue tile-lined pool with splash tiles round its edges that led on to green plastic matting. In its murky water, half submerged, I could see a couple of logs, their curved bark thick and dark brown. Then one of them turned and floated towards me.

'Meet Kaiser,' said Mr Conway.

The creature that swam over to meet me looked like an alligator or crocodile to my inexperienced eye, though maybe its tail was thicker and its snout more elongated than those reptiles. But it had similar scaly plates in brown and black covering its body. And more important as far as I was concerned, had comparable, sharp-pointed teeth, a gleaming row of which were just visible along its upper jaw that looked as capable of taking my foot off as any of its crocodilian cousins.

237

Though my toes of my feet with their yellow-thickened fungal-riddled nails were not to my taste, they might have been to a hungry caiman seeking a quick bite. So I smartly stepped back as Kaiser inched his nose out of the pool, and rested his snout on the splash tiles.

'That's his way of saying "Hello",' said Mr Conway. 'He's wanting to make friends.'

'Really?' I replied, wondering how I was expected to respond. A quick tickle under the chin before my fingers were snapped off?

Mr Conway told me that Kaiser was his best mate. He'd never fancied having a dog or cat. And that his day revolved around Kaiser, feeding, cleaning and entertaining him.

I picked up on the entertaining bit and found out Kaiser enjoyed listening to Classic FM, watching TV and resting his head in Mr Conway's lap. No mention of Max Bygraves, thank God. I wondered whether they played cards together. With Kaiser's unblinking, emotionless eyes and their yellow irises and dark slits for pupils, there was no way of sensing what was going on his mind. So he'd have been good at Poker. But there again perhaps a more obvious choice would have been 'Snap'.

Enough said. I was here because Kaiser had developed a skin problem and it was my job to diagnose what it was and how to treat it.

With a lump of liver, Kaiser was enticed out of the pool, where the lump was taken and tossed down his throat. Still fearful of him taking a lump out of me, I cautiously edged round to his tail end.

It was here, at the base of the tail, that Mr Conway had noticed the edges of some scales had turned white and had become flaky and soft.

'So what do you reckon?' asked Mr Conway, having knelt down to allow Kaiser to rest his head on his knee.

Had I been peering down at my own toes I'd have had no doubt. Onychomycosis. But in a caiman? Reptiles do suffer from similar fungal conditions to us so it was certainly a possibility. But it would require a scraping from the scales to make sure. Would Kaiser tolerate me doing such a procedure without whipping round to take my arm off as I attempted it? I wondered.

Mr Conway must have been reading my thoughts because he said, 'I can put a halti leash on him if you like, just to be on the safe side. I always do when I take him for a walk.'

He saw my incredulous look.

'Only round the garden,' he added. 'In case he suddenly decides to take off after next door's cat. You can never tell with Kaiser. One minute he's motionless. The next "Whumph" he's off.'

Thanks Mr Conway, I thought. Just what I wanted to hear.

But a halti muzzle sounded as if it might be worth trying. So while Mr Conway went and fetched it, I went out to the car via a side gate and brought back a scalpel blade and specimen collection tube.

With the halti secured over Kaiser's snout, I set to work scraping the infected scales and dropping the samples into the collection tube, well aware that Kaiser's powerful tail was still free to whip to one side and send me flying into the pool. But he remained remarkably docile; and so I managed to complete the task unscathed.

Laboratory culture of the samples grew a fungus similar to the one that had infected my toes. Treatment was via anti-fungal tablets given by mouth. Easy enough with Kaiser enjoying a daily lump of liver with the tablets disguised in them. And though it took several months of medication, the treatment was eventually successful.

'Well, I'm impressed,' said Eric when, having enquired as to how I'd got on, I told him all about my encounter with Kaiser. With a little embellishment, I have to admit.

'He was over eight feet long you say?'

'Give or take an inch,' I replied, stretching it a bit.

'And he really lunged at you?'

'Well... he certainly made for me. Yes.'

'And all that jaw snapping. Sounds terrifying.'

'It could have been.'

'Good idea of yours to muzzle him. Showed quick thinking.'

'Thanks.'

'But what a struggle you had.'

I shrugged. 'One of those things. But I managed in the end.'

'Amazing,' said Eric, clapping his hands together. 'Tell you what, I'll give Finley O'Connor a bell. He'd love this for the *Westcott Gazette*. And it would give the practice a bit of publicity. I can see it now. A picture of you grabbling with Kaiser.'

I could picture it too. A horrid 'snap' shot with one of Finley's punning headlines, *Vet Gets To Grips With Crocodile Chews*.

14

No Need To Get Upsett

Beryl hassled me just as I was settling down in the office to have my mid-morning coffee prior to starting the morning list of ops. She'd flown down from reception with remarkable speed considering her sixty-four years and stood there, black cardigan sleeves flapping from side to side, to declare that Major Fitzherbert was on the phone demanding that I should pay him a visit as soon as possible.

Major Fitzherbert was a retired army officer whose feral cat I had to deal with shortly after I'd started at Prospect House. And latterly I'd seen the Major at the hospital to give his new acquisition – a sex obsessed Cairn, Caruthers – his vaccinations. He was witness to the emergency arrival of the wallaby and was last observed escorting a lady with a poodle out to lunch.

Crystal looked up from the papers she was shifting through at the desk. 'Tell this Major, whoever he is, that he'll need to come in.'

She glanced across at me. Those cornflower blue eyes of her still had the ability to make me feel uncomfortable. Not like when I'd first started at Prospect House – giving me the urge to whisk her on to the Downs with a quick *Odl lay eee* – more like, 'You know the house rules by now, Paul. So stick to them.' 'Does he usually see you?' she queried, somewhat sharply.

'Er... Yes. As a rule.'

Eric, sitting next to me, slid down in his seat, bringing the latest edition of the *Westcott Gazette* he was reading to head height in front of him. It seemed the births, deaths, and marriages section had suddenly become of deep interest.

'Then I take it he knows he should make an appointment?'

'Er... Yes.'

'So, Beryl.' Crystal switched attention to her. 'You know what to do.'

Beryl gave one of her little coughs – one of the 'embarrassed harassed' variety – while Eric continued to hide behind his newspaper.

'Well what are you waiting for?' It seemed clear that Crystal wasn't in too good a mood this morning. Despite her surname, Sharpe, she wasn't usually this pointed.

Beryl cast her eye at me. Fortunately not her glass one as that might have popped out – Eric had told me this was liable to happen whenever Beryl got too agitated.

I decided to come to her rescue. 'I'll have a word with him if you like,' I volunteered.

'Sounds a good idea,' said Eric, finally lowering his paper.

'Who are you to say?' snapped Crystal, turning on her husband.

There was the rustle of paper as the *Gazette* was quickly raised again.

I drained my coffee, put the mug down on the edge of the desk with as heavy a thump as I dared, and got up. 'I know what the Major's like,' I said to no one in particular. 'So best if I have a quick word. Find out what's bothering him so much.'

There was a loud harrumph when I picked up the phone and apologised for keeping him waiting.

'Well, laddie, I was telling your receptionist that I need you to come out,' he barked.

'Is it a problem with Cuddles?'

'No.'

'Caruthers?'

'No. Neither of them.'

'Well how can I help then?'

'I've got a badger here, trapped at the bottom of the cellar steps. May have injured itself. Needs to be seen to.'

'Well...' I faltered, 'I'm not sure...'

The Major cut in. 'You did a splendid job catching my feral cat Leo... er... sorry... Cuddles... as I now call him.'

I remembered only too well the hunt through Major Fitzherbert's vast greenhouse, attempting to stalk and catch that untamed feline monster. But I had managed it in the end. And the Major had been impressed by my tracking skills. 'Recalls in my safari days out in Kenya,' he'd said, once the cat had been bagged, ready for treatment for a jagged wound on its shoulder.

But a badger? That would be an entirely different ball game. And one I was reluctant to play.

'So what time can I expect you?' huffed the Major.

'Sorry?'

'Your time of arrival, laddie.' There was a pause. I could hear him wheezing down the phone. 'You are coming, I take it?'

Beryl had just sidled up and slipped a note in front of me on which Eric had scrawled 'I'll cover the ops list this morning, if it's of any help'.

'Eleven, then,' I informed the Major.

'See you on the dot. Thank you, laddie.' The phone clicked dead.

'What's he got for you?' asked Beryl.

'A badger.'

'Oh really?' Beryl's eye widened. 'There was a programme about them on the TV recently. They've got awfully sharp teeth and dreadfully long claws apparently.'

Thanks Beryl, I thought. You're such a comfort.

Mind you, despite Beryl's warnings, I did have rather a soft spot for badgers – out of claw reach that is. In my mid teens I often used to go badger watching.

There was a sett a ten minute cycle ride from my home in Bournemouth; and I had many entertaining times watching the family of badgers that lived in it. I found the sett one May evening when spring fever was at its highest pitch. Blackbirds bustled in the hawthorn hedgerows white with bridal veils of blossom. Blue tits darted from bud to bud. A cuckoo's strident tones rang out across the fields, emerald fresh with young grass. As I trod softly along the lane below the bank of hawthorn in which the sett had been dug, a ball of grey shot out, bounced down the bank and careered into my ankles to divide, two badger cubs springing apart from their tussle. Moist grey snouts quivered, testing the air only inches away from my feet. Framed against a fading canvas of blue sky, a striped black and white head slipped into view at the top of the bank. I heard a low yelp. A warning cry. Alerted by their mother's call, the youngsters squeaked in alarm and bolted back up to the safety of their sett.

I was to watch that sett through the long, golden evenings of June, when the cubs – four in all – played, fought and chased each other. Up and down the bank they went. Flattened the ripening corn at the edge of the field beyond. Wore smooth the gnarled grey tangle of beech roots where king-of-the-castle was played in a boisterous tumult of squeals and squeaks. A pure pleasure to see.

Memories of those evening still made me smile. But as I drew up in Major Fitzherbert's drive, I had a feeling there would be little to smile about on this occasion.

The Major lived on the edge of Westcott, where the urban sprawl of the town met the southerly slopes of the Downs. His bungalow backed on to steps of fields and pockets of woodland that ascended the hillside behind it. Though the Major may have commanded a battalion of soldiers, making a final push through the jungles of Africa – or so he would have you believe – his battles here consisted of pushing back the banks of brambles and nettles that grew rampantly along the lower edges of the fields. Those banks of vegetation threatened to invade his garden every year, forcing the Major into an annual spring offensive before they over-ran his garden. And he did run a successful campaign, as his orderly garden proved with their serried ranks of roses – each bush strategically planted for maximum effect. Not a petal out of place. Not a leaf blemished by black spot. No mildew to be seen.

He was in that garden when I arrived, deadheading a few late September blooms, clearly waiting for me, as the secateurs he was holding were dropped into the Sussex trug by his side the moment he spotted me walking up the path. I was also spotted by Caruthers. The little Cairn suddenly sprung out of a thicket of Japanese anemones, and raced up to me, his stumpy tail wagging furiously.

Last year I had arrived five minutes late – much to the Major's annoyance – a man who I sensed was a stickler for punctuality. The waving of his secateurs on that occasion implied I could have been deadheaded along with his roses. This time I was five minutes early, so no brandishing of secateurs. I breathed a sigh of relief. At least I had a head start this time.

From the moment I had first set eyes on Major Fitzherbert, I knew that here was a man of formidable character. One who didn't mince his words. Though tall, his towering presence made him seem even taller. Exemplified by the thrust of his jaw, the hooded, translucent blue eyes, and a high furrowed forehead. From that forehead swept a carpet of white hair matched by thick white eyebrows which, when he was vexed, would knit together like two head-butting caterpillars.

'So... you've a badger for me have you?' I said, for want of a better opening gambit.

'Indeed... yes...' said the Major giving a deep throaty harrumph that set his caterpillar eyebrows whirling. 'It nearly got Caruthers here.'

He explained how he'd heard a terrible commotion the previous evening when he'd let the Cairn out for his final pee. 'An almighty ding-dong I can tell you.' He'd dashed out into the darkness wondering what the devil was going on and saw what he thought was a badger scoot away over the patio and disappear, while Caruthers came hurtling indoors, yelping.

'But the dog's okay?' I asked.

'Seems fine. Well, he is a spunky little fella. Probably gave the badger a good bollocking.'

Rather an unfortunate choice of words, I thought, knowing the Cairn's thirst for sex. But with a badger?

Major Fitzherbert scooped up the Cairn and rolled him on to his back. 'There are few scratches and a bite here on his left fore. I've put a bit of that antiseptic powder you left last year for Leo... er... Cuddles. Guess he should be all right. What do you think?'

The wounds were superficial. And Caruthers was bright and bouncy. Seems he had had a lucky escape. Would I be so lucky? I wondered.

'So where's your equipment, laddie?' said the Major, looking at my empty hands. 'You'll be needing that pole contraption you had last time if I'm not mistaken.'

'I thought it best to see what I was dealing with first,' I explained.

The Major gave another rattling harrumph and then, with a beckoning finger, told me to follow him. Having picked up his walking stick, he hobbled round the side of the bungalow past the huge greenhouse where I'd done battle with the feral cat last year, relieved that I wasn't being shunted in there to do the same with a badger. Instead, I found myself standing at the top of a steep flight of narrow brick steps at the bottom of which I could just make out a small concreted area with a door off it that I assumed gave access to a cellar. From every nook and crevice of the surrounding brick walls, sprouted tongues of green – ferns that had found footing in the crumbling mortar between the bricks and had flourished in the damp, dim conditions to produce a well of green which, in some places, obliterated the steps and partially covered the concrete of the base.

'Don't tell me...' I stuttered, turning to the Major.

'fraid so,' replied the Major. 'It's down there. I poked my walking stick through the ferns first thing and heard a growl at the bottom. Reckon it hurt itself falling down there last night and can't get out.'

'Oh great,' I groaned to myself. 'Tackling this could be my downfall as well.'

Major Fitzherbert must have noticed my hesitation, my lack of enthusiasm, because he suddenly harrumphed very loudly, insisting I should have a go as I was there anyway. 'All in the call of duty. Rise to the challenge, laddie. Take it on the chin.'

Mmm. I could literally see it happen. The badger taking me on my chin, hanging from it, his jaws locked round mine.

The Major's hooded blue eyes fixed me with a penetrating glare. 'You're not thinking of backing out are you,' he queried.

I fingered my mentally ravaged throat nervously. 'Er... No... Just that...'

'I've had to confront far worse in my time I can tell you,' the Major butted in. 'Oh, yes... Far worse. Had a charging rhino gore me once. That's how I got this gammy leg. Remember I told you last year? That's why I couldn't help you then. And can't do so now.' He tapped his right leg with his walking stick. I nodded weakly. I did remember. I also remembered a friend of Beryl's at the Health Centre telling her it was a bit of arthritis brought on by him tripping over a loose paving slab in Westcott's shopping precinct.

I was in a corner here. Much like that badger down there. And I couldn't get out of it. Much like that... Oh bloody hell. Best get on with it and stop moaning. I could do that later when my throat had been clawed to shreds – providing I had any vocal cords left.

I collected the cat catcher from the car along with leather gauntlets and a large dog-carrying crate.

'Not darting him then. Like that zoo chappie. Thought you might have learnt to do so by now.' Major Fitzherbert was eyeing my cat catcher – a metal tube through which was threaded a loop of strong cord, the idea being to lasso it over the head of the animal to be restrained and pull tight as it began to struggle.

I ignored his comment, trying to concentrate on the task ahead. The thought that I was going to try lassoing a badger rather than a cat made my throat constrict as if it were my neck – not the badger's – that was going to have the noose slipped round it.

But there was no way back now. Just down. Down those wretched slippery fern-covered steps to where awaited a...?

I up-ended the carrying crate and slid open the metal-barred door, the intention being to pop the badger in the crate once lassoed – yes... well... pigs might fly... and that badger might do likewise... fly straight for my neck.

With my gauntlets on, gripping the handle of the cat catcher between them, I began to descend the steps gingerly, placing one foot cautiously down from one step to another. The moss covered surface, the narrowness of each one half-hidden by fronds, made each a step fraught with danger. Any minute I thought I'd slip, lurch forward and plunge down into the sea of green. And I did – three steps from the bottom, when a frog sprang from an overhanging fern, and went splat into my face. I went splat on to the concrete base – from where I catapulted back up several steps on hearing a deep growl emanate from the cluster of ferns covering the far corner.

'Did you hear that, laddie?' declared Major Fitzherbert, peering down from the side of the patio, directly above the corner from where the snarling had come. 'Sounds decidedly angry, if you ask me.'

I didn't need to ask him. The fact I'd jumped back up six steps on hearing it, was proof that I knew just how angry the beast was.

'Go on, laddie,' urged the Major. 'Do your stuff.'

With one hand pressed against the slippery, wet wall for support, I leaned down with the cat catcher in the other and nervously poked the clump of ferns. Another snarl rent the air.

'Least you now know where it is,' shouted down the Major.

A little voice inside me said, 'That's very reassuring. So kind.'

There was a further rumble of rage from the ferns.

'And you know it's still alive and kicking.'

'Thanks so much,' the little voice said.

Dreading every step, I retraced every one down until I was once again on the concrete – this time standing, not sprawled on it – the cat catcher held in both hands, angled in front of me, the noose dangling over the grumbling ferns which, on being parted by the cord swishing from side to side, exposed what lay beneath them.

'Oh my... what have we here?' asked the little voice. 'Why it's Mr Brock the badger. How sweet he looks curled up in a ball.'

The black and white ball uncurled itself.

'Oh look... Mr Brock wants to say "Hello",' said the little voice.

The badger's lips turned back.

'Why... Mr Brock's smiling,' said the little voice.

Its teeth gnashed. It snarled. It lunged at me. Straight into the noose dangling in front of it.

'Got you, you little sod,' I said.

'Oh,' said the little voice and vanished abruptly.

'By George you've bagged him. Well done, laddie. Well done,' chortled Major Fitzherbert above me, waving his stick in the air.

But I hadn't 'done' yet. Not quite. There were still those slippery steps to negotiate back up again. And with a twisting, growling foaming-at-the-mouth badger at the end of a pole being dragged up behind me, threatening to yank me back down with every violent turn it made.

At one point, half-way up the badger squirmed on to his back, and it was then I noticed the tear in his groin, the skin ripped back to expose the muscles, some of which looked torn as well. That might have explained why he'd been unable to scramble up the steps and get away.

I eventually made it to the top and levering the pole up and over the carrying crate's open door, shoved the badger unceremoniously inside and, partially closing the door, released the tension on the noose. Then once the badger had shook itself free, I quickly pulled the cord out and slammed the door shut.

I slumped down on the top step. Mission completed.

Major Fitzherbert came hobbling round and stooped down to peer into the cage. 'So is he injured?' he asked. 'I can see his claws are bleeding.'

Ah... yes... of course. The injuries. His front claws were shredded from his attempts to scrabble up the walls. And though it couldn't be seen now, I explained to the Major that there was quite a tear on the inside of the animal's thigh, which would undoubtedly need stitching.

'So you're going to have to catch the bugger up again?'

I nodded.

'Rather you than me, laddie.'

And it was rather me than anyone else back at Prospect House, where nobody appeared willing to lend a hand for fear that hand would get bitten.

Mandy muttered some excuse about assisting Crystal with her consultations. Lucy just happened to be in the middle of feeding the in-patients.

'You've got a big gap in your list, Eric,' declared Beryl.

'Have I?' he muttered, giving her one of his 'I could throttle you' looks.

'Plenty of time to give Paul a hand.'

After he'd released it and his other hand from around her neck, I mused.

'Let's get the brute sorted then,' he said to me, glancing away from Beryl who had turned back to her keyboard and was innocently tapping.

She paused to remark, 'And don't let it escape like you did with that fox.' It was a reference to the fox we'd had in some months back, when Eric had inadvertently let it slip out of the crate in which it had arrived; and the subsequent mayhem caused as it was chased through the hospital. But it had been an opportunity for me to get up close and personal with Jodie in the dispensary, where the fox finally holed up, and discover what a cunning little vixen she was – Jodie not the fox.

So, as much as I liked Eric and found him to be an affable man, usually cheerful and willing, I was a little apprehensive when it came to him helping me out. A good example was the time he offered to do the anaesthesia for Mr Hargreaves' skink with a prolapsed rectum while I eased the inverted rectum back; only to discover once I'd completed the operation, he'd failed to switch the anaesthetics' machine on at the start.

'So, Paul, this is the said beast, is it?' Eric peered through the bars of the travelling crate at the rolled up badger at the back. 'Seems pretty quiet to me.' He moved the crate a little to one side with his foot. The badger didn't stir.

'It's a defence mechanism,' I warned.' Get too close and he'll uncurl like a spring and go for you.'

'Well, we'll see shall we? Here, give me those.' Eric grabbed the leather gauntlets from my hands and donned them. Then, while I knelt next to the crate holding the syringeful of sedative, he crouched down and flicked open the door.

'Oh do be careful,' said my little voice. 'Mr Brock is not going to like this.'

And Mr Brock didn't like it one bit. With Eric's arm half-way down the inside of the crate, his gauntlet splayed out almost touching the ball of fur, the badger swiftly lifted his head and lashed out, his teeth sinking into the leather finger tips.

'Bloody hell,' said Eric.

'Naughty... Naughty...' said my little voice.

Eric yanked his arm back, the badger sliding forward with it, still locked on the gauntlet, growling, his claws lashing out against the sides of the crate. With his head and shoulders half out, the badger's shoulders were pinned down by Eric's other gauntleted hand while I wedged the door against the animal's flanks. This trapped him long enough for me to inject the sedative into his thigh through the bars.

Eric let go with his right hand and pushed the badger back in with his left. The creature continued to cling on to the gauntlet which sailed off Eric's hand and went flying to the back of the crate, still in the badger's jaws.

The badger fought the sedative for several minutes, going round and round before collapsing on his side, unconscious and shivering.

'Least the bugger's now zapped,' said Eric.

'Poor Mr Brock,' said the little voice.

The rip in the badger's groin wasn't as bad as I had first feared. The muscles were bruised but intact. So having flushed out the area with saline and sprinkled in some sterile penicillin powder, I was able to stitch the skin wound up with dissolvable sutures; and having given a shot of long-acting antibiotic, I felt confident about releasing the badger, once he'd recovered from the anaesthetic. That way it would avoid any future battles with him and cause less stress all round.

'Mr Brock will be so pleased,' said my little voice.

So was Major Fitzherbert, when I returned that evening with the crate containing the now conscious badger. 'Splendid job. Well done,' he harrumphed. 'Now let me show you where to let him go.'

He waved his stick in the direction of a bank of brambles at the top of his garden, adjacent to the field that sloped up the hill. 'The other side of those brambles is a huge sett. Quite a family lives there. Have seen five or six at a time on my back lawn. They love the dog meat I put out for them. Providing Caruthers doesn't get in there first and scoff the lot. He looked down at his Cairn who was tucked under his right arm, straining to get to the crate I was carrying.

'Best if you shut him in while we release the badger,' I advised.

With Caruthers panting and running up and down up the inside of the Major's French windows, the carrying crate was placed on the lawn, a few feet away from where the garden ended and the brambles began.

'Okay, here we go,' I said, sliding back the bolt on the crate's door and swinging it open. I stood up and stepped away to stand level with the Major.

There was a snuffle from the inside. A scrabble of claws on the floor. A black and white snout appeared, sniffing the air cautiously.

Then the badger shot out and, in a blur of grey, waddled rapidly across the lawn and disappeared into the brambles.

Caruthers yapped.

The Major harrumphed.

And my little voice said, 'Bye... Bye... Mr Brock.'

15

Hark Who's Squawking

'Having trouble with your little brood again?' queried Eleanor, one July morning, peering over the garden fence as I released, yet again, one of the five swallow chicks that had hatched earlier in the summer.

'Yep, usual problem. Flapping up against the shed window,' I replied, as the young swallow swooped off down the garden and out over the open field beyond, joining up with his nesting mates, who were dive bombing through the air busy snapping up their breakfast of flies.

I'd left the shed door open day and night the past three months to give the parents free access to build their nest and raise their five-strong brood – allowing the whole family to come and go as they pleased. Only the five fledglings, having tentatively made their first excursions from the nest, were finding it rather difficult to orientate themselves and cotton on to the fact that the wide open door next to the window was their exit to the open spaces beyond.

For days, I was having to do my St Francis of Assisi act, and catch up the young swallows as they fluttered hopelessly up and down the window pane.

'One way of communing with Mother Nature,' I mused as I watched the swallows swinging effortlessly over the field with shrill *tswits* of delight.

Not that I needed to commune with her over birds. I'd been doing that ever since I'd started at Prospect House. There'd been the challenge of Lisa, the lesser sulphur crested cockatoo – presented as an oven-ready bird devoid of feathers due to her incessant self-plucking. Then of course the operation on my family's Polly, the African grey. She'd developed a tumour on her neck which threatened to asphyxiate her if not removed. In dissecting out that tumour – done on the kitchen table at my parents' house – I saved her life.

Meanwhile, Beryl, took it upon herself to guide any client with a bird in my direction.

I was presented with a steady flow of budgies' beaks and claws to clip interspersed with a couple of egg-bound birds in passing.

In between all of these, I was having to cope with the swallows at Willow Wren.

They'd certainly been a handful ever since their arrival in April. 6th of April to be precise. That day I'd spotted the first swallow or rather heard him *tswit... tswitting* on the telegraph wire than ran down the side of Willow Cottage. Looking up I smiled at the bird, and raised my hand.

'Hello, my friend. Welcome back. Hope you enjoy your new home.'

If I'd been conversant with swallow talk, I'd have realised the shrill salvo of staccato babbling that ensued was that of a very agitated avian. A very vexed bird. A bird that gazed down on an environment that had changed dramatically since last summer.

The reason being the old workshop where the swallows had nested last year no longer existed.

That building with its walk-through to a breeze-block garage, was a jerry-built structure tacked on to the side of Willow Cottage. I guessed it was added in the early 70s. Its grey corrugated-asbestos roof clashed with the red clay tiles of the 17th century cottage. And though an attempt had been made to blend the two together by sloshing a thick layer of exterior white paint on both buildings, the workshop and garage still looked like a cancerous growth bulging from the flank of the cottage. I use the word 'tacked' to describe its attachment to the cottage since that join was coming undone. The garage and workshop were gradually parting company from the cottage as if the latter was determined to reject its cancerous cousin. A gap had appeared between the two, starting up near the asbestos roof at the southern end overlooking the back garden and had been gradually broadening and spreading down in the seven months I'd lived there with Lucy the previous year. We'd split since, and it was looking like the cottage and workshop-cum-garage were also going to do likewise and part company pretty soon.

Willow Wren came with the job. Part of my contract for working at Prospect House. But it was owned by the Sharpes. So strictly speaking, any repairs required were to be reported to Crystal or Eric; and it was up to them to decide what needed to be done.

With the danger of the workshop and garage caving in on me and them losing an assistant buried under the rubble, they readily agreed to the required replacement.

Their only reservation was the timing of the rebuild.

I'd asked if it could be done in early January.

'Why then?' queried Crystal.

'It's the swallows,' I said.

'Er?' grunted Eric, his face uncomprehending.

'Well, they'll be back in April wanting to nest,' I explained.

Eric's face still looked blank.

'It would be good to have the new-build in place, ready for them.'

Eric looked at Crystal. Crystal looked at Eric. They both shrugged. 'Well, if that's what you want.'

'It's what the swallows will want,' I said, assuming that's what they'd like. Wrong assumption as it turned out.

The builder was also perplexed.

A build in the depths of winter? Dark days. Bad weather.

'It's the swallows,' I explained.

'Swallows?' he questioned looking up at the grey winter clouds.

'I see,' he added. Though clearly he didn't.

But both car port and workshop were completed on time despite weeks of rain. And they did look smart. The oak framed barn-style car port, a perfect place for the swallows to nest in.

Before, they'd used the old workshop, its doorframe askew, the door permanently jammed open, making access easy for them. And they'd been using it for years to judge by the deep layer of droppings on the workshop floor.

All that was now going to change.

The replacement workshop had a door I could keep firmly shut. To keep the swallows out. Stop them from nesting in there. They could use the new car port instead. No longer would my tools and garden equipment get constantly splattered with droppings.

But I'd underestimated the swallows' determination to nest in a similar spot as in previous years – in the replacement workshop that now stood on the site of the old one. And I certainly didn't anticipate the battle that ensued when they clearly showed who was boss. Them.

Dick Chambers was a client who also wanted to show who was boss. As Beryl explained when she booked a visit for me to see him.

'He's got this parrot who insists on being top dog.'

Beryl could be obtuse sometimes. This was one of those times.

'What do you mean exactly?' I said.

'You'll see when you get there,' she said, unhelpfully.

Oh dear. Had we another Aggie-style confrontation looming? I feared so.

The parrot in question turned out to be a yellow-naped Amazon that lived on her own planet. That planet was actually the penthouse of a high-rise block of flats tucked behind the municipal car park down on Westcott's seafront. I was to learn that she'd arrived in that apartment as a hand-reared youngster and was destined never to set claw on terra firma again. Well at least not eighteen floors down on the pavements of Westcott. 'You don't know what Aurora might pick up should I take her out into the big wide world,' said Dick Chambers, when I first met him. 'So many bugs around. Wouldn't want her to catch anything nasty.'

I wasn't sure which world Dick Chambers was referring to. Before leaving to make the visit, Beryl had told me that he was the best-selling author of science fiction – the *Star Trek* variety. His novels were set on alien, hostile planets, worlds away from planet earth. I felt as if I was stepping into one of his novels the moment I stepped into the lift with its mirrored walls and found myself being transported up to the top floor and jettisoned into a chrome fitted hallway. Talk about 'Beam me up Scotty'.

Dick Chambers had been the proud owner of Aurora for eight weeks when I was first summoned to see her. That call set the scene for subsequent voyages up to his flat.

'Please ensure the vet dons the over-suit in the hallway before entering,' he'd instructed Beryl over the phone. 'And he mustn't forget the over-boots,' he added. Instructions Beryl didn't tell me about until I was just about to set off. Making me all the more baffled as to where in the world I was going.

Both items I found neatly stacked next to the front door of his apartment. Well, at least I don't have to strip and shower first, I thought, as I struggled into the suit. And there's no space helmet to contend with.

Dick Chambers was a short, portly guy with a complexion mimicking a lunar landscape. Pock marked and cratered from the ravages of adolescent acne. He was dressed in a close fitting silver-grey tunic top and matching leather-belted trousers. Very Trekkie-style.

'That's Aurora,' he said, pointing across the room to where the Amazon was perched on the back of a chrome and black swivel chair, looking lost in front of a vast console, which flashed and beeped with a multitude of red and green lights.

Dick Chambers saw me looking at the lit-up panel.

'My communications centre,' he said, as if that explained everything.

It didn't. Communications with whom? I wondered. Or indeed with what? Was I on the Starship Enterprise, reaching across the final frontiers to Vulcans and Cardassians on planets in the outer galaxies?

Apparently not. As Dick Chambers explained. Just Internet access to fellow Trekkies around planet Earth. Aurora continued to give me a beady-eyed look, the red rims of her irises reflecting the twinkling red lights on the panel behind her.

'So what seems to be the problem?' I asked.

'I can't communicate,' said Dick Chambers without hesitation.

'Well it does take time to form a bond with a parrot. Especially a youngster like Aurora.'

'No... No... Not with her. With the outside world.' He waved his hands wildly above his head.

What planet was this man on? I wondered. He seemed several thousand light years from this one. Clearly my bewilderment showed as Dick Chambers clasped his hands together and tutted.

'Aurora's made that chair her territory. She won't let me get near the console. I'm losing touch with Captain Kirk and Co.'

'And clearly losing touch with reality by the sound of it,' I was tempted to say. But resisted.

'What on earth can I do,' he wailed, his beaming face on my arrival now having disintegrated into meltdown, all blubbery lips and moist pink eyelids. 'It's not as if she's got nowhere to go. I had that beautiful cage over there made specially for her.' He pointed at a large, gleaming stainless steel structure which towered from floor to ceiling, bristling with fins and turrets, and which dominated one corner of the living room.

'She went in it when she first arrived,' he continued. 'But she was constantly clamouring to

263

be let out. So I did. Now she won't go back. And I can't get to my console.' He held up a bandaged finger. 'She bites me whenever I try to get her off the chair.'

As if to emphasise the point, Aurora emitted a deep growl as I stepped towards her. I stepped back smartly. Though Aurora was no alien species, I didn't see the point of doing a Captain Kirk and go where one man had gone before just to get bitten in the process. Not an 'Enterprise' I'd relished. And I certainly wasn't 'Intrepid' enough to try.

'What about tempting her back with tit-bits?' I asked, lamely.

Arched eyebrows arching even higher gave me the answer without the need for words. As did the small piles of nuts and banana leading up to the cage door.

'Of course, the longer you let her stay out, the less likely she'll ever want to return,' I went on, stating the obvious.

The eyebrows remained arched. Clearly I was light years away from impressing Dick Chambers. Action needed to be beamed in. A final frontier reached.

'A towel,' I said, snapping my fingers while Aurora's eyes lit up at the sight of my wiggling appendages. Moments later her lights were dimmed as I smothered her in the pink fluffy towel Dick Chambers had handed me; and she was transported back to base. Back in her cage.

I suggested Aurora be given some toys to play with.

Plastic Darth Vaders and Obi-Wans sprung to mind. But no. That was just me getting confused with *Star Wars*.

'Try letting her out at set times, so she gets to know when this will be.' Parrots have a very good sense of time and I knew Aurora would soon get to know when those times were. But as to getting her back in her cage again. Well...

A subsequent visit to his planet to clip Aurora's nails gave me the answer. Before entering the living room, Dick Chambers carefully inspected my oversuit to ensure my cargo of earthly bugs was kept at bay. Well under cover. On seeing Aurora, I had visions of her about to launch into space. Outer space.

She was sitting in what looked like the cockpit of a flying saucer screwed to the top of a stand. Overhead, shone a chrome dome from which hung plastic antennae, many twisted and distorted from the ravages of Aurora's beak.

'I dreamt this up to keep her off my console,' explained Dick Chambers. 'Her very own PlayStation. And it's worked a treat.'

'Uhm...' I muttered to myself, as with nail clippers in my hand, I advanced on a growling Aurora. PlayStation eh? I wonder what game you've in mind. Beak-a-boo? To judge from the menacing mandibles in front of me I was going to be Spock-on.

Yet another dismal failure on my part. I'd not been assertive enough.

The same was happening with the wretched swallows.

And it had reached the point where one of the swallows had dived down with an angry chatter and skimmed through my hair, its claws grazing my scalp. I'd broken into a run, heading back into the kitchen, with the bird chasing me. With another agitated *tswit-tswit*, it looped ahead of me and disappeared through the back door. I raced in to find it zooming round the kitchen before it veered off to the hall with me in hot pursuit. Up in the bedroom, the swallow circled round my bed, dropping several deposits on my pillow. Then with a final barrage of avian abuse, it made its escape via an open window.

Eleanor broke into one of her hearty hoots when she popped round and I told her what had happened.

'Perhaps you shouldn't have tried blocking its nesting site,' she said, as she watched me stuff my soiled bed linen in the washing machine. 'I reckon it was getting its own back.' She gave another snort of laughter.

I was almost inclined to believe her, and felt rather guilty at what I had been trying to do over the last couple of days. Stop them nesting in the new workshop. After all, they'd travelled thousands of miles across Africa, survived the searing heat of the Sahara, struggled over mountains, sea and forests in order to reach their final destination and raise a family where they were accustomed to. In the old workshop. The one that no longer existed.

But I hadn't reckoned on their strong sense of place and the determination to nest in precisely that same place as in other years. That place was still going to be the workshop. The new one.

Hence the battle of wits which ensued.

I might have sensed their annoyance in the angry *tswit-tswit* that echoed through the air soon after two arrived, when they circled the new car port, chose to ignore it and bombed the new workshop door now firmly closed and strictly out of bounds. But I had to open the door sometime.

As soon as I did, both swallows seemed to appear from nowhere and with a gleeful whoosh over my head, zoom in before me.

'Just make sure you always keep the door closed,' declared Eleanor when I brought her up-to-date with developments.

Easier said than done, when staggering out with armfuls of gardening tools or a heavy chain saw. Whenever I elbowed my way out, the swallows elbowed their way in.

Early one morning, I stomped back into the kitchen and sat down heavily.

'I just don't believe it,' I said, addressing Emily. 'There's a swallow in the workshop already.'

She cocked her head to one side – she was always a good listener.

'I know what you're thinking,' I said. 'I must have left the door open overnight. But I didn't, Emily. I didn't. Honest. I've just unlocked it. And I swear it was empty last night. No swallows in it. I checked it out before locking it. Just to make sure.'

Emily cocked her head the other way, clearly as puzzled as I was.

A close inspection of the new workshop solved the mystery. There was a two inch gap running round the eaves. In the swallows' determination to gain access to their old nesting site, one had squeezed in through the gap at dawn.

I thought I could put paid to that by plugging the gaps with balls of newspaper. I was wrong. The balls were found rolling round the yard the next day, the swallows having plucked them out to get back in again. Bin bag liners suffered the same fate. As did plastic netting. I found that netting hanging down the outside wall of the workshop, the swallows twittering cheerfully inside, behind a locked door.

In a fit of pique, I charged in and brandished my extendable paint roller at them, as they sat chirruping in the highest corner of the sloping ceiling.

That's when one of the swallows launched its scalp-raking attack.

'Give in. Let them nest where they want to,' judged Eleanor, peering over the fence as I stomped round the garden.

So I did give in. Reluctantly. I left the door of my lovely pristine workshop open and watched as the swallows swooped in and out with beakfuls of mud.

Unfortunately, they opted to build their nest over the door.

Just the spot where I had to stop to switch on the light of an evening.

Just the spot where piles of droppings would accumulate, perfectly placed for me to tread in during the ensuing months.

It was a busy summer for those birds. The male was in and out daily to feed the female as she sat on her eggs for two weeks. When they hatched, the toing and froing increased as five hungry chicks had to be fed. I'd read that such a brood consumed over 500 insects a day. That meant a lot of zooming in and out.

When the fledglings began to test their wings, there was much hopping over my pots of paint, swaying unsteadily on the handles of my spades and forks and flapping against the window pane, the youngsters unfamiliar with the open door adjacent to it.

That's when my Francis of Assisi act came to the fore – scooping up a struggling fledgling to release it out on the lawn.

Of course they all came back to roost each night. Sometimes crowding on the edge of the nest. Sometimes choosing the tops of my now droppings-splattered work cabinets.

Then, as if to spite me, another nest was built, another brood reared. By mid-summer, I had thirteen birds careering over the cottage and garden all day, before swarming into the workshop to roost in a noisy bustling flock.

'But it's nice to see them flying around, isn't it?' said Eleanor.

I grunted. Personally, I could have wrung their chestnut necks with all the mess they made. Heaven help me if I required something from the workshop late at night. Switching the light on produced a frenzy of flapping wings and a cloud of swirling feathers. It was like a scene from Hitchcock's *The Birds*. I soon learnt that anything needed was best left till the morning. Meanwhile, Beryl made sure I had plenty more birds to flap around me at Prospect House. And in doing so, get me in a flap as well. She did this by booking in several appointments for a man by the name of Mike Masters.

'You and he should get on like a house on fire,' she said.

'Why, is he a fireman?' I said hopefully.

Beryl shook her head. 'Don't know what gets into you sometimes.' She gave me one of her bashed-with-a-brick owl looks.

If only she knew.

Beryl filled me in before I met this Mike Masters. And no, he wasn't a fireman... shame... but a retired RSPCA Inspector who had moved to Westcott with his wife, Debbie, and had set up a sanctuary for birds called WARS – Westcott Avian Rescue Society.

I was a little apprehensive of meeting this guy, who probably knew more about birds and how to treat them than I did.

And when Mike Masters marched into my consulting room, I felt even more uneasy. Here was a man who knew what he was about. He had a military bearing that made you want to stand to attention immediately. From his dark blue uniform with their gleaming buttons down to his black shoes with their shiny toecaps, it suggested someone who not only applied exacting standards to his appearance but also applied similar standards to his dealings with the birds he and his wife rescued. Everything carried out with military precision.

'Please to meet you, Mr Mitchell,' he said crisply, shaking my hand having slid a large plastic container on to the table. 'I'm told you're the bird expert round here.' He stood back, removed the peaked cap he was wearing and tucked it under his arm. I felt uncomfortable by the way he was staring at me. His mottled grey eyes seemed to question, their greyness like gathering clouds before a storm. A colour matched by that of his neatly cut hair and trim moustache.

'I have got an interest,' I murmured, my confidence draining the more Mike Masters stared at me.

'In which case you'll be interested in what I've got here.' Mike pushed the container across the table and I stared in through the bars of the door at a large bundle of tawny feathers. A ruffled brown head swivelled round to stare back at me with defiant yellow eyes.

'Well I never,' I blurted out, wondering what the hell I was supposed to say.

'Thought you'd be surprised. Don't see many of these. Especially round these parts.'

'No you don't,' I stuttered. Too true, I thought. You don't see many. In fact I'd never seen any before. This was an owl obviously. But what species? I hadn't a clue. I hoped to be given one when I asked, 'Where was it found?'

'Over on East Barton golf course. Probably hit by a car. Sort of thing that can happen to these low flying owls. As you'll no doubt know.'

I sensed Mike was testing me, so quickly decided to get on safer ground by asking, 'I understand it's broken its wing?'

'Yes. Let me show you.' Mike pointed to a towel hanging next to the instrument trolley. 'If you can give me that I'll hike the owl out for you.'

He proceeded to extract it with great expertise, the owl's talons buried safely in the towel, and stretched its right wing out across the table. 'There. See. A fractured humerus. Hope you can pin it. Shame to put down such a rare bird, otherwise.' He gently eased the owl back into the container. 'Would it be your first?'

I wondered what he was referring to. First time I'd seen this type of owl? Or first time I'd pinned a bird's wing? I kept to safe ground again and told him I had pinned a couple of birds' wings, so avoiding any question of identifying the species of owl I was going to operate on.

'Let's hope all goes well, then,' said Mike.

Well, so did I.

And it did.

Once the owl was anaesthetised and the wing clipped and the ends of the bone exposed, a long sterile needle was pushed up through the shaft of the humerus and manipulated back down into the lower fragment of bone, enabling me to stabilise the break.

'Well, that was a hoot,' said Lucy, as she carried the tray of used operating instruments through to the prep room, while I placed the recovering owl on a wodge of paper towelling inside its carrying container, ready for Mike Masters to collect.

'Ouch, Luce, leave the horrible puns to me,' I said, glancing at her retreating back and suddenly realising I'd used my pet name for her – 'Luce'. She briefly looked over her shoulder and for a split second I thought I saw a twinkle in those hazel eyes of hers. Then she turned back – back to being the composed, but detached and distant nurse she'd become since returning to live up in the nurses' flat.

'Oh, by the way,' I called out, 'would you happen to know the whereabouts of East Barton golf course?'

I saw her pause by the prep room sink and then say, 'It's to the east of Westcott, along the coast before you get to Stanport. Where the sand dunes start. Why?'

'It's where this owl was found.'

Lucy turned her attention to tipping the tray of dirty instruments into a bowl ready for scrubbing. Nothing more was said.

But her mention of 'sand dunes' nudged a vague recollection. Didn't one species of UK owl live in that sort of area? A Google trawl of UK owls and sand dunes came up with Little Owls, the Green Owl pub opposite some sand dunes with six fully ensuite rooms, and a British Trust for Ornithology's description of a short-eared owl. Mottled brown body. Pale underparts. Barred tail and wings. Yellow eyes. My owl had more orange than yellow eyes but otherwise fitted the description given.

So when Mike Masters came in to collect the owl and take it back to his sanctuary to recuperate before being released, I was able to say with some confidence, 'This short-eared owl should make a good recovery.'

'Please to hear that,' said Mike. 'Only one thing...'

'Oh?'

'It's not a short-eared owl.'

'Ah...'

Mike shook his head. 'No... it's actually a long-eared owl. One that's way off its normal territory. But not to worry. An easy mistake to make as this bird hasn't raised its ear tufts all the while it's been in. And the main thing is that you were able to pin its wing. Thanks.' He gave my hand a formal shake. 'I'm sure we'll meet again,' he added, before briskly marching out with his owl.

I was left with my own long ears burning and thankful to discover my next patient was a budgie.

And he was right. We did meet again. Only this time he saved me the embarrassment of guessing what the bird was, as he told Beryl in advance, when he booked the appointment.

'You're having a shag,' she informed me, her thick pan of make–up unmoved – a mask hiding any implied innuendo, though there was a suggestive glint in her eye when she said it.

In one meaning of the word, I wished I was having a shag. Jodie had flown off to Goa with some mates – having grown tired of the limited delights Westcott had to offer – which I suspect had included me. Guess there's only so many times you can have your cake and feel stuffed before it goes stale on you. As for Lucy, to judge from her continuing cool demeanour, any thoughts I had of getting back with her were clearly half-baked.

So the only shag I got was another meaning of the word – not shreds of tobacco – but a sea bird – a smaller version of a cormorant – which Mike

Masters pulled out of the canvas bag he'd heaved on to my consulting table, its long hooked beak firmly shut, a length of cotton bandage tied round it.

'It would go for you otherwise,' Mike informed me, pinning the shag to his side with his elbow and pressing down on its back to stop its legs scrabbling on the table top. But it didn't prevent the bird lunging in my direction, croaking loudly, its long snake-like neck whipping towards me – a demonic action which Mike quickly stopped by grasping the shag by its throat and pulling its head to his chest.

Mike told me it had been found on the beach flapping and rolling around, tangled up in a length of nylon fishing line.

'It was literally tied in knots,' said Mike. 'The wretched line coiled round its wings and legs. I've managed to cut that away. But it trailed up to its beak. So I suspect it swallowed a fish with a hook in it and that hook's now stuck in its gullet. Seen it happen before.'

The shag gave another angry croak and squirmed violently.

'Steady on old boy, we're only trying to help,' Mike muttered as the writhing bird wagged its tail and jettisoned a stream of green liquid faeces across the table.

'Tell you what. Let me sedate it and then take a look,' I said. 'Wait here a mo and I'll go and get some Ketamine.'

I returned from the prep room with what I hoped would be the approximate dose to put the shag under and slipped it into the bird's thigh. It went out like a light – rather too quickly for my liking. I just prayed I hadn't overdosed it.

'Okay, Mike, let's get it down to the prep room and see what's up.'

It was actually what was down that concerned me. A fish hook down the bird's gullet, if Mike was correct.

Both Mandy and Lucy did ask if we'd need any help, but I felt sure with all of Mike's expertise we'd manage without them. So they left us to it.

Mike laid the shag on the prep room counter and stretched it out its by now flaccid neck, while I cut off the bandage tied round its beak and opened it wide to reveal a small length of the fishing line looped over the tongue and disappearing down the throat. I gave it a gentle tug.

Mike put out a restraining hand. 'Er... no Paul... I shouldn't if I were you,' he said quietly. 'I'll only drag on the hook. May I?'

'Sure... of course,' I said, stepping away to watch as Mike carefully felt down the shag's neck, a finger and thumb either side of the windpipe.

'Ah... got it,' he said, stopping half-way down. 'Here... feel it?' He retracted his fingers to allow me to palpate the spot. And yes... I could feel the outline of a hook resting beneath the loose skin of the shag's throat. 'Right,' he said. 'Now find the back of the hook. Any luck?'

I nodded.

'Okay. Angle it so the point is facing you and then push it through the skin.'

I did as instructed and found that the fish hook slid out quite easily, though I had to pull a bit harder to get the end knotted to the line out.

It was then simply a matter of snipping the line and drawing it back out through the shag's beak. Job done.

It might have been the end of the line for the shag, but it was the beginning of a long line of

275

cases that Mike and I worked on together in the future.

Meanwhile, my swallows had lined themselves up on the telegraph pole outside Willow Wren. It was early September, the family getting ready to leave. A row of chattering, lively youngsters and their parents. Begrudgingly, I had to admire those parents. They'd fought and won their battle against me. Now they had another battle to overcome in their arduous migration south.

'Safe journey,' I whispered as the little flock rose and, with a final chorus of calls, circled the workshop and disappeared over the fields.

'You were sad to see them go then?' said Eleanor, later.

I suppose I was. Especially as it reminded me of someone else who had flown the nest – one she and I had built together at to Willow Wren. Lucy. And I still found that very hard to swallow.

16

Let Us Bray

When the call came through that the Jacantha Stokes required a vet, I attempted to make myself scarce. Fat chance with Beryl on the loose. She could ferret you out quicker than one up your trouser leg, and the effect of being grabbed by the genitals was the same.

I'd heard Beryl say on the phone, 'Good morning, Jacantha. What can we do for you?' At which point, I bolted down the corridor (rabbit hole) and disappeared into the dispensary (warren) intent on getting some wormers for a puppy only to find Lucy was already making up the prescription. She gave the merest upturn of her lips as, over my shoulder, I heard Beryl calling my name. 'Think you're wanted,' she said, turning back to the bottle of worming tablets, snapping its lid shut with a sharp twist of her wrist – a gesture which left a 'but not by me' hanging in the air.

'Ah, there you, Paul,' said Beryl, catching up with me by the dispensary door, eye-balling Lucy over my shoulder, her false eye swivelling like a CCTV lens. 'Hope I'm not interrupting anything.'

'No... No... Nothing,' I replied, rather wishing she had, and made to move past her.

'Ah... not so fast Paul,' said Beryl putting out a restraining hand. 'I've Jacantha Stokes on the line, wanting a visit. Doug's done himself a nasty.'

'Well, can't Eric do it?' I queried, walking back down the corridor. Undaunted, Beryl scuttled behind me, her habitually worn black cardigan loose over her shoulder, its arms fanning out like a bat's wings.

'But she insists on having you,' she said. 'She says you know Doug's wily ways and how to deal with them.'

She was certainly right about Doug's 'wily ways' as Jacantha called them. I did know them only too well. And that was precisely why I was trying to get out of the visit.

Doug was a miniature donkey – one of a pair – the other being Daisy. Whereas Daisy was a dun-coloured sweetie with all the good characteristics expected of a miniature – good tempered, affectionate, easy to handle and loved a cuddle – Doug was the complete antithesis. It was as if, when the characteristics for a good donkey were being drawn from the gene pool, it were the dregs left lurking at the bottom that surfaced in Doug. Like us humans, every animal has its good traits. Only with Doug, those traits were desperately difficult to locate; and try as I might, I never did find them.

To look at, he was an impressive little donkey. Standing at three feet tall, he was a spotted skewbald – mainly white with some grey patches over the cross on his shoulders, and with black tips to his huge, upright ears. It's probably what attracted Jacantha Stokes to him in the first place. She was an artist and sculptress with the temperament associated with people of that ilk. She relished having her life filled with things that had dramatic impact. Positively flourished on the challenges they provided. They fanned the flames of her creativity. Dealings with Doug didn't disappoint. She was constantly on fire – in a burning rage at his misdemeanours.

And I'd been witness to one such conflagration earlier in the summer. Then I'd been quite happy to make the visit unaware of what I was letting myself in for. In addition, Beryl's description of Jacantha Stokes painted an interesting picture of the woman I'd be meeting.

'She creates things out of bits of scrap metal,' she told me. 'There was a chicken of hers on display in Westcott Library. Can't say it was my cup of tea.' Beryl paused to scratch the mole on her chin. Then added, 'Just looked like a jumble of rusty nuts and bolts. But you'll see for yourself when you visit, as her garden's littered with her work.'

Jacantha Stokes lived in the grounds of Chawcombe Court – Lord and Lady Derwent's residence – in what must have originally been a keeper's cottage. It was tucked away on the edge of the estate's park, and I had to negotiate a bumpy, unmade road through a grove of silver birch and larch to find it. After the gloom of the shadowy ten minute drive down that track, to burst out into the sunlit glade in which Dingly Dell sat made me blink. The cottage itself also made me blink. It was so Hansel and Gretel – tiny, thatched, with timbered, ivy-clad walls – that I almost expected a wicked witch to sally forth as I stopped outside its front door. Instead, I got Jacantha Stokes. And what a colourful character she was – certainly in terms of what she was wearing. Jacob's coat of many colours was no match for what festooned her frame. She billowed out of Dingley Dell, a tie-dyed kaftan in reds and blues swirling round her diminutive frame, while from her neck trailed a long silk scarf in greens and yellows. With the addition of a bandana of orange and purple tied round her orange hair, its knotted ends looped over her left ear, the overall impression created was of a psychedelic pixie high on magic mushrooms.

'Mr Mitchell... Mr Mitchell... so pleased to meet you, and welcome to Dingley Dell,' she gushed, flinging both arms out to grasp my hand. 'You found me okay? I am rather hidden away down here.'

'Well you're certainly off the beaten track,' I remarked, gazing round the garden, which consisted of a maze of yellow-bricked paths that weaved by beds of shrubs and meandered through a sparse coppice of trees before losing themselves in the denser woods beyond. I half-expected Scarecrow, the Cowardly Lion and Tin Man, accompanied by a troupe of Munchkins from *The Wizard of Oz* to be skipping along them. Instead, along the paths at varying distances from each other, was an assortment of rusty looking objects which I took to be the results of Jacantha's artistic dabblings. I recognised a chicken and something that vaguely resembled a pig. It had four metal pipes as legs. A circle of thick, entwined strands of cable with two large nuts wired in its centre as a snout. And, at what I took to be the rear end, a large coiled spring which presumably was meant to be a tail. Several similar pieces revealed themselves as Jacantha took me round to the back of the cottage where I was introduced to Doug and Daisy, their heads pushed through the lower bars of a wooden field gate, curious to see who this stranger in their midst might be. The skewbald rolled his eyes, pulled back his head and trotted off across the paddock behind him with a loud snort.

'That was Doug,' said Jacantha. 'While this is Daisy.' She reached down to the donkey that still had her head through and rubbed her ears. 'She's very affectionate. You can do anything with her. But it's Doug I want you to see.'

Yet it was clear Doug didn't want to be seen, and had disappeared into a field shelter over the far side of the paddock from which he emitted a loud 'Hee-Haw' – his equivalent of 'Come and get me if you can.'

That's when the fun and games began.

Jacantha lifted a halter and lead off the gate post. ''fraid he's not very well halter-trained,' she confessed. 'But maybe we'll manage.'

Daisy walked sedately alongside as we made our way towards the field shelter, one side of which faced us, and from which Doug's head poked out, watching our approach, no doubt planning his next move.

'Right little fella, no messing around, eh?' I said, as we drew level with the entrance and I stepped slowly towards him, my knees slightly bent, my arms held out wide.

Chance was a fine fling when Doug took his chance to dodge me and attempted a giant leap for donkey-kind. I saw this barrel of equine flesh become airborne and fly towards me like Pegasus on Speed.

His chest connected with mine and we both collapsed to the ground with him on top of me. As he scrabbled to his feet, I lunged up and threw my arms round his hindquarters in a rugby tackle, only to find myself being dragged several yards across the paddock, before my weight forced him to the ground again, where he began to thrash. At which point, Jacantha sailed across like a multi-coloured balloon holding out the halter and attached lead rope. Now astride Doug, I turned to snatch them from her. As I did so, a searing pain shot through my left hand.

'Ouch!' I roared, looking down to discover my whole hand was in Doug's mouth, his incisors clamped to it.

'Why you bugger,' I shouted, pulling my hand free. I forced the halter over his muzzle and secured it. I then rolled off him and staggered to my feet. He did likewise. We both stood there, quivering, our chests heaving, both done in, knackered. Meanwhile, Daisy had quietly walked away, clearly embarrassed by her companion's bad behaviour.

And all this because Jacantha was wondering whether Doug had a touch of Sweet Itch and wanted someone to take a look.

I certainly had a sweet itch. A strong desire to throttle Doug with the lead rope I was holding. But it would have needed two hands, and my left one was swollen and bleeding.

In my rugby tackle of Doug, I had come up close and personal to the base of his tail, and had been virtually eye to eye with some small patches of hair loss with scaliness and thickening of the area. Not quite the way I'd normally examine a pony's skin. Nevertheless, that, combined with the symptoms Jacantha described – swishing his tail, swinging round on himself and rubbing his rump on the gate posts – was suggestive of Sweet Itch. As the condition was an allergic reaction brought on by midgy bites, I told her to get Doug a lightweight summer rug.

'Make sure it's one that will cover his neck and belly,' I advised. 'And buy a good insect repellent.

One that you'll only need to apply weekly. I realise it will be a bit of a challenge.'

Doug's ears shot up.

Jacantha gave me a quizzical look.

I shrugged.

I was shrugging now, having strode into reception and spun round the day book and the visits booked in it. Eric had three visits that afternoon. I had none. Seems there was no escape from another confrontation with Doug. Unless I dug my heels in.

Beryl had slid back on to her stool behind the reception desk and pulled her cardigan tightly across her chest – an action I'd witnessed many times before. A danger signal. A sign of cross words to come.

'Jacantha is being very insistent.'

I sighed.

Beryl was ready to put me in my place. But I already feared I knew where that place was. Dingley Dell.

Beryl continued to reason, a little less abrasively.

'Sorry, Paul. I know that little donkey is a real pain but Jacantha said he's ripped himself on some barbed wire. So he really does need to be seen now.'

'Okay. Ring her back and tell her I'll be over as soon as I can.'

'I already have. She's expecting you within the next half hour.'

Grr... Beryl had won, hands down. I raised mine in surrender.

But Beryl still hadn't finished. 'I reckoned you'd need some help. So I asked Mandy...'

No, surely not? Mandy would never willingly go out on a visit unless it was to accompany Crystal, in which case she'd go at the drop of a hat.

'She said it would be fine. She'd cope.'

'Really? Mandy's coming with me?' I was dumbfounded.

Beryl shook her head vigorously. 'No... No... She's letting Lucy go.'

Oh Lord. That risked stirring up memories of last year's visit to the Richardson's, when Lucy assisted me in the delivery of a foal. And all the consequences of that visit which ensued.

But the decision had been made for me. I had no choice.

Thank you Beryl.

So it was with Lucy in the passenger seat, that I drove over the Downs heading for the outskirts of Ashton, passing the turning down to Willow Wren – made without any comment – though I saw Lucy glance down the lane to the cottage and did wonder what she was thinking. After all she had lived with me there for nearly seven months.

When she did speak, it was to enquire about the miniature donkey.

I told her what a handful he was and that his owner, Jacantha Stokes, was useless when it came to handling him. She was one of those airy-fairy artist types. Pleasant enough, but a bit scatterbrained.

'So that's why you asked me to come along, is it?'

I caught her eye in the rear view mirror and found myself blushing.

'Ah... I see. It wasn't your choice.' Lucy slid her hands down her jeans and interlinked them tightly over her knees.

The journey continued in silence.

Broken only when we arrived and caught sight of Jacantha skipping down her yellow brick path to greet us, engulfed from neck to ankle in overlapping bands of silk, each band dyed in such a radiant hue that Judy Garland would have been stunned into silence. Jacantha's raiment was more than somewhere over her rainbow. It was way over the top of it.

'My... I see what you mean,' was Lucy's comment, as we clambered out of the car.

'Thank goodness you've arrived. I'm so worried about poor Doug,' Jacantha gasped, the sleeves of her garb blowing in the wind. 'Please hurry.'

Lucy and I hastily donned boots and snatched up smocks, ropes, bags of surgical instruments, and with me clutching my black bag in my free hand, chased after the retreating figure of Jacantha as she skipped down one of her yellow-bricked paths and disappeared round the corner of Dingley Dell.

Having skipped round as well, we caught up with her opening the field gate and gesticulating wildly across the paddock to where I'd previously battled with Doug.

At the far side, on the edge of the woods, I saw Daisy standing over a mound of white, half hidden in a bracken-filled ditch. It just had to be Doug.

'That's him... yes...' confirmed Jacantha. 'He was grazing over there when a fallow buck from the herd in the park came charging out of the woods, roaring at him. It's their rutting season. Maybe he saw him as a threat. Anyway it spooked poor Doug.'

We were now half-way across the paddock, Jacantha looking oddly out of place as she bounced along in her tube of silks, rather like a multi-coloured chipolata dancing over hot coals. 'I saw him rear up and twist sideways,' she continued. 'Then the next thing I knew he was down in the ditch, struggling to get up.'

Daisy looked up at us as we reached her. And then gazed back down at Doug's body, lying stretched out in a mat of churned up fern roots, a loop of barbed wire from some old fencing wrapped round his left thigh, pulled tight where he'd tried to drag himself free. You could see he'd been scrabbling to extricate himself to no avail, and now lay exhausted, breathing rapidly, panic showing in the whites of his rolling eyes.

'Okay little fella, let's see if we can sort you out,' I said with as much confidence as I could muster. The thigh looked a mess. The white hair was matted with blood where the wire encircling Doug's leg had acted as a sharp cheese cutter, slicing through his skin to bury itself deep in the underlying muscles.

Sedation of Doug was going to be necessary before I could do anything else. That was easy to give as he was so exhausted he barely flinched as I injected him in his neck, and he gradually relaxed and went to sleep.

Meanwhile, anticipating the task ahead, Lucy had unpacked the set of sterile instruments, wound dressings and antiseptic scrub, and lain them out on a green drape in the flattened bracken, next to Doug's hind leg.

'Damn,' I suddenly declared. 'I forgot the wire cutters.'

Lucy reached across the instruments she was laying out, and lifted up a pair. 'I didn't,' she said quietly.

'Well done, Lucy. Thank goodness someone was on the ball,' I replied, smiling at her. She didn't smile back. Merely gave a slight shrug of her shoulders.

I took the cutters from her and snipped off the two twisted lengths of barbed wire that snaked away into the soil of the bank, where they'd been partially buried in the bracken. I then used the cutters to gently ease the remaining length out of Doug's thigh, tracing it round the front and on to the inner surface. It was here most damage had been done, the skin torn away in a jagged flap. Without any prompting Lucy set to work, methodically washing away tiny flecks of soil and debris from the exposed tissues, flushing the area with saline solution squeezed from a bag and gently dabbing clean the edges of the skin where the hair was caked in clotted blood. She worked swiftly and efficiently, knowing exactly what she was doing. Jacantha watched silently from the top of the ditch, a fist held tightly to her lips.

I lifted the flap of skin with forceps and scraped the edge of it with a scalpel blade. Fresh blood oozed from it, showing it was still viable and could be stitched across the exposed muscles. I then carefully examined those muscles while Lucy held Doug's leg out and twisted slightly back to give me better visibility. Again, done without me having to prompt her. One of the main muscles was torn. A major artery throbbed beneath it. Thankfully, it hadn't been ruptured, otherwise Doug would have been dead by now, his life blood having ebbed away.

Lucy handed me a suture needle already threaded with suitably sized catgut and I proceeded to stitch the body of the muscle mass back together – a relatively easy task. But I needed to make sure I inserted as many sutures as possible to avoid any breakdown once Doug was back on his feet.

Otherwise, his weight might have torn the muscle open again. The skin edges were secured with nylon stitches which would need removing in ten days or so. I dreaded to think how we'd cope doing that, but somehow we'd manage. Perhaps with Lucy's help again? I could but hope.

Once finished, and a long acting antibiotic injection and tetanus booster given, I leaned across and flicked the corner of Doug's eyelid. His long black eyelashes flickered in response. The anaesthetic was beginning to wear off. He was starting to come round. Good.

While he did so, Lucy and I helped Jacantha construct a temporary holding pen out of some larch-lap fencing panels in the field shelter, into which a groggy but manageable Doug was eventually led.

Then it was back to Prospect House. Our route took us high over the Downs again. The view as ever over to the estuary of the Ouze and the sea beyond spectacular – lit up today in early autumn sunshine. A view that Lucy and I had shared last year on returning from the Richardsons' foaling. A view then cast in the colours of a rising sun. A time that heralded the dawn of our relationship, when I stopped to admire the scene and slipped my hand in hers.

On a sudden impulse, as we were about to pass the same lay-by where we'd stopped that early morning, I swerved into it and cut the engine. A silence settled on us only broken by the thrump of cars and lorries thundering by.

I eventually said, 'I much appreciated your help this morning, Luce. Thank you.'

She didn't reply. Just continued to gaze out at the rolling hills, white-peppered with sheep.

'And Luce...' I paused. 'Luce... I'm sorry for the way I've treated you. You deserved better.'

Only then did she turn to me and speak. 'Do you really mean that, Paul?' Her soft hazel eyes searched mine, questioning.

'I do... really... from the bottom of my heart.'

I saw Lucy hunch her shoulders and purse her lips. Lips that I'd kissed so many times before. Precious lips of a girl whom I now realised was still precious to me. I yearned to lean across, put my arm round her shoulder, and draw those precious lips to mine.

But when Lucy said, 'I think we'd better get back. Mandy's expecting me,' the moment was lost.

Would I ever get another chance?

17

Going Crackers At Christmas

That time of year was approaching again. That time of Ho... Ho... Ho... Here we go. Kisses under the mistletoe. Last year, I'd had the bright idea of installing a Christmas tree in the waiting room - against the protestations of Mandy who had visualised all sorts of problems with falling needles and dogs cocking their legs against its trunk. In the event, it wasn't so much falling needles as a falling tree that caused such uproar on Christmas Eve.

And I almost caused a falling out with Beryl over another bright idea of mine – sending her that Internet Christmas card of Santa Claus on a red-tiled roof, a bag of presents slung over his shoulder. By clicking on the bag he sprang on to the chimney pot. But instead of popping down it, he peed down it. I thought it hilarious. Beryl definitely didn't. It peed her off considerably.

So it was a no-no to any bright ideas I might have come up with this Christmas as they could have resulted in woe... woe... woe... at Prospect House this time round.

But for kids of course, the approaching festive season was one to be anticipated. The Christmas lights, the presents, the pantos and that perennial favourite – for parents anyway – the spectre of the school nativity play looming up.

At that play, there'll be the usual pushy parents wondering why their little Jonnie wasn't given the part of Joseph and ended up being the rear end of a donkey instead. And others agog to see whether this year's Mary is less stroppy than last year's when that one sat down heavily on her stool and threw the plastic baby Jesus into the orange-box crib with such force that his head popped off. I was told about this by Mrs Jennings, the teacher from Westcott's Primary School over the other side of the Green from Prospect House. She owned a cat whose booster I'd given earlier in the summer. And I was seeing her again now, only not with a cat, but with a group of eight pupils from the school.

'Sounds like a charabanc party,' I whispered to Beryl, as I listened to the chatter of voices emanating from the waiting room.

The babble stopped abruptly when I marched into the room and ground to a halt self-consciously, as eight little faces peered up at me from the circle that surrounded Mrs Jennings. It was a very seasonal-looking circle. Five lads were in dressing gowns, with red-chequered tea towels wrapped round their heads. A couple of girls had white cardboard wings attached to their backs. And the remaining lad was virtually invisible, swamped by an oversized sheepskin coat, inside out, with its sleeves hanging down to his knees and the collar over his head – shepherd or one of his flock I couldn't quite decide.

'We've just been doing a dress rehearsal,' said Mrs Jennings, by way of explanation.

'I'm one of the five wise men,' said a tea-towelled boy proudly, peering up at me through heavy black-rimmed pebble glasses.

'Five?' I queried, looking at Mrs Jennings.

She shrugged. 'We had difficulty in finding parts for everyone.'

The boy with the glasses turned to one of the angels who was clutching a small cardboard box, her thumbs keeping the lid firmly in place.

'Well, go on, Emma,' he said, pushing her forward, crushing her wings, 'show him Furry.'

'Leave off, Gavin,' said the girl, pushing him back with her elbow in a very un-angelic fashion.

Mrs Jennings hastily intervened. 'Now... Now... Behave yourselves, you two.'

'Er... let's go through to the consulting room, shall we?' I said.

'Can we all come?' said a muffled voice from the depths of the sheepskin.

'Only if everyone's on their best behaviour. Understand?' said Mrs Jennings.

Tea towels nodded, angel wings flapped and the sheepskin coat wagged its sleeves, as their teacher ushered them through, Emma elbowing her way to the front with the cardboard box.

She lifted it on to the consulting table and seven anxious faces and a headless coat clustered round as I cautiously took the lid off.

Inside, curled up on a cushion of cotton wool was a brown and white rodent, not much bigger than a mouse, but with much longer legs and a very long black-tipped tail. The creature lay on its side, motionless, with no visible signs of life.

Gavin stood on tip-toe and peered into the box, his pebble spectacles, sliding down his nose. 'I reckon he's a goner,' he declared, giving the box a vigorous poke.

'Don't do that,' said Emma crossly, smacking his hand. 'You'll frighten Furry.'

'Not if he's snuffed it, I won't,' retorted Gavin, pushing his spectacles back up his nose.

I didn't like to say it but I happened to think Gavin was right. But the sudden jolt made the rodent's whiskers twitch. So it hadn't passed on. Not yet. But I thought I'd better warn them of the likely outcome.

'He's a very poorly gerbil,' I said quietly.

'He's a jerboa,' piped up a voice from the inside the sheepskin coat.

Carefully I lifted out the prostrate creature. I could see a smear of blood on the white fur of its belly. Parting the fur, a tear in the skin was clearly visible.

'Can anyone tell me what happened?' I asked.

There was silence for a moment. Then, a rush of words from Emma.

'I was on the computer when Gavin said that no one had checked the jerboas today.'

'That's cos it was your turn and you forgot,' said Gavin, accusingly.

Tears welled up in Emma's eyes. Furiously wiping them away, she continued, 'I went and looked at them and saw Furry was sick. He was lying in a corner of the cage, not moving.

'I called Mrs Jennings and she said Furry was injured and that we ought to take him to the vet's.'

'So here we are,' said Mrs Jennings. 'A few more of us than intended. But they all wanted to see if you could save Furry.'

'It was his fault,' said the sheepskin coat. 'The other jerboa attacked him.'

'They shouldn't have been together,' said Gavin, knowingly. 'Males fight. Says so in my pet book.'

'Can you do anything for him, Mr Vet?' sobbed Emma, sniffing back a tear.

'Naw... he's had his chips,' said Gavin gruffly, giving the box another poke.

'I'll try stitching him up,' I said, pulling the box out of Gavin's reach.

'Right, children,' said Mrs Jennings. 'I suggest we all go home now and let Mr Mitchell do his best to save Furry.'

'It's a dead loss,' said Gavin, as he was bundled out.

What a charming little lad.

Once the children had trooped out, I took the jerboa down to the prep room. Mandy was the duty nurse that afternoon and she bustled in, her starched green uniform crackling. 'Emergency is it?' she sniffed, not quite able to keep the sarcasm out of her voice.

But with her customary efficiency, she picked the cardboard box up and marched into the operating theatre, where she tipped the jerboa out, still on its pad of cotton wool, flicked on the anaesthetic machine and eased the face mask over its whiskers.

It didn't take long to clip the hair away from the wound, clean it up and insert two dissolvable sutures.

Furry was collected by a delighted delegation, devoid of their nativity wear, the following day.

'Didn't snuff it, then,' said Gavin, pushing his spectacles up his nose. I could have rammed them down his throat.

A week later, two weeks before Christmas, Beryl flapped a large brown envelope in my face. 'From the school, addressed to you,' she declared.

Inside were eighteen hand-made Christmas cards from all the pupils in the class. One in particular made me smile.

Dear Mr Vet,

Thank you for saving Furry. I was very worried he might have died or something worse might have happened.

Lots of love from Emma.

I took the cards home with me and pinned them up on the timber beams that divided the dining area from the kitchen.

'Well, Emily,' I said, reaching down to stroke my spaniel's ears. 'Just look at that. Eighteen cards already and there's still two weeks to go.'

Christmas cards were a big thing with my dad, He would draw up a neat list of the people to whom they had sent cards and one for the people from whom they had received cards. Each list had the dates cards were sent or received, with cross references to determine whether or not to send cards to those who hadn't sent one last year, and whether or not to send cards next year to those who hadn't sent one this year. Completely baffling to Mum and me, but Dad seemed to know what he was doing.

Displaying the cards received was also carried out with Dad's military precision. This involved the hanging of red-ribbon strips pinned to the living room's picture rail, equidistant from each other. The pin holes were circled in pencil for easy location the following Christmas. The number of cards threaded through these ribbons and their position in relation to others alongside was dependent on their height, width and scenes depicted (old masters were not permitted to jostle next to blessed virgins, and jolly cardinals roasting their chestnuts in front of a roaring fire, were kept away from rosy-cheeked choir boys singing in their stalls). Dad got quite riled one year when, having threaded through the ribbons all fifty-five cards so far received, his carefully planned and executed sequences got thrown out of the window when five festive robins simultaneously plopped on the front door mat Christmas Eve.

As for me, I wouldn't have minded how many Santas with their reindeers, mufflered mice or puffed-cheeked Dickensian trumpeters I received, if in amongst them was going to be a card from Lucy. But I wasn't holding my breath.

But I was certainly trying to, when a few days later, I was presented with one of the hazards that occur over the festive period. The family pet gaining access to some of the rich pickings on offer – intentionally if the owners think Fido deserves a Christmas dinner like theirs with all the trimmings or unintentionally when Fido whips the giblets off the kitchen table behind their backs.

This particular Fido was actually a Jack Russell called Ossie; and that particular afternoon his presence could be smelt rather than felt due to the ingestion of a large pile of turkey giblets. They had barely seen the light of day from being pulled out of the turkey's rear before they disappeared down Ossie's throat. I'd told the owner, Mrs Birchell, over the phone the previous night when I was on duty, that she'd better bring him the next day for a check-up in case it upset his tummy.

'Phew, who's let off?' said Eric, breezing into reception, his hand clasped across his nose and mouth.

'Well, don't look at me,' replied Beryl indignantly. 'It's all Paul's doing.'

'Really?' Eric said swinging round on me. 'The curried beans were too much for you were they?'

'What's that ghastly smell?' This from Crystal who had strode in, waving her hand across her face.

'It's Paul,' declared Eric, pointing an accusing finger at me. 'He's been on the beans.'

'I don't care who's been on what, we need some fresh air in here. Beryl, open a window. And where's that Summer Bouquet you're always squirting round the place?'

'Sorry Crystal, but I've just run out.'

As Beryl spoke, the waiting room door crashed open and out piled three clients with their pets. 'Sorry,' one man gasped, 'but would you mind if we wait out here? It's getting a bit stuffy in there.' As he spoke, a loud fart echoed out from waiting room.

'That will your next appointment, Paul,' said Beryl, her voice muffled behind her hand.

'Well for heaven's sake see it before we're all gassed out,' snapped Crystal.

I hurried down the corridor to the door that led off the waiting room across to my consulting room. I opened it and was hit by a blast of fetid air and another loud fart. Across the room sat Mrs Birchell and alongside her a brown, black and white Jack Russell, trembling slightly, his head lowered, with what could only be described as a 'Sorry but I can't help it' guilty look on his face as another gust of wind erupted from under his tail. Several more exploded from him as he trotted across to the consulting room, where he hardly needed lifting on to the table as enough gas was being emitted from his rear end to jet-propel him up there. I felt sure if I'd lit a match under his tail he would have rocketed into space.

Mrs Birchell was extremely apologetic. 'Ossie does tend to scavenge. But usually gets away with just a minor tummy upset. But this time...' Another fart from the Jack Russell emphasised the point she was making.

Checking his temperature, rolling the thermometer up his bottom, elicited yet another.

Palpating his abdomen, released two more.

And when I patted him on the head and said what a good boy he'd been, he wagged his stumpy tail and fanned a final fart in my face.

An anti-spasmolytic injection to settle the guts, a rice and lamb diet for a few days and I felt Ossie would be sorted.

I had no wish for him to wind up here again.

Within twenty-four hours, another Christmas hazard blew up in my face. Only this time it wasn't a blast of wind but a surge of electricity that was the cause of me examining a shocked toy poodle.

It was Topsy, the toy poodle belonging to a Mrs Guthridge – the lady who had fainted into Major Fitzherbert's arms on being told a giant African rat had just been admitted to the hospital. Seems that having knocked into each other on that occasion, they'd hit it off ever since.

As the Major explained in agitated tones when he and Mrs Guthridge arrived in reception with an inert Topsy in his arms, and a crying Mrs Guthridge clinging to his side, he'd been helping her to hang the Christmas lights on her tree. Caruthers, his Cairn, had been chasing Topsy round the base of the tree (I suspect the randy so-and-so was going crackers hoping to pull her) when she'd careered into the lights' trailing flex and yanked it free from its plug.

'There was this sudden flash,' boomed the Major, 'and an almighty yelp from Topsy here. She spun over and collapsed.' He slid the inert poodle into my arms.

'Right, take a seat in the waiting room both of you,' I instructed, before hammering down to the operating theatre with Topsy, shouting for a nurse as I did so. Mandy ran in as I was ramming the face mask over the poodle's nose and flicking on the oxygen from the anaesthetic machine.

I looked at her rib cage.

No movement.

I felt each side of her chest with a finger and thumb.

No heartbeat.

I briefly lifted the mask away and peeled back her upper lip.

No colour.

I looked up at Mandy and shook my head.

No life.

Oh how I hated those times when I had to inform an owner their pet had died. A time to understand their anguish. A time to empathise with their loss. I had lost dear little Nelson. Crushed to death under that car wheel – a sudden loss like with Topsy here. It had torn my heart out. As did Topsy's loss with Mrs Guthridge. Her grief overwhelmed her. In a torrent of tears she crumpled into Major Fitzherbert's arms. 'My poor, poor Topsy, I'm going to miss you so much,' she cried, burying her face in the Major's sleeve, while he softly stroked her hair, his eyes glistening with tears; and Caruthers laid subdued between them, his head between his paws.

At least it must have been of some comfort to Mrs Guthridge to have the support and friendship of Major Fitzherbert. In much the same way as Beryl had been a support to Ernie Entwhistle when his beloved collie, Ben, had to be put to sleep. She and Ernie had been good friends ever since. Festive evidence of that friendship appeared on the reception desk next to Beryl's computer.

'Ernie's signed up to evening classes in crafts,' she said. 'And he made this just for me. What do you think of it?'

I had to think very hard and be careful of what I said so as not to offend Beryl. There were four legs made out of bamboo – one noticeably shorter than the others, jeopardising the creature's stability – rectified by Beryl wedging a matchbox under the offending limb. The head was made of woven straw with a cork for the nose and two black beads for eyes. The body, likewise, was a matted bundle of yellow straw with a tail made out of a pipe cleaner. The main clue to its identity were two lop-sided antlers made out of twigs in various thicknesses and various shapes, that had glued to them, balls of screwed up sweet wrappers in red, blue and green.

Beryl watched with her one beady eye, sensing my bewilderment, as I studied what I guessed was meant to be a reindeer.

'Not bad for a first try, is it?' she declared.

'Excellent... yes...' I said, lying through my teeth.

But that's often the way with presents – Christmas presents in particular. People make the effort to give you something. You have to make the effort to show pleasure in what you've been given.

Ties you'll never wear. Socks to add to the drawerful you've already got. A shirt in the wrong colour, wrong collar design and several sizes too big with, 'I've kept the receipt in case you want to change it,' from Aunt Hilda while you desperately try to inject some enthusiasm in your, 'Thank you... just what I wanted.'

Mind you, I did give Lucy a whopping big 'Thank you' last Christmas when she presented me with several pairs of boxer shorts. I was particularly enamoured by the pair depicting a charging bull elephant with his trunk raised. An action which I later emulated for her during the Queen's Speech.

It was early December, already nearly dark, tea-break time, when the subject of the forthcoming Pet Blessing came up.

Beryl leaned across from where she was sitting with her mug of tea, and said, 'I guess you'll take Emily along, won't you, Paul?'

I nodded. 'And will you be going?' I knew Beryl hadn't got a pet of her own, but wasn't surprised when she told me she would attend with Ernie and his new young collie, Bess.

Crystal and Eric didn't have any pets either, so I didn't think they'd be coming along.

'Er... no...' replied Eric, reddening, when I asked him.

Likewise Mandy.

But Lucy? Had she still be living at Willow Wren with me she'd have had plenty of pets to choose from. But she'd returned to Prospect House with only her cat, Queenie and rabbit, Bugsie. Nevertheless, I'd have welcomed one or both along if it meant she'd turn up as well.

Besides it was all in a good cause. There'd be a collection afterwards to raise funds for WARS.

The idea had been mooted by Eleanor Venables after she'd met and got to know Mike Masters when he came out to rescue a buzzard fledgling that had been abandoned by its parents.

'Such a worthy cause, don't you think,' she'd said to me. 'And with your love of birds, I'm sure you'll support it.'

It seemed like a good idea. Mike Masters was a decent bloke and anything to help his charity I would certainly support. Eleanor dragged me along to meet Reverend James and seek his approval to have the blessing in St Mary's.

'My dears,' he said, 'that does sound like a very good use of the church. It will encourage the means by which a worthy continues to help our avian brethren be restored to good health and enable them be released back into their world,' James paused briefly for breath, before adding, 'Rather like you did with your swallows, Paul.'

'So you'll be happy to conduct a blessing?' asked Eleanor, unsure of what Reverend James had been on about.

I quickly intervened. 'That's what James is saying in so many words.' Too many as usual, I thought, while giving him a friendly smile. My smile faltered when the reverend started up again.

'I think the occasion would be a very charming way to express our feelings and appreciation for all the good things that come from our close relationship with the creatures we take under our wing and demonstrate how their place in our lives is so justly deserved.'

Eleanor looked perplexed. 'Is that a "Yes" then?'

I intervened again, to translate the James-speak into normal English. 'Yes it is,' I said.

Eleanor clapped her hands with glee. 'Oh, jolly good show,' she cried. 'It will be so much fun.'

I wasn't so sure.

'Well, Emily, today's the day,' I declared on the morning of the Blessing. 'You looking forward to it?' Emily pricked her ears and tilted her head to one side. 'Just make sure you're on your best behaviour.' Emily responded with a grizzle. 'Yes, I'm sure you will, sunshine.'

Not that there was going to be any actual sun about. The sky was heavy with voluminous banks of grey cloud, threatening the snow which was

303

forecast that morning and which, by eight o'clock, started to float down in powdery flakes. I watched them swirl and drift past my front bedroom window to settle on the lawns and shrubs until they gradually disappeared from view – buried under a soft mantle of snow. Across at St Mary's, the headstones in the churchyard donned caps of white, the beech trees alongside the rectory garden, sleeves of white, while in the upper branches of those trees, rooks hunkered down in their white-rimmed nests.

St Mary's was only a matter of a few minutes' walk across from Willow Wren, so I thought it unnecessary to venture over until a few minutes before the start of the service, due to begin at eleven o'clock.

As that time approached, the snow gradually stopped falling, leaving the outside transformed into a winter wonderland. Any moment, I expected a red-coated Father Christmas to fly into the church's car park, ahead of having Rudolph blessed, while fairies skated down the snow-covered tiles of the church roof and elves played peek-a-boo between the snow-covered tombs of the churchyard.

With twenty minutes to go, I saw the first car drive up the lane, followed by two more, the noise of their engines muffled by the blanket of snow surrounding them.

'Okay, Emily, better make a move, eh?' I said, as people now began streaming into the church with pets of all shapes and sizes. She responded by racing to the front door at the side of the cottage with an excited woof.

I had struggled into a thick windcheater and was crossing the living room about to don some wellies by the door, when a terrible commotion erupted immediately outside the front of the cottage. Startled, I sharply turned to glance out of the front window just as a head reared up in front of it. A head that was white with long black-fringed ears and which emitted a very loud Hee... Haw... on peering in and catching sight of me.

'Bloody hell,' I exclaimed, recognising the head as belonging to Jacantha's miniature donkey, Doug. Behind and some distance away, heaving herself through the snow-covered grass which divided the cottage from St Mary's, was a figure festooned in what appeared to be soggy red sacks topped by a woolly, red and white pom-pommed hat with sprigs of holly sticking out of it. Jacantha Stokes.

I hurriedly pulled on my wellies and floundered through the snow round to the front. Doug, upon seeing me, bared his teeth, gave another loud Hee... Haw... and then jumped the low mound of white which was the buried hedge that separated Willow Wren from Mill Cottage. He crunched smartly across Eleanor's front garden just as she was coming out of her front door. The two of them collided. The cat basket Eleanor was carrying got knocked out of her hand. It crashed into the snow, the door sprang open, and a terrified Tammy sprang out and sprang up the nearest tree. Snow showered off the branches as she clawed her way up from one to another until, half-way up, she lost her footing, slipped and came slithering back down the trunk. With her front legs outstretched above her, her claws scoring the slippery bark, she hurtled back down to earth emitting a loud yowl as she did so.

The sight and sound of this rapidly descending fur ball was too much for Doug.

He jumped in the air, spooked.

Then twisted round and shot up the path like a demented snow plough.

He churned through the snow, straight past the feebly flapping arms of Jacantha and, with a speed worthy of a Grand National winner, sailed over the white-covered hedge bordering St Mary's graveyard, slipped and slid through the gravestones up to the porch and vanished inside.

At which point all hell erupted from within.

The organ had just struck up 'All Things Bright and Beautiful'. That came to a grinding halt, petering out on high note that sounded like bagpipes being garrotted. It was replaced by a cacophony of neighs, bellows, bleats, yelps and howls.

I waded towards the porch door as fast as I could, just as two pygmy goats came charging out, with a very flustered Graham Merriweather in hot pursuit; to be followed by a squealing Miss Piggy, liquid turds streaming from her. At the door, a Jack Russell scooted between my legs, farting furiously, and I got hit in the face by a clucking, flying chicken.

'So sorry,' crowed chicken-costumed Anna Hutchinson, who came waddling out behind it. 'That was Martha.'

At the entrance to the aisle, I saw Doug bucking and kicking his way down it, people in the pews to each side diving out of reach of his flailing hooves. A giant white rabbit was hopping furiously ahead of him, trying to avoid his teeth which were bared and snapping at his fluffy tail.

A small group of terrified children were huddled by the font, the protective arms of Mrs Jennings round them. From under one of her arms peered the bespectacled face of Gavin, who pushed the specs up his nose and yelled at the rabbit-chasing Doug, 'Go on... Punch his lights out.'

Up in the pulpit, quaked Reverend James, crossing himself feverishly. While behind him, perched on top of the altar cross, an African grey parrot shrieked, 'Look out... Look out... There's a croc about.' This evoked more screams from the kids and a mass exodus from the pews, as people scrabbled and clawed their way over them, access to the aisle being blocked by the rampaging pony and the possibilities of a crocodile slithering up it.

It was the arrival of Mike Masters – albeit it a little late on the scene – who marshalled everyone together and restored order. It was he who ascertained there was no crocodile lurking amongst the prayer mats. Verified by close questioning of a man who smelt of rats. At that point, Reverend James felt it safe to descend from the pulpit and dispense a few words of comfort and condolence amongst the remaining few – the rest having made their rapid departures in advance of his impending verbosity.

Only as things settled down, Doug reined in, goats rounded up, dogs retrieved, and the African grey enticed down with a wafer from the sacristy, did I notice one particular person missing. The one person who I hoped would have been there. Lucy.

Beryl, who had witnessed all the shenanigans with her eyeballs on stalks – well certainly her good eye had been on one – told me as she walked back to Ernie's car, her arm linked in his, Bess trotting by his side, that Lucy had given every intention of attending. 'Only hope nothing's happened to her with all this snow about,' she said quietly.

I began to worry. I tried her mobile. No reply. Back in the cottage I tried again. Still nothing. Maybe she'd broken down. Worse, been involved in an accident. The road over the Downs had several black spots. Drivers were forever being injured; and there had been one fatality in the time I'd lived there.

By mid-day I'd really worked myself into a stew. A call through to Mandy verified that Lucy had indeed left earlier to come over for the service though she'd decided not to take Queenie or Bugsie. I had half-a-mind to get in my car and make the journey over to Westcott just to see if I could spot her car on the way. But what if I came on the scene of an accident? Saw her car smashed on the side of the dual carriageway. A crumpled shell in the snow, from which her mangled body would have been pulled out. I realised then, with my imagination set on fire, just how much I still felt for her. How much passion still smouldered deep inside me. I needed her to rekindle it. And in lighting it, to prove that deep down inside her, a similar flame also burned.

The muffled sound of a car engine, tyres crunching on snow, out front made me leap to my feet.

Yes. It was Lucy. I ran out to meet her.

'Lucy...' I faltered. 'I thought you'd had an accident.'

'A puncture,' she explained. 'Luckily, I wasn't going too fast and managed to skid on to the hard shoulder. But the AA took ages to come out.' She must have seen the relief flood my face. 'I did try phoning but couldn't get a signal.' She looked across at the now deserted church, the snow on the paths around it mashed to a dirty mush. 'Seems I've missed all the fun.' She shrugged. 'Not that I brought any of my menagerie to be blessed. Just thought I'd support WARS and help swell numbers.'

'You've no idea...' I managed to blurt out, shaking my head.

'Oh well, not to worry. Another time, maybe.' Lucy made to open the car door again.

'No, wait,' I said. 'There's someone who deserves a blessing.' I looked at Lucy and then down at Emily, who was gazing up at us both, her stumpy tail wagging furiously as ever. 'After all, if it hadn't been for you, Emily wouldn't be here with me now. That in itself is a blessing. Come on. Let's go over.' I held out my hand. 'Please.'

It seemed like hours before she slowly stretched out her hand and tentatively allowed me to clasp it.

Slowly, silently, we crossed the white front lawn. St Mary's was now haloed in watery sunshine which turned the snow on its roof into a diadem of crystals that flashed and gleamed above us. Ahead, Emily dashed and spun round with excited leaps, glittering snow icicles showering into the air around her.

I let go of Lucy's hand and quickly bent down to cup some snow into a ball.

'Oh... no you don't,' shrieked Lucy, ploughing ahead of me, giggling.

I threw the snowball. But missed her.

She scooped some from the top of a headstone and aimed it at me. I ducked but still got showered. Laughing, I packed some more together and chased after her, flinging the snowball as she drew up her arms to shield herself. This one hit her shoulder, powdering it in white.

'Beast,' she yelped, sending one back that smacked my cheek. 'Gotcha,' she said, her laughter ringing out. A peal of gleeful happiness.

I grabbed her hand and pulled her into the porch and threw my arm round her waist, drawing her to me. Both of us were rosy cheeked. Both of us catching our breath. Clouds of it hung in the air.

As did the words I uttered.

'Lucy...' I gasped, searching her face. 'I do love you... you know.' I ran a finger gently across her lips.

As the sun dipped behind the rectory beeches, an amber shaft cut between the branches and caught Lucy's face, lighting it in soft pinks, sparkling in her hazel eyes.

There was a pause. A hesitation. Then, she answered softly, 'And I love you too.'

Our lips touched. And then we kissed. A deep, long, lingering kiss.

A kiss that's to be repeated in that same place. In that same porch. On a warm May day, five months later.

While wedding bells ring out.

While cherry blossom drifts down on us.

While:

White fluffy clouds in a cluster will be *Hanging on a breeze to dry.*

Yes. Thank you, Max.

And thanks also, to Crystal, Eric, Mandy and Beryl, who wish us well in our new life together.

And not forgetting dear, sweet Emily as she dances round our feet and gives a woof of sheer joy.

****